BAUMGARTNER'S
BOMBAY

BAUMGARTNER'S
BOMBAY

Anita Desai

ALFRED A. KNOPF   NEW YORK
1989

THIS IS A BORZOI BOOK
PUBLISHED BY ALFRED A. KNOPF, INC.

Library of Congress Cataloging-in-Publication Data

Desai, Anita
Baumgartner's Bombay.

I. Title.
PR9499.3.D465B38   1989   823   88-25753
ISBN 0-394-57229-7

Manufactured in the United States of America

FIRST AMERICAN EDITION

I wish to express my gratitude to Girton College, Cambridge, for having provided me with a year of perfect conditions for work.

●●●●●●●●●●●●●●●●●●

I would also like to acknowledge my debt to Professor Alex Aronson and Sir Denis Forman for reading Chapter 4 and making many helpful comments and suggestions; to Sybil Oldfield of the University of Sussex for providing me with much detailed information, and to Alicia Yerburgh for her patience and sympathy with yet another book.

In my beginning is my end. In succession
Houses rise and fall, crumble, are extended,
Are removed, destroyed, restored . . .

—*T. S. Eliot,*
'East Coker'

ONE

Although she had fled the blood-spattered scene and fled the collected crowd of identical individuals – one-legged, nose-picking, vigilant-eyed – and hurried down the street at a speed uncommon for her, a speed no one would have thought possible on those high red heels that were no longer firm but wobbled drunkenly under the weight of her thick, purple-veined legs, Lotte slowed as she neared her door. Her body seemed to thicken and clot, her actions slowed till she was nearly at a standstill. She opened the door with fumbling, ineffective movements as though she had forgotten its grammar, her fingers numb, tongue-tied as it were. Entering the room, she shut the door behind her heavily, taking great care with the locks and bolts and chains, afraid the crowd might follow her, may even now be approaching her room, preparing to shoulder its way into it. When every lock was in place, she leant against the door in the theatrical manner that came naturally to her – pressing a packet of letters to her breast as years ago she had pressed a flower against a bosom still plump and warm, flounced with white lace and spotted with red spots, singing all the while to the stage-lights, her mouth open, a tunnel of red from which might issue either a trill or a howl. Pressing the bits of paper to her now shrunken and flabby bosom, she breathed long harsh breaths that rasped her throat.

They slowed themselves till her breath caught and snarled

itself in a sob. Then she moved, putting down the packet on the table and feeling her way to the stove. There she lit the gas flame and put on the small, dented kettle. While she did so she had something on which to concentrate, her lip held by one front tooth, and she did not need to think of anything. Not Hugo. Not God. Nothing. Her face drew towards its centre, all the lines around the eyes, the nose, the mouth, concentrating in a frown, as she found the coffee, measured it into a cup, laid it out on the table beside the packet of paper. Touching that with her small finger which she could not quite control, which gave a jerk outwards, wilfully, she let out the sob she had been holding inside her: Hugo, Hugo, *mein Gott*, Hugo, what's happened, *was ist dann, wie kannst du* . . . then bit her lip, brought all her fingers together, on to the kettle handle, lifted that and filled her cup. She warmed milk in a pan. She found the sugar bowl. Then put them all together – cup, coffee, milk, sugar – concentrating on her movements, not allowing another jerk, another sob.

Finally she lowered herself on to her chair at the table, to drink. But did not drink. The cup waited, the coffee steamed, together they invited. But Lotte had pushed the cup aside, swung violently round in her chair to the shelf by the table, let her hands hunt through the objects there, greasy and used and familiar, dropping and pushing them away till her fingers found the bottle she wanted. Wrenching off the top, she brought it close to her with one hand, found a stained, smeared glass into which she poured some gin, and drank, holding the bottle and the glass close to her breast to keep them from shaking or falling. Lotte's mouth, now crumpled and wet and quavering, and the glass and bottle, all held close to each other, for company, as if hunted, as if in hiding.

But finally she put them away from her, very carefully, on the table. Then picked up the packet and clumsily slipped off the narrow pink ribbon that held together the cards. For those were not letters, they were postcards except for one or two that had been folded for so long that the several sheets formed a single thickness, like a card. The writing was so faint, so spidery, it formed a kind of skein or web, on the yellowed paper, and seemed closer to the drawing of an intricate plan than the lines of a language. She had to turn to the shelf again and from amongst the fallen and cluttered objects find the spectacles she hardly ever used because they pinched the top of her nose and left sore marks behind.

As she hooked them over her ears, cursing them out of custom, she told herself: look at the dates, first look at the dates. Yes, as was to be expected from the appearance of the stiff, brittle bits of paper, the dates were of long ago, the long ago that Lotte hardly remembered – thirty-nine, forty, forty-one – just as she thought, suspected. They made her bunch her fingers, clutch her neck, as if she were choking. Then she had to settle the spectacles on her nose, so she could read.

'*Meine kleine Maus,*' '*Mein Häschen,*' '*Liebchen* . . .' she murmured the unfamiliar, unaccustomed German, those forgotten endearments, the antiquated baby-language, feeling them on her tongue like crystals of sugar. Her teeth shrank from impact with them. She read on and each line seemed like the other, each card alike: 'Are you well, my rabbit? Do not worry yourself. I am well. I have enough. But have you enough, my mouse, my darling? Do not worry . . .'

Do not worry, do not worry, Lotte mocked, spitting out those pieces of sugar as if they were glass and cut her. With the spit came laughter, and sobs. Little Mouse, *Mäuschen*, do not worry, I am well, I am well. She began to rub the back of her hand against her mouth, rub harder and harder till it hurt, and through the pain and the cries the words continued to come: *Meine kleine Maus, mein Hugo, Geliebter*, I am well and do not worry . . .

When she pulled herself together and saw what she was doing, what she had done, she found everything in a mess, reflecting her face, reflecting herself. The coffee spilt, the cards scattered, the bottle emptied, the glass lying on its side. A scene, in miniature, copying the scene at Hugo's that she had fled.

Getting up from the chair, she stood over it and stared, furious and frightened. She could not allow that here – Hugo had, *mein Gott*, Hugo – but she could not, she must learn, be careful, not allow . . . Forcing back her sobs and cries, she made herself pick up the cup, the glass, the bottle, put them away, wipe the table, pick up the cards, collect them in a packet, and sit down with them on her lap, as calmly, as soberly as she could.

She no longer looked at them. She stared out of the window, at the six panes of glass in three rows, two to each one. She stared at the view she faced every day over her coffee, her gin – the building across the court, its grey concrete walls ribbed with black drain-pipes, the doors opening on to balconies hung with washing, stacked with tins and boxes. Right at the top, a layer of sky. A blank sky, as always, with neither colour nor form. Empty. Afternoon light. Daylight. Perpetual light. And blankness. Even the sounds were perpetual, constant – the radio that blared, the woman that screamed, the children that played, the pots and pans that clanged. They made a wall themselves – of metal, always in commotion.

Lotte's mouth drooped. At the corners, moisture gathered, formed drops, slowly began to slide down her chin, adhesively. The chin shook, dissolved. Lotte began to shake. Her fingers tightened on the cards. Looking down, in order to avoid that sky, that window, that blankness, she tried to pick out the words from the spider's nest of ancient writing. She ought at least to find out who had written them, to Hugo. Sucking at her lips, she stared at the bottom of the first card, the second card, the third. Some were signed 'Mama'. Others 'Mutti'. Some 'Mü'.

Lotte pressed her fingers to her lips, to her eyes, to her ears, trying to prevent those words, that language, from entering her, invading her. Its sweetness, the assault of sweetness, cramming her mouth, her eyes, her ears, drowning her in its sugar. The language she wanted not to hear or speak. It was pummelling her, pushing against her and into her, and with

her mouth stuffed she moaned, '*Nein, nein, nein*, Hugo, no.'
Her teeth bit on the crystals and her nerves screamed at their
sweetness. All the marzipan, all the barley sugar, the chocolates and toffees of childhood descended on her with their soft,
sticking, suffocating sweetness. Enough to embrace her,
enough to stifle her, enough to obliterate her. Sugary, treacly,
warm, oozing love, childhood love, little mice and bunny
rabbits of love – sweet, warm, choking, childish love. Lotte
wept and drowned.

●●●●●●●●●●●●●●●●●

When Baumgartner shut the door and came out on the
landing, he had to take great care the cats did not slip out.
Fritzi, still dragging his battered hind leg and with blood
turned to a black and shining crust where his ear once was, had
been indicating with increased impatience that he was ready
for the streets again and tried to hobble out from between
Baumgartner's legs, but was scraped up and returned to the
dimness and safety of the flat, while Mimi had made a swift
dart like a cobra's head for the exit but been pressed back
gently with a murmur: 'Now you wait here, *mein Liebchen*,
and I bring you something tasty – a piece of sausage, hah?
Blutwurst, Leberwurst, Bratwurst – was willst du?' He laughed at
his daily joke so that the warts on his nose all bunched together
in a purplish lump that wobbled and his eyes disappeared in
nests of wrinkles. Mimi was not amused, she was hungry and
bit him sharply in the thumb. '*Ach, Liebchen*,' he moaned,
drawing back the thumb and nursing it in his fist, 'that was
naughty, was it not?' She withdrew, her back still arched in
outrage, and he shut the door on her, assuring her through the
crack, 'Something I will bring back for you, so be good now,
please, for a little,' and made his way down the stairs.

They were ancient stairs, worn into hollows at the centre,
and each heavy tread raised dust. He felt carefully for the safe
hollow of each board as he went down, holding an empty
plastic bag in his hand, reminding himself to be careful, not to

fall and cause trouble in his old age. Down in the hall which was unfurnished but for the cooking smells of the building that collected and boiled and steamed within its green walls, the watchman on his stool shifted his legs to let Baumgartner pass, smiling faintly out of politeness but with a twist of distaste at the corner of his mouth. The plastic bag was empty but the watchman knew how it would stink when he returned. Also, Baumgartner rarely washed his clothes; they emanated a thick, cloudy odour that he himself found comforting in its familiarity but some considered offensive. His eyes were short-sighted and blinked half-shut against the glare that thrust itself in at the door and so he did not notice that watchman's expression as he passed him on his perch under the wooden board that bore the tenants' names – Hiramani, Taraporevala, Barodekar, Coelho, da Silva, Patel – mumbled 'Good morning, *salaam*', and went down the steps into the street with his bag, uncertain as ever of which language to employ. After fifty years, still uncertain. Baumgartner, *du Dummkopf*.

The glare came from the sea, down at the end of the street, glittering solder in the morning heat and heavy and sullen at low tide, but Baumgartner did not turn his face in its direction. He had to look down and watch his feet as he picked his way past the family that lived on the pavement in front of Hira Niwas. They worked constantly at reinforcing the shelter they had built here, flattening out packing-cases for walls and tin cans for the roof, attaching rags to the railing around Hira Niwas and stretching them on to their own rooftop; yet it remained tremulously impermanent and Baumgartner took care not to run into one of the sticks that propped it up or the rope on which the washing hung. He had to avoid the gnarled and rotting feet of the man who always lay in a drunken stupor at this time of the morning, his head inside the shelter and his legs outside, like pieces of wood flung down, as well as the pile of cooking pots that the woman washed in the gutter so that they shone like crumpled tinfoil in the glare, and the heaps of faeces that the children left along the same gutter, and the squares of greasy paper from which they had eaten their food the night before. It was a familiar sight to Baumgartner, as he was to them, with his plastic bag in his hand and his shoes slit at the sides for comfort, but they still had to watch each other, to be vigilant.

The woman, washing, automatically edged her sari over her face with a twitch of her wet hand as she did in the presence of any male; actually she hardly thought of Baumgartner, a lump in grey pants, as one: the gesture was a conditioned one, now instinctive. The child that had the straw-coloured and straw-textured hair of the famine-struck standing about its head like Struwwelpeter's in Baumgartner's nursery book, sat on its haunches, straining to defecate. It looked up at Baumgartner as it looked at all passers-by, its face clenched with the problem: should it sing out for money, for *baksheesh*, or not waste its small, painfully hoarded energy? In the case of Baumgartner, the problem was easily solved: he clearly had nothing to give, they all knew that, the family on the pavement that watched him set out daily with his plastic bag. So she drew the snot on her upper lip back into her nostrils with a contemptuous snort and began to wail for her mother who cursed her casually, simply as a comment on life, on all their lives.

Baumgartner knew that family as well as a devout Christian is familiar with the Holy Family in the cattle stall; he knew all the looks, the voices and words in their gamut. But he never walked past them, never turned his back without feeling the hairs on the back of his neck rise, a brief prickle of – not exactly fear, but unease, an apprehension. He knew the absolute degradation of their lives; he knew the violence it bred – the brawling in the night, the beating, the weeping. Now the effect of it all had become dulled, but in the beginning it had appalled, and he remembered that – how he had returned to Hira Niwas one night, soon after they had set up abode on the pavement, a part of the migrant wave from the drought-stricken countryside, refugees from famine, or riots, and the woman had been screaming as though run over by an automobile. He had found a crowd of onlookers already gathered there, watching the man beat his wife with his fists and then kick her down, grab her by her hair and drag her up the street, swearing. 'What is happen?' asked the concerned Baumgartner of the watchman at the door. 'Is murdering her? Is police not come?' The watchman had shrugged – he did not consider Baumgartner worth talking to – but some of the onlookers turned round with amused looks and explained, 'Drunk man saying his wife behaving badly with other men, so he is beating her.' 'He is killing her,' Baumgartner bleated, wondering at their nonchalance. 'We better call police.' But no one moved. When the man began to beat his wife's head against the pavement so that the blood spilt and gushed he hurried up to him and caught him by his shoulder only to be flung off and hurled against the wall. Some in the crowd helped him to his feet, saying, 'Don't trouble, sir, no good people. Both drinking too much.' Baumgartner tottered to his feet and allowed them to push him away. He did nothing more, knowing himself incapable of anything, but although the man had been too blind with liquor and fury to know what he was doing, Baumgartner was sure he had taken note of his intervention. After so many years and so many similar scenes, he remembered the look that the man had flung over his shoulder at him when he had tried to intervene, and the yellow, blood-streaked eye of the drunkard, murderous. It still brought out the prickle, those beads of sweat on his neck, and he walked by, hunching his shoulders protectively, fearing them. They watched him fearlessly – to them he was nobody, an old man with an empty bag. Finishing with the pots, the woman spat into the gutter, then bent to pick them up.

Baumgartner did not turn towards the sea. That was for the evening, when the breeze came up with the tide, and the sun fell headlong into the waves, livid and melodramatic in its orange and purple flames, and people strolled, for pleasure, buying themselves peanuts to eat or coconuts to drink from, and one was not conspicuous if one loitered too. But now everyone was out on business – cars and people had a purpose, everyone bustled, the vehicles became entangled in their hurry and horns hooted in furious impatience. The morning scene had no tropical languor for all that it was hot; the Bombay style was brisk, Baumgartner thought regretfully, brisk and businesslike.

He was very aware of his lack of business; if he were ashamed of it, he was relieved too, relieved not to join the crowd, the traffic, but to amble alone into the lanes and alleys that made off from the main road, and shuffle past the old dingy houses that no one bothered to paint, that stood perpetually in the shadows, and where life washed up in drifts, like debris. Scuffing through that litter, he turned into the dark doorway of the quiet and nearly empty Café de Paris.

Here he met with the first smile of the day, but so slight and sardonic and well concealed behind a bush of tobacco-coloured moustache, that he did not see it. Nor did the café proprietor's eyes reflect it; they were the bottomless pits of a cynic and a melancholic and so the smile was no more than a grimace. Baumgartner did not mind; he did not see, being still dazzled by the light of the streets, that explosion of light that his weak eyes could hardly tolerate. Groping for a chair, he lowered himself on to its comfortless tin seat by a marble-topped table, placing his hands on it for coolness and grateful for the green murk of the Café de Paris: Farrokh wasted little money on electricity.

'Tea, *sahib*? Coffee?' he asked as he came across since the waiter was still in the kitchen, noisily preparing the cutlery and the crockery for the day's custom. He leaned over the table, placing his raw, meaty hands on its edge and frowning at a smear of grease on the marble that he wiped with the napkin he carried on his shoulder.

'Och, Farrokh, so good. Yes, tea, pliss, tea is nice,' sighed Baumgartner, feeling the perspiration trickle down his neck and back, almost audibly. 'And something for the pussy-cats, yes? You have something from last night, Farrokh?' he coaxed, edging the plastic bag across the table at him.

Farrokh gave another of his dour smiles that failed to light his eyes. He took the bag from Baumgartner resignedly and went to the kitchen door with it, handing it to one of the boys who worked there in striped underpants and tattered vests and with towels flung over their shoulders. Then he called back to Baumgartner, 'I'll have it ready for you later, I told them keep fish curry for you. It's hot. Your cats like *masala*, spice, chilli, turmeric, *jeera*, bay leaf?'

Baumgartner had no option but to smile and nod. He was in debt to Farrokh and the other restaurateurs who filled his bag for him with the remains of the food cooked the night before. Without their help he could not feed the cats that flocked to him in the alleys, knowing him to be the Madman of the Cats, the Billéwallah Pagal, or the sick and maimed ones he picked up from the streets and carried home to nurse, telling them they would have to leave when they were cured but never finding the heart to turn them out.

In return, he gave them his custom. He could not really afford to patronise cafés, however third-rate their quality and competitive their rates, but it was necessary to remain a customer, not to slip down to being a beggar. Baumgartner was not as unconscious as one might think of the dividing line. Planting himself heavily at the table and grasping the glass of thick, milky tea that had been set before him by the waiter's wet and dripping hand, he made himself play the role of customer. It would not do to smile and thank the waiter, he had to remember he was paying for what he got, remind them also that he would pay. In that comfortable knowledge he could raise his head after the first gulp and look across to the counter where, behind glass cases containing livid yellow queen cakes with pink icing and plates of fried salted savouries, Farrokh stood swatting flies. Over his head the tinsel garland he had hung around the tinted portrait of his god Zoroaster stirred and twinkled like a ring of bluebottles in the shadows. It was almost

impossible to read the faded sign he had hung beneath it: TRUST
IN GOD, or the handwritten label attached to the sign: *Terms
Strictly Cash.*

'Mmm.' Baumgartner tried to show his appreciation of the
hot, the thick, the suffocatingly sweet tea. He tried to think of
some repartee he might have with the dour Farrokh. There
was a time when he had enjoyed every opportunity to talk,
even to strangers, particularly to strangers since all acquaintance with them, however quick, however warm, had to be
fleeting, leaving him to go on alone. Now the habits of a
hermit were growing upon him like some crustaceous
effluent; it required an effort, an almost physical effort, to
crack it, to break through to the liquidity and flow and shift
and kinesis of language. Crustaceous – crab – ungainly
turtle: that was how he thought of himself, that was how
he saw himself – an old turtle trudging through dusty Indian
soil.

On this morning he was still struggling to find some item of
news that he might discuss with Farrokh – for Farrokh read a
Gujarati newspaper spread on the counter before him with
ferocious attention and could always be roused by mentioning
the name of a politician or referring to any political situation,
being at heart a suppressed and thwarted leader of men like
every other Indian he had ever met – when Farrokh folded up
the grease-yellowed paper, leant across with his elbows on it,
between the case with the sponge cakes and the case with the
fried samosas, and jerked his unshaven chin gloomily in the
direction of the far end of the room. 'D'you see that one there?'
he asked conspiratorially. 'He was here last night, we had to
turn him out when we closed, then found him in the doorway
when we opened up this morning. Back he is here, and I don't
know what to do with him – throw him out?' He made the
appropriate gestures with his powerful arms and no one could
have mistaken his intention.

Baumgartner could not twist his neck any longer; it had
long ago become set; he had to turn himself right around on
the small swivel of the tin chair and look into the dark corner at

which Farrokh so balefully glared. There he could make out nothing at first but what seemed like a bag of pale fur on the table; it might have been a cat. He found himself giving an involuntary twitch that started in his neck and ran down his shoulder and through his arm, making his hand turn over on the table in a flutter of excitement: could Farrokh have found him a cat, a homeless one? In his amazement he opened his small, watery eyes wide to take in its condition, and made out two solid baked brick-red arms of human flesh that lay on either side of it, protectively. It was only another human being, another – but here Baumgartner pulled himself together: it was too easy to use the coarse language everyone else used these days, to be uncharitable. And it might be a fellow countryman, although of another generation, for the head, covered with such a mass of blond curls, surely was youthful. Nordic possibly, it was so pale – if not Teutonic. It lay helplessly on the table-top, like something carelessly left behind, the arms that sprawled about it sunburnt to a raw, meaty red on which the bracelets he wore seemed incongruous in their delicacy, their femininity. Angel-child, raw meaty man, helpless lass – he was all three. That was how young men were now, Baumgartner knew – they saw no difference between what was considered masculine or feminine, and, as for Baumgartner himself, he was too old for it to matter.

Having taken in all the details he could gather, and failed to add them together into a known quantity, he turned back to Farrokh for further information. To his surprise, Farrokh abandoned the familiar weapon of the newspaper and the safe barrier of the counter and came out from behind it, tying up his pyjama strings under the long loose white vest he wore, and sat down on a chair at Baumgartner's table, a rare act of confidence. Clearly he was under some pressure that made him behave so uncharacteristically since Farrokh, for all his squalor and sourness, was also a dignified man who made much of wearing the sacred thread, of reading the scriptures and remaining aloof from all those of an inferior race, to him a mass of *mleccha*. For all the kindness shown him, Baumgartner had always felt he belonged to the latter.

Today he chose to display a different persona to the bemused Baumgartner. Touching him on the shoulder with an un-accustomed familiarity, pressing his thick white fingertips into Baumgartner's unresisting shoulder, he lisped, 'You – you and I, we are of a different age. Not that one's –' letting go of Baumgartner's shoulder, he flipped his hand in the direction of the slumped young man with the utmost derision. 'He, he belongs to this new race – men who remain children, like pygmies, dwarfs. Yes, I know they are very tall – I know they are growing bigger and bigger, these jungly heathens of today. Eat and sleep and lie about in the sun all day, they grow like turnips you leave in the ground – *too* big.' He made a ferocious noise through the many hairs in his nostrils. 'But what is there inside all that big, strong flesh and bones? Hanh?' he queried threateningly. 'Anything there? No? You are right. Nothing. Empty. Hollow. Hah!'

His enormous, thick, white hand plucked another gesture out of the air above Baumgartner's head. It commanded the waiter in the kitchen door to bring more tea for Baumgartner, for all that Baumgartner weakly protested, uneasy at the thought of paying for more tea than he wanted. 'To you – I am ready to give more tea,' Farrokh assured him, plucking at the vest on his chest as if offering that as well, with all its holes and stains, magnanimously. 'But for *that* one – why should I bend my back, dirty my hands? Hah? What for? For a kick from his boot – the boot in which he climbed Himalaya, I suppose. Already he has kicked his parents in the face, I think – rich parents, giving their son motor bike, motor car, watch, money, ticket to India, everything. Then what do they get? Boot in the face, goodbye and get off. Hah? That is how they come – to Afghanistan, to Nepal, to India. Tell their parents they don't want job, they don't want work. Tell them big big lies about Hindu gods, say they love Buddha, say they want to visit temples, live in ashrams. Yes, they visit temples and live in ashrams alright,' Farrokh sneered, 'but do they look at Buddha – or at Rama, or Krishna or any other god? I know what they do. *You* know what they do, Bommgarter *sahib*? Get drugs in these ashrams, drugs from those pundits and other people like them. *That* is why they come to India, and Nepal, and Afghanistan. I say let them take drugs – let them kill themselves – why not? I care? I just call police and tell them remove them, throw them into gaol, into city morgue. But what I don't like, Bommgarter *sahib*, is how they come to India, spoil Bombay, spoil Goa, spoil holy temples, spoil my restaurant. Why for? Have we invited them? No! Then why they come? And what do they give in return, hah? Do they pay my bill? No. When Rashid goes to them with the bill, then they pull out pockets, show the big holes, say, "No money, no pay." Just like that.' Farrokh slapped the table with his hand, making Baumgartner draw back. 'Just like that. And what you can do? Call police because boy has not paid bill for two rupees? No, you have to forget. Then they go to shop – I have seen them myself, picking up bread, picking up bananas, saying, "I am hungry, no money, my mummy-daddy no send money, please give me," and you know what kind of people we are in India, Bommgarter *sahib*, can we refuse food to anybody?' Baumgartner obediently shook his head, thinking of his plastic bag with shame, with a pang. But Farrokh was not referring to him at all, he was going along in the full flood of his indignant rhetoric. 'All the time we are giving, giving – to bull walking in the street like a lord every morning, to the beggar, to the leper, to the fakir who comes to my restaurant with tin can and marigold garland and snake round his neck so I give, give him money to go away and not trouble my customers. To all – give, give. My religion says: give, give. *Yes*, but that is enough. Why must I give to rich, bad children from England, from America? Is it we who must give them or their own people, their mummies and daddies, rich-rich uncle-aunties in *foren*?'

Farrokh was so incensed that his hand kept slapping the marble table-top again and again, smacking it as he might smack the cheek of an offender. Bubbles of spit grew on his moist red underlip and were caught in the bush of his moustache from which they fell in drops. Baumgartner looked from them to the hand on the table, slapping and slapping, till his own cheek felt worn and numbed.

'Kick them all out, kick them over the sea, I say – hanh? But how? They have no money for ticket, they say. They come here very grand – tickets, rucksacks, trekking boots, everything. Then everything goes – in Afghanistan, in Nepal already it starts to go, so they can buy hashish, buy *ganja*, all those powders they have to take like babies take milk. So when they come here nothing is left – rucksack empty, feet bare. What to do? Bommgarter *sahib*, what to do?'

As requested, Baumgartner shook his head silently.

'Go to Goa, that is what,' Farrokh bawled violently, leaning forward as if to throw Baumgartner backwards. Forced to raise his hand and wipe his face of flying spit bubbles, Baumgartner pretended to be smoothing down his hair instead, politely. 'Goa they all hear about, you can be sure. Golden sand, palm trees, cheap *feni* to drink, music on the beach, dancing naked – you know what goes on there?'

No, Baumgartner indicated.

'No, I also not. Such things were not in my day. I only knew school, shop, work, wife, children – that is my life. But these – these baby-men who come now from America, from England, they know another kind of life, Bommgarter *sahib*, they have other life. Music they have to have, hashish they have to have, women they have to have – not wife, not like my wife, but *women*. And all in Goa they can get, under coconut tree, under moon and star. So there they go. Pay fisherman ten rupees to build hut with coconut palm leaf. Crawl in with woman, with hashish, not come out for two day, three day, five day even.' A note of envy had entered Farrokh's voice. It slowed, came to a standstill, exhausting itself in a sigh. His chin sank down into the mat of black hair on his chest. 'Such a life,' he sighed, and Baumgartner felt that regret had overtaken the censure in his tone. Perhaps he could now excuse himself and slip away?

But Farrokh clenched his hands, knitted together the fingers on which small hairs grew in tufts, and roared, 'How long it go on, hanh? How long? Soon they need money. Go to post office. Has letter come from my dear mummy, my darling daddy? No? Must have, please look, look again, they must send! No, no letter, no money. Then they begin to scream – shout filthy language, abuse – begin to cry, sit in post office and howl like babies. Friends come, take them away, give them hashish. Next day, again post office, again: My money come? No? Look again, you pig, you swine, you Indian ass, they shout, my money must come, my daddy will send, he love me, my mummy love me. But no letter – Monday, Tuesday, Wednesday, no letter. So then they go to Anjuna beach, sell rucksack, sell watch, sell everything. Just like fisherwomen,' Farrokh laughed with contempt, 'fisher-women selling prawn, pomfret, in basket, on head. Then they have little money, buy ticket for Bombay, come here, say they will buy ticket and go home. But how? How to get money in Bombay, Bommgarter *sahib*? You know?'

Baumgartner licked his lips, trying to smile, wishing Farrokh's diatribe did not have these personal references.

'You don't know,' Farrokh said, with satisfaction, as if he had always suspected Baumgartner of such basic ignorance. 'No, and he also not know. Then – then,' he went on, his voice picking up power, 'they begin *stealing*. Yes, pickpocket in cinema house, pickpocket in market. Burglary in old people's home. In shops. Even killing, even murdering. Police tell me – I know many police – they tell me how much murder is going on in Bombay. No longer black man killing white man for money, Bommgarter *sahib*, it is now white man killing and robbing black man. And white man killing white man too.' He glared into Baumgartner's face with ugly triumph, defying him to challenge his claim.

Baumgartner could not look into Farrokh's face any more. He looked down at his own feet, shuffled them uneasily. He had no intention of standing up for the white man's reputation here in Farrokh's café while he had his morning tea and his cats got their food, none whatsoever. It embarrassed him that any-one should think he ought to or would try to protect the white man.

Farrokh's voice dropped to the level of reasonableness. 'So when they come here, to my Café de Paris, do you think I will say welcome, welcome, *sahib*, lord, master, come and do me the honour of eating in my café? Let me give you tea, cake, omelette, what you want. Not Farrokh Cama,' he shook his head and beamed at the strength of his moral stand, his ability to withstand moral rot. 'I, Farrokh Cama, go tell my waiters, tell Rashid and Domingo, no cake, no tea, no omelette. Push them out. Out, into the gutter. Tell them, go and beg in the market-place, go live like lepers in the street, but not come to Café de Paris please.'

Having turned out the foreign scum, at least verbally, at least in his imagination, Farrokh sat in silence for a while, seemingly satisfied. But then he began to drum those flat, thickened fingertips on the table in impatience, with the sound of large flies drumming on a windowpane. 'Not always listening to me, Domingo and Rashid,' he sighed. 'So when I come in this morning – little bit late, last night big party for my sister's grandson, big Navjote party in Parsee gymkhana, so little bit late today – I find Café de Paris already open, Rashid and Domingo cleaning, sweeping, washing – and that fellow sitting there.' He glared over Baumgartner's shoulder into the far dark corner. 'Just sitting, sleeping. I think, let him rest, I will do my accounts, have my cake and omelette, read my paper. But still the boy is sleeping. No waking. What is matter? Is he sick? No. I know what is matter, Bommgarter *sahib*. He – is – DRUG – ADDICT!' Farrokh hissed into Baumgartner's ear, rolling up his fists as if to crush the life out of such a worm.

An involuntary sound came from Baumgartner's mouth – of anger, of alarm, of commiseration – he allowed Farrokh to interpret it as he liked. He felt nothing for either Farrokh's dilemma or the boy's, only that he was pressed between the two, against his will, miserably.

At that moment another customer came in. Fortunately a known, old one, and a Parsi as well. As Baumgartner hoped, Farrokh rose to his feet, pulled up the loose pyjamas and shuffled towards his friend to whom he could unburden himself in the ease and expansiveness of his own language.

'Kem cho, Farrokhbhai?' 'Kem cho, Pesi, Kem cho?' Baumgartner heard the delighted greetings under cover of which he could at last rise and flee. He stopped long enough to place some coins beside his glass, glance into the murky corner at the pile of flesh and fur still carelessly spread in a crumpled heap – a furred carcass before it disintegrated – and then made his escape.

Escape – a funny word to use of the Colaba streets, he smiled to himself, rubbing one ear as if Farrokh's talk had made it sore. How did one escape, caught in the traffic like a fish in a net teeming with a million other fish? So much naked skin, oiled and slithering with perspiration, the piscine bulge and stare of so many eyes – he made his way, thinking tiredly how familiar it all was, how he scarcely noticed any of it, merely glanced to see if everything was as it had always been: the juice-*wallah* at the corner, down the pavement from Farrokh's café, dressed in a piece of checked cotton round his waist and a white singlet, feeding sweet limes into a mincing machine and pouring into a red glass jug the frothing liquid in which seeds rose like bubbles, then scraping up and throwing handfuls of pith and peel into the plastic bucket at his feet, all his movements co-ordinated and regular for all their casual carelessness; then the shops on the Causeway, most of them hung with bolts of cascading cloth, nylon and silk and georgette and cotton that smelt of mills, of chemicals, of everything man-made; the cheap, ready-made garments spread on the pavements for display, just out of reach of the feet that shuffled past hurriedly; the shoe and sandal stalls, desultorily flicked at with dusters by gloomy salesmen, the fruit stalls and the snack stalls decorated with red chillies, yellow lemons and lilac onion-rings. There was the bird-man who always positioned his cages of rose-ringed parakeets, Himalayan talking mynahs and dotted munia birds that had been cunningly brightened up in buckets of scarlet dye outside the jewellery stores that were frequented by Arabs, for they loved birds too, and Baumgartner had often stood beside him, watching a man in a *burnoose* or a woman in a *chador* choosing from amongst the twittering cages while the bird-man sweated profusely in anticipation of gold bars and lavish cheques. There was a goldfish man too but the fish that floated in his globes of water were of paper and only desired by spoilt children. Also the fortune-teller who hoped someone would have the time of day to stop for a consultation but erred in coming out so early, at a time when people were still hurrying to go to work and had not yet been thrown out of the government offices or the courts or banks to find solace and hope at the soothsayer's who spread his amulets, his 'lucky gems', his playing cards and other tools of his trade on a soiled red rag in the dust, waiting to welcome them; Baumgartner had never stopped and the man always had a malevolent look for him as he passed. Beggars hopped with agility in and out of the crowds, spotting the likeliest benefactors with their brilliant, darting eyes, stretching out a fingerless hand for a coin here and raising a ravaged face to the window of a stalled taxi there. How oriental, how exotic, Baumgartner used to think, smiling the abashed smile of one who did not belong, but today he felt only their weight upon him, the pressure of their bodies, their needs, demands, greed and hunger which left so little space for him, so narrow a passage through which to shoulder his way.

He had lived in this land for fifty years – or if not fifty then so nearly as to make no difference – and it no longer seemed fantastic and exotic; it was more utterly familiar now than any other landscape on earth. Yet the eyes of the people who passed by glanced at him who was still strange and unfamiliar to them, and all said: *Firanghi*, foreigner. For the Indian sun had not been good to his skin, it had not tanned and roasted him to the colour of a native. What was the colour of a native anyway? To begin with, everyone had seemed to him 'dark' but after all these years he separated them into boot-black like the juice-*wallah* with his oranges and pith and pulp, sallow yellow like Farrokh in his tubercular café, dusky chocolate, coffee-bean, tea-leaf, peanut-shell, leprous purple, shade merging into shade till all blurred into brown. He was none of these: his face blazed like an over-ripe tomato in the sun on which warts gathered like flies. His hair would not turn dark; it stood out around the bald centre like a white ruff, stained somewhat yellow. Even if he had used hair-dye and boot-polish, what could he have done about his eyes? It was not that they were blue – far from it; his mother, holding him on her knee and clapping hands in a game, had called them 'dark eyes, *dunkele Augen*', but Indians did not seem to think them so. Their faces sneered '*firanghi*, foreigner', however good-naturedly, however lacking in malice. Still, the word, the name struck coldly and he winced, hunching his shoulders and trying to avoid the contact he knew they hated because contact contaminated. Accepting – but not accepted; that was the story of his life, the one thread that ran through it all. In Germany he had been dark – his darkness had marked him the Jew, *der Jude*. In India he was fair – and that marked him the *firanghi*. In both lands, the unacceptable. Perhaps even where his cats were concerned, he was that – man, not feline, not theirs. He nodded thoughtfully; *ja*, the cats, they always knew. Still, it was a long time since he had felt so acutely aware of his outlandishness. It had come to him at some moments, in a drenching of terror that he could remember even now, but for a long time it had not been as it was today. Today he was disturbed in a new way. Strangely, his over-familiarity with the scene had served to wipe out its colours, its effects, leaving it dull, unworthy of notice. On it was imposed an image with a marvellous sharpness – the image of the boy, the sick boy slumped across the table. He did not know why. He was not concerned about him, why should he be? What did the boy mean to him with his filthy yellow curls and his ridiculous silver bracelet? There was no reason why he should be stirred by his fairness or his filth, or his misfortune. Let Farrokh boot him out on the street to make his way to the docks, to the railway station, to the consulate, or even go back to Goa for another round of hashish. If things were worse, let the police deal with him, or call an ambulance. Baumgartner would not involve himself with any of it, Baumgartner knew better than to do that. Then why should he continue to think of that fallen head, that helpless posture when there was so much to distract him, so much colour and sound and business and life to demand his attention?

Well, he knew. He might try to hurry away and rid himself of the fact but it was there: the boy was German, was he not? Yes, that was it. A German from Germany. He had sensed, he had *smelt* the German in him like a cat might smell another and know its history, its territory. Farrokh had told him nothing – to Farrokh they were just *firanghi*. No one had mentioned Germany – and had not needed to; one German could tell another always. In the camp, they had looked at each other covertly, and not only was German-ness stamped like a number on each, but further information as well – that one was a Jew, another Aryan. The looks they had exchanged had been the blades of knives slid quickly and quietly between the ribs, with the silence of guilt.

There had been no such exchange in the café, there was no longer a reason for such an exchange, Baumgartner reminded himself, hitting his thigh with his fist as he hurried. That fair hair, that peeled flesh and the flash on the wrist – it was a certain type that Baumgartner had escaped, forgotten. Then why had this boy to come after him, in lederhosen, in marching boots, striding over the mountains to the sound of the *Wandervogels Lied*? The *Lieder* and the campfire. The campfire and the beer. The beer and the yodelling. The yodelling and the marching. The marching and the shooting. The shooting and the killing. The killing and the killing and the killing.

Baumgartner was running. Beginning with a march, as

ordered, left–right, left–right–left, he broke and ran – or would have had he not been bumped into and shoved aside and hindered. The crowd opposed him, opposed his escape, but protected him too, covered up for him as well. He blundered through it, without seeing it any more. Colaba Causeway, its crowds and smells and noise, all drew back into a morning shadow. A grey and hazy sea rose and obliterated them, draining them of colour and substance. Out of the grey wash, other images emerged.

TWO

His father. When he walked, there was no obstacle, and no hesitation. He strode, he paraded – his head held high, his hat gleaming like the wing of an airborne beetle. His waistcoat gleamed too, now black, now green, like a bottle of dried ink, and the spats on his shoes were like the ears of a soft animal laid close against the leather. His walking-stick with the ivory knob tapped the Berlin streets with authority – pleasantly, light-heartedly on a Sunday afternoon, but still with authority. Hugo tried to ally himself with that by touching the signet ring on his father's finger as he allowed his hand to be rolled into a round moist ball like a half-eaten roll, and held – again lightly but with authority. He tried to match his steps to his father's, and did not even notice as they passed the familiar landmarks of their street – the apothecary's bow-shaped window in which sat a paste-pink denture and a jar of blue dentifrice; the bakery with its baskets of croissants and rolls dusted with salt or with poppyseeds, the tea cakes decorated with pieces of walnut or of orange; the dwarf in the white raincoat and the dark glasses who mumbled, '*Zigarren, Zigaretten*', in a monotonous undertone beside the newspaper kiosk which had buckets of flowers on its floor – and went further and further out of their own territory.

He realised they were out of it when they sat on a tram, when he heard the bell ping, the wheels slither, and felt himself reeling through the Sunday streets, as empty as the ocean. At

Roseneck the light turned yellow, turned green. It was as thin as beer, then thick as honey. 'Hurrah', he shouted – that was what little boys shouted, he knew – as he broke away from his father's hold and ran down the sandy path under the birch trees. It was the foliage on the birches, and their bark that affected the light so botanically – but Hugo did not notice; his feet in the square brown boots were pounding the sand now that he knew where his father was taking him. It could only be on fine Sundays – on such a Sunday – that they would sit at one of the wooden tables outside the café, at some distance from the band which played, invisibly, the medley of Strauss waltzes that trickled through the leaves on to their table like pollen sifting through the sunlight, like honey circulating through the hive. Then the waiter brought a mug of hot chocolate for Hugo, flakes of chocolate flecking the cream that floated like an island on its dark surface, and for his father a mug of beer. Smiling at the disbelieving look in his eyes, the hesitation that held his upper lip rigid, his father slid the mug of beer towards him. 'No one's looking,' he said with a wink, 'quick now', and Hugo climbed on to his knees – they were fat and the edge of the bench made two welts across them – and bent over the pewter mug to draw the froth in through his lips. It was cold, bitter, smelt of wet straw and tasted of steel. Its gleaming metal knife cut across his tongue and made him gasp and withdraw, froth-moustached, to make his father laugh as he never laughed at home. He seemed to need to come away in order to laugh out loud – coarsely, perhaps – to push his hat back from his forehead and turn terracotta with laughter. Hugo was a little frightened by its loudness, its coarseness, and sat back, subdued, first licking the froth off his lips and then turning to the hot chocolate, dipping into and sipping its richness, its sweetness as secretly, as privately as a mouse. He had been made a fool of, he had been the butt, but it had turned out well and the reward was sweet.

It was late when they walked back towards the tram-stop, and even his father's feet were slow and unsure in the shadows of the pines that lay like long strips of felt on the sandy path. Twilight stood blue between the tree trunks, and around the café the trees were already wearing garlands of coloured lights although night was still far away – 'Of course you will be home by bedtime, you booby,' his father said contemptuously – and the band was swirling through *Die Fledermaus* and *The Merry Widow* in reckless, intoxicated circles. His father had still not done with laughter but, to top it off, suddenly removed his hat from his head and, snatching the cap off Hugo's, exchanged their headgear so that Hugo's small head almost vanished, turning him into a headless gnome while his little cap flew up and perched like a saucer between his father's scarlet jug-ears, as he tittered with mirth.

> *'Hopp, hopp, hopp,*
> *Pferdchen lauf galopp'*

sang his father irrepressibly and his knees jumped up and outwards to reproduce the sound in action. Hugo was awed by so much of the ridiculous and when passers-by, a gentleman with a lady on each arm, hurrying, almost running towards the music and the dance, burst into shrieks and bellows of laughter, turning again and again to look at the comic pair, Hugo was glad for the hat tilting over his eyes and concealing his face from the brassy world.

> *'Über Stock und über Steine,*
> *Aber brich dir nicht die Beine!*
> *Hopp, hopp, hopp,*
> *Pferdchen lauf galopp.'*

When they walked down their own street, there was only decorum in his father's behaviour. Pride, ownership, status, yes, but above all decorum. He held his arm stiffly in a triangle at his side for his wife to hold with the lightest touch of a gloved hand, her feet whispering along in shoes like two grey velvet mice, and when they stopped at the flower stall to buy her a bunch of Parma violets – violets were said to be 'her' flowers, Hugo did not know why but accepted the undeniable – she would protest in her lowest murmur, then smile the same smile weekly as she pinned them to the lapel of her cape. That, too, was one of her distinctive marks – that she did not wear a coat but that sweeping, enfolding black cape – in winter with a length of fur wrapped at the neck. Like the bunch of violets, they were as much 'her' as the signature that she wrote in long, spidery flourishes with the steel nib of her long green lacquered pen.

At home, Hugo skittered back and forth between the apartment and his father's showroom, the staircase in between a place of perilous choice, the no man's land where he might be summoned and drawn by either. Downstairs there was the large, open, unnerving space of the showroom in which elegantly languorous *chaises-longues* in carved mahogany or consoles in blonde wood with gilded scrolls basked in the light from the floor-to-ceiling windows, while the more sober, less opulent pieces of furniture stood quietly along the walls as if biding their time. Here his father was ruler, moving gracefully from one piece to another with the pride of a connoisseur or artist – putting out his hand to smooth the satined surface of a sofa here, spreading out his fingers and pressing them into a pouffe of buttoned velvet there. As clamorous of attention as the 'Empire suites' and the 'boudoir sets' that occupied the floor space were the mirrors that hung on the walls in their gilded rococo frames and the lamps shaded with mosaics of glass, cut and patterned. Mystifying and alarming were the three-piece mirrors that sat on the dressing tables and showed you unfamiliar aspects of your head, turning you into a stranger before your own eyes as you slowly rotated to find the recognisable.

The opulence of the interior made Hugo hesitate on the stairs, hug the newel post and fear to descend. From between the banisters he watched his father's employees polish and dust and shift according to his father's orders, or carry out pieces into the delivery vans that waited at the curb, events that made his father fold his hands behind his back and hum with a special air of prosperity and satisfaction – like a bee that has stored much honey, Hugo thought.

His mother did not like him to watch these commercial transactions. Whenever there was such a sale or delivery going on, she would send Berthe out on the landing to call him. He thought it was because she feared the delivery men in their large, navy blue, wool coats as he too, a little, feared them. He went up with a mixture of relief and reluctance that gave him a stoic air.

'Upstairs' was her realm even if invaded and occupied to a large degree by his father's merchandise – or 'creations', he corrected himself – so that the objects could be divided, even by a child, into 'his' belongings and 'hers'. Obviously the ashtray in the form of a Prussian helmet and the onyx case that held cigarettes were 'his' and so of course was the barometer shaped like a pistol that hung on the wall between the two french windows, and less obviously the great mirror in its scrolled and convoluted gilt frame that held the whole room slightly tilted on its calm and shining surface. The table lamps with their domes of orange silk, fringed, bobbled and tasselled, that susurrated as one walked past, the shelves of leather-bound volumes of Goethe, Schiller and Heine – his or hers? The engraving of Rembrandt's self-portrait on the green wall of the drawing-room might have been chosen by his father but Hugo was certain that of Dürer's hands that hung in their prayerful attitude, grey and blue, in the arch formed by the two swathes of silk that hung over their brass bedstead in the bedroom could only be hers, his mother's. He mused often on how, when one came down to it, 'her' objects were actually few but for Hugo they were the ones that contained a living quality that prevented the rooms from becoming showrooms: the lamps and the books could be brought to life by her touch, just like 'her' piano at which she sat and played on Sunday evenings when they had returned from Roseneck and she from visiting her friends in Grüne-wald. And the rubber tree in its pot, military as it was in its erectness and the manner in which it put one leaf to the left, then one to the right, all the way up to its wick of shocking, naked pink, became hers because she tended it, while the more graceful and wayward tendrils of ivy in baskets above the window were quite naturally and obviously hers.

Hugo, sitting on the window-seat under them, did not know what made him bite his knee, lifted up to prop his chin, and give a shiver as if he had bitten on a stone when she sang. The cause lay somewhere within the precarious sweetness of her thin voice singing:

> *'Kommt ein Vogel geflogen,*
> *Setzt sich nieder mein Fuss,*
> *hat ein Brieflein im Schnabel,*
> *von der Mutter ein Gruss.'*

Not always was it like spun sugar, like sugar being drawn out of him, in glossy threads. When he brought home the hedgehog in his pocket, having found it struggling through the rank grass and soiled newspaper on a roadside verge, it had become a lament. Ach, *du kleiner Dummkopf,* you little silly, how could you take it away from its poor *Mutti?* And what are we to do with it? How can we keep the smelly thing in Berthe's beautifully cleaned house? Who will clean, who will feed – ? I, I, I, he howled, drumming his heels on the shining parquet floor and beating his chest like a wild man of the jungles. And he did. With a dropper, steaming with warm milk, he fed and fed the infant hedgehog in its cradle of cottonwool inside a matchbox till it swelled like a football being pumped with air. Its very quills filled with milk. Milk was oozing out of the limp, unprotesting bag of flesh when Berthe proclaimed it dead, killed by overfeeding. Then all the sweetness in the air had shattered into splinters of glass. Everyone had screamed; in the midst of all the screams, the hedgehog disappeared – into the dustbin? Out of the window? Hugo howled and howled but they would not tell him. His mother only scolded and scolded: 'See what you did, *du kleiner Affe,* killed Mama Hedgehog's baby. So silly, *so ungehorsam . . .'*

And Hugo bit the muddy flesh of his knee to keep from crying out when she sang, with such ineffable sweetness,

'Lieber Vogel, flieg weiter,
Nimm ein Gruss mit, einer Kuss,
Denn ich kann dich nicht begleiten,
Weil ich hierbleiben muss.'

Yes, that was what was wrong, he shivered – the sweetness always ended in a quaver. It drew together and produced a teardrop. The teardrop hung suspended, glinting in the light from the window, and Hugo watched, mesmerised, waiting for it to explode and drop. Tear-drop, pear-drop. Silver-light, gold-flesh. And then – the fall.

'Hugo, *Liebling*, here is a little money; will you run and buy a pat of butter for our supper.'

He pushed out his lower lip in ready protest: why could he not stay with her, why could Berthe not go instead? Because Berthe had left – on what was said to be her annual holiday in the Harz from where she came but from where she had not returned. (In the way in which his mother's lips became tight and pale when he questioned her, he sensed that she knew more about the disappearance than she said.) So he reluctantly slid off the window-seat, the warm, perspiring backs of his knees making a rude sound as they came unstuck from the wood, held out his hand, '*Gib mir dein kleines Pfötchen*', for the money, and dawdled down the stairs into the street, reluctant even when she laughed over the banister, 'And buy yourself a little chocolate with the change to make the errand sweeter.'

The street was not the sunlit, delicate, precious scene it had seemed when framed by their window upstairs. Coming loose from the window-frame, it had crashed two storeys into darkness. Down between the shut houses with their chocolate and liver-coloured façades, it was already twilight. The only figures to be seen on it were somehow threatening – the collars of their overcoats turned up and caps pulled down low over their eyes as if they wished to be faceless; a man who abruptly withdrew into the doorway of a closed warehouse, ostensibly to open a newspaper out of the wind but looking steadily over the top at Hugo; a woman with a raddled puce face who walked by without noticing him but muttering to herself crazily while waving invisible flies from her mouth . . . how was it that Hugo never saw such people when he was out walking with his father or hand-in-hand with Berthe, by daylight? He kept his eyes on the shop windows as he passed them, hoping to draw comfort from the familiarity of the objects displayed season after season, but found them lacking in colour and interest – it might have been a trick of the light but they all seemed covered by a layer of dust. The bared fangs of the denture, so pink and white, seemed fierce rather than comic now, and the mouth-wash disgusting with the line of sediment rimming the jar in which it had stood for so long; at the tobacconist, the row of pipes were held choked and throttled by a wooden stand like a vice between the tins of tobacco that smelt musty and damp even through the pane of yellow glass; the newspaper kiosk had no flowers today, for some reason.

Hugo was hurrying faster than he knew, the coins slipping inside his fist wet with perspiration, and as he rushed into the grocer's shop he bumped into a woman coming out with an armful of parcels from which the top of a celery and the neck of a goose protruded grotesquely. '*Kannst nicht sehen?* Can't you see?' she scolded as Hugo disentangled himself from the swampy odour of her damp loden coat and edged past the two stands loaded with boiled sweets to the counter where he handed over the money entrusted to him. 'Two hundred grammes of butter, please,' he managed to croak, but could think of no further qualifications when the grocer demanded, 'White or yellow? Salty or unsalted?' He stood silent, shamed, till the man finally said, 'You are Frau Baumgartner's little boy? Ah then, I know,' and sighed as he shifted his pink and porcine bulk to the stand where he kept butter, cream and eggs. He wore woollen socks that were unravelling around the pressed-down heels of his slippers and gave off an odour very like eggs.

When Hugo came out into the street with the brown paper

parcel, already disagreeably greasy in his hands, it had grown darker, and the darkness continued to congeal as he made his way back, heaving for breath as if against obstacles although he could not have said what they were. Strangely, the young man with the *Welt am Abend* newspaper was still hiding in the doorway, still looking furtively over the top. And worse, the madwoman who imagined flies had not disappeared but instead collapsed on a bench under a plane tree where she sat with her legs so wide apart that she could only mean Hugo to see her torn and ragged undergarments. She let out a sudden shriek as he walked past that could have been a curse, he could not tell. The lamps were lit to look like thumbprints of butter on the blackness but threw no light, only created shadows.

By the time he returned to No. 56, he was so unnerved that he did not notice the state of the butter in his hand which had become one with the scrap of brown paper. He was clutching at its oily ooze as if it provided some kind of security. And the worst was to come – the staircase, from the hall to their apartment over the showroom. In the dark, it was no longer a place to linger; there was no light and nothing to watch. There was a switch by the door, placed conveniently for him to switch on so that the bulb over the landing in its Chinese hat of pink china lit up but he knew its habit of going out before he could reach his own door, no matter how fast he pounded up the stairs. He knew it always went out when there were still half a dozen steps to the landing, and then he would have to grope his way up that last flight to his apartment door.

This evening it went out so soon and so abruptly that Hugo was convinced of its malevolence, of its connivance with some evil conspirator who sat by some hidden spyhole on the staircase and watched. He knew about those men who lurked in the shadows, waiting for the right moment to fling the noose, whip out the knife, bring down the cosh . . . he had even seen the man waiting – much further down the road, with his newspaper, but he could have followed Hugo – Hugo never turned to look back over his shoulder – or even overtaken him in the dark. Now he would be waiting at his own door, barring his entry into safety, protection and light. Waiting for Hugo. Hugo knew he was waiting – and lunged forward with a howl, throwing himself at the door and feeling his hands close not upon its solid brass knob but instead on something soft, warm, yielding. Instantly, his hands recoiled – and the object loomed up at him, pale, round, loose, dead; there had been no feel of life at his fingertips, the face was as flabby and relaxed as in death, when rot has set in.

At last a sound emerged from Hugo's open mouth – like a train emerging from a tunnel, it roared and shrieked into the open. The door flew open, a shaft of yellow light slanted through in which his mother stood, thunderstruck, and the cloth bag that hung on the door knob for the baker to fill with rolls in the morning swung hilariously from side to side.

How she laughed when she understood what had happened, how she twittered and chuckled. She was still chuckling when she undressed him for bed that night, unbuttoning the viyella vest from the viyella underpants with her quick, cold fingers. 'And the butter!' she exclaimed again. 'And the coins rolling down the stairs – pit, pit, pit! Did not even buy himself a bar of chocolate with the change, my little hero. Your tongue lost its taste for sweets in the dark, did it?'

> '*O du lieber Augustin,*
> *alles ist hin!*
> *Geld ist weg,*
> *Beutel ist weg,*
> *Augustin liegt auch im Dreck,*
> *O du lieber Augustin,*
> *alles ist hin!*'

Yet she was there holding the traditional cone of bonbons, wrapped in gold foil and decorated with rustling silver streamers, at the door of his school at the end of the first day. He had been so afraid she would not be. All the other children had talked of the bonbons their parents had promised to bring to school – already ordered, already bought, they said ecstatically – and he had stood silent, so consumed by fear that she would not meet him with a similar prize that he could not concentrate on building blue blocks into one tower and red ones into another or listen to the story about the wolf and the seven little kids told by the long-toothed teacher whose hair kept escaping from its tortoiseshell clasp and dangling beside her ear like a misplaced tail. So he had not run out after the others, but stayed to the last and sidled out, hoping the others had all left before he came out to face his ignominy. Then there she was, with violets pinned to her new blouse, holding out to him a gilt cone with silver streamers, smiling the smile she smiled for no one but him. '*Mein kleines Häschen*,' she said, 'Here's my little rabbit'. Before she could shame him with an embrace, he had snatched the cone out of her hand in jubilation and held it up for the others to see. But there was no one, the other children were vanishing down the street in a flood of chocolate and toffee, licking and smacking their lips and oozing with spittle. No one saw his triumph.

His mouth full of toffee, his tongue blamed his mother. 'You came so late,' and then, 'You don't look like everyone else's mother,' he complained. 'Why don't you look like the other mothers?'

Left alone with her, left behind by his father, he kicked at her with savagery, pummelled her chest with his fists, furiously. He blamed her, blamed her entirely. When she put her arms around him and tried to draw him to her, it was that encirclement of soft, sweet-smelling arms that he blamed for his imprisonment in this flat, this house.

'I want to go with Papa!' he roared, drumming his heels on the floorboards. 'I want to see the *horses*,' and struck at her with his fists, 'not *you*.'

'I know, I know, I know,' she murmured, trying to make her voice soothe him since her touch could not.

'You don't!' he shouted. 'You *don't* know!'

So she was quiet.

The whole flat filled with quiet like a well in which they sat drowning.

That was the end of his pleading, his demanding. It would not have come about if Herr Pfuehl had not come the evening before, if Hugo had not heard them make plans to go to the races together. He would not have known what they were, but he heard them speak the horses' names: Summer Lightning, Tutankhamen, Turkish Delight, Carolina, Prince de Galles, Puerto Rico, Sweet Sensation . . . The names like flags, or streamers, the cigars, the laughter, the tinge of red coming out on his father's face, the gleaming shoe tapping, more laughter, more names – Abyssinia, Trocadero, Indian Chief, Marzipan . . . and Hugo was gripping his father's knees, staring at his father's face, saying, 'Take me, Papa, *take me.*'

His father's knee gave a twitch, his kneecap moved out of Hugo's grasp. 'Mutti,' he called, 'take the child away, why is he still up?'

'But Papa, I want to go,' he lunged again before being carried away. He brooded that night, planning his plans under the tent of his quilt, certain the night would yield and tomorrow would come, with horses. How could it not when he had performed all the magic he knew? Held his left thumb in his right hand, his right toe in his left hand, said, 'Mick-muck-mo, Make-it-so,' even knelt by his bed and said a prayer as he had seen the Christian children in school pray to '*Lieber* Jesus'?

When his father left the apartment, dressed for the races, in his hat and with his ivory-topped cane, Hugo could not believe. For a long time, his mouth remained open, and he watched the door, certain it would open again and his father would come to fetch him. How could he not be taken to share a treat? The minutes passed, the footsteps on the stairs receded till they could not be heard any more. The door slammed. Then Hugo moved, with a roar. He ran to the window and beat on the glass as if to break it, so that his mother had to hold him away even if she were kicked and beaten.

'Hugo,' she said at last, kneeling there with her hands in her lap, 'Hugo, I have never been either.'
He looked at her with the hatred of one prisoner for another.
'*Hoppe, hoppe, Reiter,*
wenn er fällt, dann schreit er.
Fällt er in die Hecken,
fressen ihn die Schnecken,
fällt er in den Klee,
schreit er gleich: O weh . . .'

Another time, when triumph had come his way, he had not been able to accept. The school was holding its Christmas party. For days before, the class had cut out stars of silver paper, linked chains of pink crêpe paper, fashioned figures out of blonde straw and raffia, and watched Fräulein Klutke pin them to the tree on the dais. The night before the party, however, fairies had come with gifts, she informed them, and there were the unexpected presents hung from the branches of the fir tree in wrappings of red and yellow tissue paper. Now the children stood in rows beside the piano, threw back their heads and roared:
'*O Tannenbaum, O Tannenbaum,*
Wie grün sind deine Blätter!'
Then there were the buns, the mugs of cocoa to be downed, if the tight little muscle in the throat allowed such a passage. For Hugo's part, it did not; he held the bun in one hand, the mug of cocoa in the other, but his eyes and heart and mouth remained fixed on the tree glittering in its finery, the candle flames darting at the shiny surfaces, turning it to a thing of fire and stars fallen out of the sky. Most of all, they remained fixed on its topmost ornament – a great ball of red glass in which all the light gathered together and danced, tantalising him as nothing else ever had, this ball that was made of fire, that could not be played with, only regarded. He clutched his thumbs inside his fists, thinking that if he owned that red glass globe, then he was the owner of the whole world, like a magician.

Uneaten, undrunk, his treat had to be replaced on the table for now all the children were being ringed around the tree, and Fräulein was climbing on to a stool to unpin and hand out the gifts. 'Walter Loewe!' she called, holding out a bulky parcel from which a horse's head on a long stick looked at its new owner with a long-lashed wink, and then, 'Annelise Hauptmann!' So the children were called out one by one to receive the presents that their parents had sent in for them – though this neither Hugo knew nor his parents. He stood waiting to the end of the whole roll-call, locked into a terrible urgency to pass water, and now Fräulein was looking at him, the only one without a Christmas gift, and now she was reaching up to the top of the prickly fir tree, now she had her hands around the glass globe, quite delicately as if she too saw its extraordinary worth, now she was smiling directly at him and calling – yes, she called, 'Hugo Baumgartner', she did.

And Hugo could not move. Not one step. Not even his hands would stretch forwards. Instead, he locked them behind his back. Then, when the other children began to chant, 'Hugo, it's for you – it's yours, Hugo,' he hung his head and stared at his shoes, for nothing, nothing would persuade him that the twinkling glass globe was his. He knew that it was not – that Fräulein Klutke had made it up on seeing that there was no other gift for him. The other children began to push and shove him towards the waiting Fräulein but this brought him so close to tears that she was obliged to call out, 'Stop pushing him, children. If he doesn't want it, we shall find another child to take it. Who is the smallest? Elizabeth Klein?' and she handed it to her favourite.

Then the agony was over and he could collapse into the dark ditch of his shame. What was the shame? The sense that he did not belong to the picture-book world of the fir tree, the gifts and the celebration? But no one had said that. Was it just that he sensed he did not belong to the radiant, the triumphant of the world? A strange sensation, surely, for a child. He could not understand it himself, or explain it. It baffled him, and frightened him even – as if he realised that at that moment he had wilfully chosen to turn from the step up and taken the step down.

> *'Schlaf, Kindlein, schlaf!*
> *Da draussen gehn zwei Schaf!*
> *Ein schwarzes und ein weisses,*
> *und wenn das Kind nicht schlafen will,*
> *dann kommt das Schwarz und beisst es.*
> *Schlaf, Kindlein, Schlaf!'*

It would have been difficult to return to school after such an ignominious scene. Of course there were the Christmas holidays in between, when the children might have forgotten, but Hugo had not and that was what mattered.

Then, as it happened, he never returned to that school. In the new year, speaking to him with an artificial, brittle lightness of manner, his mother took him on the tram a long, long way into the city instead, on a grey, grizzling morning, with office-goers and shop and factory-workers hemming them in with folds of dark, damp wool, all the way to the other end of the city, he felt, and then delivered him up to what seemed a warehouse with no windows or lights, only a mass of squirming, frantic children and a teacher who had a face like curdled milk in a pan and was called Reb Benjamin; Hugo recoiled from his grease-lined collar and patched and odorous jacket; strange, large volumes lay open on his desk from which he read in a harsh and melodramatic tone in a language Hugo had never heard before. The boys who shared a wooden bench with Hugo spent the morning trying to shove him off so that he had to grip the edge of the seat to keep from falling off. '*Was ist los*, Baumgartner? What's the matter?' the teacher asked. 'Is it the bathroom you need already?' and the children grew pinched and blue in the face with laughter.

It was in this school for Jewish children, oddly enough, that Hugo first had a remark directed at his nose. When he went out into the yard where the mud was frozen and broke under his shoes, he heard around him a chant that came from all the children as they jumped, hopped and clapped their hands to keep warm: '*Baumgartner, Baum, hat ein Nase wie ein Daum!* Baumgartner's dumb, has a nose like a thumb!'

He fell to fingering it nervously, trying to discover the relation between his nose and his thumb, a habit that never left him.

When his mother, standing and waiting at the gate for him, asked him how it had been, he said nothing. He pushed out his lip, frowned and looked away. One morning in the school had taught him the tactics for surviving.

> '*Hänschen klein, geht allein,*
> *in die weite Welt hinein,*
> *Stock und Hut stehn ihm gut,*
> *ist ganz wohlgemut.*
> *Doch die Mutter weinet sehr,*
> *hat ja nun kein Hänschen mehr . . .*'

She woke him in the mornings, a grey shawl over her shoulders, switching on the harsh white electric light and making him wince. She brought him his shoes that she had polished because Berthe had not returned and not been replaced either. At night, his mother's gentle stories of the Red Rose and the White Rose lulled him to sleep too quickly, so that he woke a little later and missed Berthe's stories of war and violence that had kept his nights lively. She would have been able better to share his experiences at the new school, he felt. His mother was in any case too busy doing Berthe's work; he resented seeing her arms red with the soapwater in the tubs of washing, and he was distracted by seeing her leap up from the table to fetch dishes from the kitchen and carry them out. His father, too, frowned and fidgeted when she did that. 'Can't you sit through a meal?' he complained, and she threw him an exasperated look that said, as clearly as words, 'And who will serve us then?'

> '*Es tanzt ein Bi-ba-butzemann*
> *in unserem Haus herum, didum,*

es tanzt ein Bi-ba-butzemann
in unserem Haus herum.
Er rüttelt sich, er schüttelt sich,
er wirft sein Säckchen hinter sich,
es tanzt ein Bi-ba-butzemann
in unserem Haus herum.'

Perhaps because she could not cope with all the work, the apartment gradually lost its waxy gloss, its air of comfortable opulence. So many small economies combined to construct a shabbiness that one could not quite put one's finger on what was at fault – everything had lost, everything seemed diminished. When Hugo loudly sucked a stick of barley sugar he had bought on the way back from school no one objected – there was no dark expensive chocolate to give him instead. When he pulled out an old red woollen cap she had not allowed him to wear earlier, he found no one objected to it any longer, and was mystified – studied the loose knitting and the mothy texture to see what transformation had taken place to make it acceptable now.

Downstairs in the showroom all was not well either. Hugo was not aware but his father knew that the wealthy Jews who had patronised the place, buying whole suites of furniture when a daughter married or a son set up house, no longer were interested in anything so difficult to transport as furniture. They had put their money into moveable assets, or else emigrated – to England, to Holland, to Canada. As for the 'Aryans' they must have had their own shops and dealers to patronise, they did not come to Baumgartner's. The long yellow vans no longer lined up at the door for deliveries, and the delivery boys and the cart drivers vanished from Hugo's boyhood, taking with them the secret pleasures of terror and suspicion. There was no one to flick the dust out of the gilt scrolls around the mirrors or keep the table-tops of mahogany glowing. In Hugo's dreams, the brilliant mirrors tipped out their highly coloured and illuminated reflections like pools of water from unsteady basins, then slipped out of their frames and crashed. But on the floor there were no shards of glass, only soft heaps of dust, like cloth bags filled with baker's rolls, on which he trod warily for his father was angry if he wandered in with questions that he could not answer. He sat at his desk in the backroom, biting his moustache with anger. The telephone no longer rang.

Almost his only visitor was the timber merchant from Hamburg who had always supplied Herr Baumgartner with quality wood for his furniture. Once or twice he was brought up to supper. Hugo's mother would be pale with the effort to cover the table with dishes and lift off their lids to reveal meat and fish in gravy and sauces. The Gentleman from Hamburg, far from being impressed, wagged his finger at her and said, *'Nein, nein,* this is not the way to live any longer. We must learn to save, to be sparse, to prepare – hah? You understand? It is no longer easy to find customers for Herr Baumgartner's beautiful furniture, and let me tell you – it will not grow easier.' But he did not like Frau Baumgartner to look dismayed or frown with worry. When she did, he would spring up and go to the piano and say, 'Come, play for us. Let us have a song as in the old days. All might still go well.' How could she sing after that? She sat with her napkin pressed to her mouth, choking, and Hugo stared at them as though they were actors on a stage, he the uncomprehending spectator.

Yet they were not as poor as others were. Unlike the men who searched the dustbins for chicken bones and slept on benches under sheets of *Berliner Zeitung,* or the women who stood on the streets because there was nowhere else to go, their scent reeking of cheapness, the Baumgartners did not starve. Somehow Herr Baumgartner brought in money; sometimes from the racecourse to which he still went, whenever the Gentleman from Hamburg came and sometimes even without him – but without that debonair air of twirling his moustache or his ivory-topped cane – merely thoughtfully, worriedly or guiltily. Hugo no longer asked to accompany him; he did not like the looks their neighbours threw them when they left the house, and knew it would be worse on the racecourse; he wished his father did not go. He sat on the window-seat, watching, till he returned, and then left the room so as not to hear his parents' conversation.

'But Siegfried,' he once heard his mother whisper, 'in this we are not alone.'

'Who is there? Who is there?' his father asked dramatically, not whispering at all. He was opening and closing his fists as though to catch a fly.

His mother named them but, like flies, they seemed to escape and disappear. Her own parents had left years ago, her father to take up a chair in German in a university in a northern country. Hugo had known them on those brief visits his mother made to her home town, and thought them like two flakes of grey ash upon their hearth, weighed down by the weight of the books they read to him. They had a great fondness for reading aloud, Hugo none for listening. Once when he cried in protest, his grandmother rose, went to the kitchen and returned with a tomato. She held it out with a smiling certainty that a small boy could not but like a tomato. Her daughter, knowing better, smiled and took it from her hand, saying she would keep it for later. In the garden, tomatoes glistened like bubbles of rusty paint on the blackened stalks that held them up in the rain. At the *Shabbos* dinner, candles stood aslant in the pewter candlesticks and wax ran like a gutter on to the tablecloth. Hugo was pleased when he heard his father refuse to join his book-reading, prayer-saying parents-in-law in their provincial university in a distant country.

'What – you think they will have room for me?' he answered, pawing the ground as if to break through the boards and gallop off.

He did go, on a visit, to his own parents, still on their farm which he had fled as a boy, only to return and inform them that the times were bad there as well: the land was stripped, they were starving, eating roots now that the potatoes had gone; no wonder his sister Esther had left, with her husband, a horsedealer, for Paris where she was trying to get tickets for America. His mother, who had told Hugo about the churns of butter, the pans of milk – could not believe. 'And their hens, Siegfried? The eggs? The cows? The horses? And wheat?' and Hugo joined in by asking, 'Have they been robbed? Or was there a fire?' till his father shouted an order for silence.

> '*Eija, Popeija,*
> *was raschelt im Stroh?*
> *Die Gänse gehn barfuss*
> *und haben kein Schuh.*
> *Der Schuster hat Leder,*
> *kein Leisten dazu,*
> *drum gehen die lieben Gänschen*
> *und haben keine Schuh.*'

In the night the noises on the street were so hideous that Hugo stirred but only to slip deeper into his bed. He woke when his mother sank silently down at his bedside. 'Don't look,' she told him, 'don't get up', and he obediently pulled up his quilt, burrowed under its protection and breathed in the darkness. Next morning he saw the letters JUDE painted in red on the showroom window. His father was standing in the hall and staring out, immobile. He made no move to wipe it off. When Hugo spoke to him, he answered in a kind of hiss that frightened Hugo so much, he ran.

The next night the noise increased – glass splintered, crashed, slid all over the floor in slanting, shining heaps. Men lifted tables, commodes, *armoires, chaises-longues* and the mirrors off the walls: it sounded as if the house, the whole street were being evacuated. His father stood at the window upstairs and watched, cursing, but his mother held Hugo by his arm and would not let him go near. 'If they see you, they will stone you,' she warned, sternly enough to stall him. 'Hide, we must hide, Siegfried.' Hugo found himself shamefully willing to do so, even the broom cupboard seemed a haven on that night.

Herr Weiss from upstairs rang their doorbell. When they did not open the door, he called through the letter-box, 'It is only I, Weiss. Frau Baumgartner, have no fear. Will you not come up to us? My wife has sent me to fetch you, you will be safe with us.' Frau Baumgartner looked to Herr Baumgartner for a reply; he made none but stood at the window as if turned to salt.

The next day they came to take him away. It happened very quickly, very efficiently – the police car drew up at the curb, stilling its honking hooter, the stormtroopers in brown walked in, simply lifted Herr Baumgartner off his chair and carried him out; the hooting began again and the police car disappeared. Hugo might have been playing a game with his toy soldiers, marching them up, then marching them down. It was only that his father had disappeared that was not play, not accountable. For two weeks there was no news. All day Hugo waited in the flat while his mother ran from one police station to another to find him, or news of him, returning with her face and hands blue with cold. Hugo boiled water in the kettle so she could hold a mug with hot water in it. To warm her fingers. They did not speak, or look at each other.

Till he returned, a fortnight later, from Dachau. In that early year, it was still possible to leave Dachau. His mother ran to greet him with her arms thrown up in an abandon of relief, but his father turned away, he did not want her embrace, or Hugo's. He turned his back to them, shoulders hunched in his thin green jacket, and did not want to speak. He would say nothing about Dachau. When they came near him, he began to shiver – the shiver started in the back of his neck, making his head jerk like a hen's, and then ran down into his shoulders so that they shook. He had to go to bed and they pulled on quilt after quilt, trying to make him stop shivering. Even his face twitched on the pillow, pulled in every direction. Eventually he turned on to his side and stared at the wall. Now and then a remnant of that shiver made the quilts suddenly heave, subside.

The Gentleman from Hamburg came. He sat in the chair beside the Prussian helmet ashtray and the onyx cigarette-case that everyone knew was the father's chair. His right leg lifted over his left knee, he made expansive gestures as he explained it all to Frau Baumgartner, smoothing the air before him with his manicured hands. When his voice boomed too loudly, Frau Baumgartner looked worriedly at the door to the bedroom, and he dropped his voice in consideration. 'You see?' he said softly, leaning forward. 'You agree? You will persuade him to sell?'

> 'Fuchs, du hast die Gans gestohlen,
> gib sie wieder her!
> Sonst wird dich der Jäger holen
> mit dem Schiessgewehr.'

They sat together on a narrow seat at the back of the tram, surrounded by coffin-faces, watery and grey from having been indoors all winter. While his mother drooped, as though still weak from the lack of sunshine, Hugo himself was ebullient, excited by the names of the streets on their white signposts – Larchenweg, Terrassenstrasse – by seeing new foliage a pale yellow on the roadside trees, the women in elegant coats walking their dachshunds on leather leashes, the delivery boys on bicycles with baskets loaded with goods, the bells ringing as clear and sharp as cracked glass in the spring air. Here the sun was not only tangible but visible, a jolly blur both circular and incandescent over the rooftops, as it never was in their own dreary street. The warmth of it on the tram roof made him itch inside his coat that had in any case grown too small for him and felt like diseased fur after a winter's perpetual use. 'Don't be so impatient, child,' she warned, 'it is a long way to the Grünewald.'

They were both travel-sick when they got there, but the Friedmanns seemed to have anticipated that: on the wooden table under the cherry tree in their small garden stood a tray with tall glasses and a jug. They were made to sit there in the sunshine that slanted in through the flowering branches ('Come and see the cherry tree flowering once more,' they had written) while the young Frau Friedmann ran to fetch cakes and the old Frau Friedmann sat with her mittened hands on her lap and smiled at him coaxingly, saying, 'In a little while Albert will come home and he will take Hugo to see the swans.'

Hugo did not want to be taken away; he wanted to sit under the black twigs and the white blossom, and drink slowly from the glass of blackberry wine and nibble another biscuit dusted with cinnamon, and see the remarkable sight of his mother flowering in the company of her friends, the friends who she had been in the habit of slipping off to see and visit alone when his father would take Hugo out for a few hours; somehow she had not liked them to meet these friends of her girlhood, from her home town where they had been neighbours and old Dr Friedmann a colleague of her father's at the university. Then Hugo had not cared; he had revelled in the masculine atmosphere created by his father – the somewhat roguish, slightly inebriated air of gentlemen on the town. Today he sat on the garden bench, taking in the sight of a pair of white butterflies lighting upon a grey bush, the cherry blossoms falling silently on the table, and listening to his mother's voice lift and fly with lightheartedness and relief, and he wondered why she did not come oftener if it made her so happy. Laughing, she was saying, 'And Adele, the time we went to the Max Reinhardt production together – it was *Lohengrin* wasn't it? And we had gone straight from school, in our navy blue pinafores, and were sitting up with the pigeons, in the cheapest seats, when that gentleman in tails and a top hat came running up the aisle, gave us two tickets and said' – she imitated his voice – ' "Excuse me, Fräulein – I am forced to leave early – my seats are free – will you not kindly take these tickets and enjoy the music from a good seat." ' Adele joined her in the disbelieving laughter, and nodded. '*Ja,*' she told

Hugo, 'and we went up, up, up, right to the front, right up to the stage nearly, and sat there amongst the ladies in their furs and the men in their tails, wearing our navy blue pinafores. And mine had chalk dust all over it.' She raised her hands to her red cheeks as she laughed at the remembered embarrassment, now become a treasure. Hugo, instead, remembered the figure of his father, left behind in a wrapping of blankets; he felt uneasy, sensing a rift, a break between his parents that might have existed for all these years but of which he was only now really aware. He kept his eye on his mother, suddenly so much younger and, he felt, exposed and vulnerable.

Then the son Albert appeared and, at old Frau Friedmann's insistence, took Hugo and their beautiful King Charles spaniel, who was of course called Charles, out of the little gate at the bottom of the garden and down a sandy path criss-crossed by the roots of the pine trees to the lake to see the swans. Hugo was a little hurt by the way his mother eagerly saw him off and turned to her friends as though she had been waiting for this moment. By the lake's edge he watched Albert break some stale rolls and toss them over the water towards the swans that swerved and glided towards them and noted the way their feathers knitted together like chain-mail, holding off the drops of black and icy water, but somehow they reminded him of his father's rococo mirrors, gliding as they did upon the shining glass of their reflections in the still water, and he was silenced by the knowledge of their transience. Strangely, Albert's thoughts seemed to have run on the same lines for he told the swans, '*Ja*, take these rolls – they may be the last we have to give you.' Then he turned to Hugo and said, a little sharply, 'Your shoes are getting wet – don't go so close to the water,' and Hugo realised he was bored with his company and therefore refused when asked, 'Shall I take you out in a boat? Would you like to row?' For a while they clambered over the rocks and roots around the lake, a streaming Charles running ahead of them, tearing their trouser legs on blackberry thorns while Albert told him of the deer that came to drink at the lake and the hares in the forest. To Hugo it seemed he was stumbling through the illustrations of a book of fairy stories, the forest where Hansel and Gretel followed a trail of breadcrumbs, or in which Sleeping Beauty lay hidden by a wall of thorns – beautiful, hushed and vaguely sinister.

Holding aside a thorny branch, Albert stood still, looking at the lake on which the fir trees had laid their long shadows in strokes of black paint. He said, as if making conversation, 'But if we will ever see them again, I – really – don't – know,' and then led the way up the sandy path to the garden gate, his shoulders sloping and looking as dejected as the wet and muddy dog.

They found the garden overtaken by a chilly shadow; the ladies had gone in. Inside a room that seemed to Hugo like a peasant's with its rough timber furniture, its bowls of garden flowers, its painted china and worn rugs, he found his mother in a flushed state of animation at a cottage piano on which she was playing a duet with the young Frau Friedmann, a dark woman with two long plaits of red hair over her shawl. She smiled at Hugo when he came in but did not stop playing. Instead, she sang, together with her friend:

'*Kennst du das Land*
wo die Zitronen blühn?
Im dunkeln Laub
die Gold-Orangen glühn . . .
Dahin! Dahin!
Möcht' ich mit dir,
O mein Geliebter ziehn!'

Hugo stood under the globe lamp of red paper that hung from the ceiling, transfixed by the reckless gaiety in her voice, the words that had a wild gypsy ring to them and filled him with unease and foreboding.

Later that evening, when they sat at the peasant table, eating a potato soup and some rather watery rolls for which old Frau Friedmann apologised over and over again while the younger simply laughed deprecatingly, the talk that lapped around the stolidly munching Hugo turned to new poets and their work. Frau Friedmann described a strange Indian poet whose work she had been reading, a sage with a long white beard and long hair and piercing, hypnotic eyes. 'A sage from Bengal,' she explained to Hugo's entranced mother, while Hugo puzzled over the name which he associated with *bengalische Lichte*, the fireworks he had seen exploding in the dark on some festive night while wrapped comfortingly in his father's arms. After the table was cleared, a book of poems was brought for them to see; it had a pale blue cover and its title was meaningless to Hugo – *Gitanjali* – but he leant across to look at the photograph to which they turned and found the poet-sage's face as the old lady described. Somehow its outlandishness connected with the song he had just heard his mother singing, and Hugo squirmed at the unfamiliarity of it all. He thought it had to do with poetry – an element in his mother's life that he understood as little as his father did, something they put down to her youth in a university town while they were two masculine city-dwellers. Reminded of his father, he felt an urge to return to him, to what was his own world – or what remained of it – but heard his mother say, 'Now Adele, show me your own work, your new verse, it is yours I want to see, and Albert's', and then ribbon-bound portfolios of their verse were brought out and read aloud, verses about linden trees in spring, about swallows in autumn skies, about butterflies, frost, children playing and, of course, the flowering cherry tree.

They might have gone on all night, intoxicated by their views of spring and beauty and art – one poem was dedicated to the Indian sage and was called 'On Reading Tagore' – while Hugo stood at the window, watching the greying of the light till a desperation overtook him: he could not allow his mother to continue with her pretence that she had returned to her youth, that her adulthood could be ignored. Seeing her so childishly irresponsible and irresponsibly blithe, he was driven to an adult decision. Turning around, he saw them listening admiringly to Albert reading a poem about the deer by the lake that he called 'The Kaiser of the Woods', and blurted out 'Mama, *komm*, we must go back to Papa now.'

In the tram, lifting her face out of a fold of her cape, she accused him in mortified tones, 'How could you, Hugo, in the middle of such a beautiful poem?'

Then, the door opening, her scream: '*Was ist los?* What's happened? Hugo, *das Gas!*' They ran, shedding coats and capes on the way, down the passage to the kitchen. The door was shut but there was no doubt, the sickening, sweet, cloudy odour poured through its cracks. They threw themselves on it as though the gas were a physical, concrete barrier, and were astonished when the door burst open. The gas was like cushions and quilts of anaesthesia piled up, all around, swaddling the limp figure that sprawled on the linoleum, the body sagging out of the open oven door. When they lifted him, the head waggled helplessly out of their arms. For a moment, his open eyes misled them to cry out in relief but in a moment it turned to a wail.

> '*O du lieber Augustin,*
> *alles ist weg!*
> *Geld ist weg,*
> *Beutel ist weg,*
> *Augustin liegt in Dreck,*
> *O du lieber Augustin,*
> *alles ist hin!*'

They never left each other, or the flat. Nothing was said, but Hugo understood his mother wanted him beside her, he could not leave her, and so he stopped going to school. It was a relief to him that this meant the end of those endless tram rides, the mud and the ice in the yard into which the children pushed each other, the hysterical teacher who tore out his own hair and theirs by the handful, the strange language in which he recognised only every third or fourth word, and the forbidding sound of the Torah. Unfortunately it also meant the end of the friendships he had begun to make: he was sorry not to see Eddie Wallfisch any more, or go skating with him. He realised now that the school had had an element of robust reality that appealed to him, that he had been learning to deal with and even enjoy, and that he missed in the hushed pallor of his own home.

He spent too many hours with old tattered copies of *Der Gute Kamerad* which now seemed pure fantasy, its stories of camping in the forest and journeys on the sea no more relevant to his life than a dream is to daytime. His mother gave him her own copy of the Kaiserbuch which she said had come out in honor of the Emperor Franz Josef in 1906; she pointed out to him the gold-embossed portrait of the Kaiser, then closed its thick brown covers, ran her hand lovingly – even pridefully – over the imperial motto in its flowery scroll: *Viribus Unitis*. But when he took it in his hands, Hugo thought it looked and felt exactly like a coffin, the coffin into which they had closed his father. Instead of poring over it with her nostalgic fascination, he took recourse to the schoolboy's totem – his penknife – and spent the silent hours whittling instead. Sometimes on the window-seat by the piano, sometimes on his bed, sometimes out on the landing, simply to be out of the house. Whenever he heard a step, he got up and went back into the flat that was beginning to resemble that Kaiser-coffin of a book.

Their lives fell into a groove and remained there: they might have been an old married couple, Hugo and his mother, seldom leaving the apartment, looking after each other with stricken concern. Some of the neighbours dropped in occasionally, bringing them magazines, bringing them rolls, or jam they had made. Never butter; there was no butter. Never newspapers, it was better not to see them. The Gentleman from Hamburg installed himself in the shop downstairs, his own name – his good, sound, Teutonic name – painted on the new shop-window in letters of black, edged with gold. When he came up to call on them, he was concerned, polite, helpful over the tea Frau Baumgartner served on a tray. Then she would go to the roll-top desk, open it and go through the papers in it with him, her voice a murmur Hugo could barely overhear from his corner by the bookshelf. Generally, after such a visit, some object or the other would be removed from its place and carried downstairs – the Prussian helmet in the shape of an ashtray, the pistol-shaped barometer from between the french windows, and even the wooden negro who held umbrellas in the hall – the ivory-topped cane had already vanished. Hugo was astounded to see it uproot itself after so many years of standing stock-still and inscrutable, and watched its shining black head bob down the stairs in disbelief. Eventually the piano went too. When Hugo opened his mouth to protest, his mother laid her finger on her lips and whispered the old saying, 'Stepchildren must behave doubly well.' Silently he turned the words over in his mind: '*Stiefkinder müssen doppelt artig sein.*' The apartment became strangely empty, and this emptiness matched the silence into which they sank.

The Gentleman from Hamburg began to bluster. 'A young man who is not pursuing his education, what chance has he in this world?' he demanded of Hugo after drinking a cup of coffee with them, the coffee ground from bitter beans that made their mouths pucker and gave their speech an edge. 'Frau Baumgartner, you cannot imagine he will be fit for employment – '

'What employment, Herr Pfuehl? What employment can you think of for him?' she replied with some asperity. She used her coffee cup only for warming her hands.

Herr Pfuehl continued to bluster. 'At least send him down to learn something in the office. We can't have the late Herr Baumgartner's only son grow up uneducated and unemployed, can we?'

'That,' said Frau Baumgartner, setting down her coffee cup, 'he can certainly do. Thank you, Herr Pfuehl, I will see that he does that,' and left Hugo gaping at his first lesson in the stiffening effect of hardship.

It seemed to Hugo that he entered the small office at the back of the showroom and never left it again. To begin with, he sat at his father's old desk, going through the bills, endlessly doing calculations or tapping out business letters on an ancient typewriter, and then he brought blankets down so that he could sleep on the sagging green sofa by the radiator and a kettle so that he could boil himself some soup or *ersatz* coffee on the gas ring.

Eventually his mother moved in as well, the apartment upstairs surrendered to Herr Pfuehl when his family arrived from Hamburg. 'It is too big for us now,' she apologised to Hugo, looking away. She tried to keep out of his way. 'But where do you go, Mutti?' he wanted to know, and she laughed and told him how she had been visiting her favourite pictures in the museum – 'One must make sure they keep the helmet well polished for Herr Rembrandt,' she joked – or insisted it had been a fine day in the park although the rain had streamed down the office window. She tried to keep out all day while he was working and returned only when the showroom closed and the delivery boys left and Herr Pfuehl mounted the stairs to dine with his family. What did it matter if his wife, Frau Pfuehl, who wore a hat made of two birds' wings, one over either ear, and hid her eyes behind a strip of netting, spat after her when they met at the entrance, one shaking her umbrella on entering and the other shaking it open on leaving? 'Hugo, Frau Pfuehl, she spat at me! *Sie hat auf mir gespuckt!*' his mother cried, coming in with her face flushed. '*Ja, gespuckt* – like a guttersnipe. Can you believe it of Herr Pfuehl's wife?' Hugo looked up from the accounts, his eyes so blurred by the endless figures that he could not see or interpret her expression. Frau Pfuehl? For a moment he could not take in who she meant and, when he did, his mother had already started talking of something else, the eggs she had managed to buy in the market, and their absurd, idiotic price. 'For two eggs,' she mocked, holding them up in her hands, 'the size of a pigeon's. A very small pigeon's,' she laughed, and boiled them for their supper that they ate sitting side by side on the sofa.

'Why not go and spend a day with the Friedmanns again, Mutti?' Hugo suggested, wiping his mouth of egg. She said

nothing. 'You should keep in touch, Mutti,' he urged. 'How?'
she replied, and told him they had gone to the countryside in
the belief they would be safe there.

> *'Haslein in der Grube sass und schlief.*
> *Armer Haslein, bist du krank,*
> *dass du nicht mehr hupfen kannst?*
> *Haslein hupf!'*

'In India he may begin a new life!' the Gentleman from
Hamburg thundered, walking up and down with his hands
under the tails of his new, striped coat. 'Yes, you may think of
it as an ancient and backward land, my good Frau Baumgartner, the land of snakes and fakirs, but have you not heard of the
British Empire? Don't you know, Hugo, that it is a colony of
our neighbours in Britain? I have reasons for thinking of it as a
promising place and so should you, Hugo, now that you have
taken over my clerical work. You ought to know how much
of my timber comes from there, all the finest mahogany and
rosewood, and all the fancy pieces of sandalwood – where else
but from the East, from India and Burma and Malaya? So
don't dismiss my suggestion with that look,' he warned them,
removing his hand from under his coat and giving it an
admonitory wave, having noticed how the two on the sofa
had exchanged looks and how Frau Baumgartner had raised
her handkerchief to her lips to conceal her laughter. 'I can get
him a passage on a boat of the Peninsular and Oriental Lines
that leaves for the East from Venice. We will get him on to a
train to Venice – quickly, before the trains stop –'
'The trains stop?' she spluttered.
He gave her an exasperated look; what was one to do with
these hysterical Jewesses? 'Not easy to get a ticket any more,
but I will manage it, and also give him a letter of recommendation to my acquaintance in the timber trade in India – I have
been doing business with him for many years now, always
satisfactorily. Why not think over it, Hugo, before you say
no? I have heard that "no" enough.'

'Herr Pfuehl,' Hugo's mother murmured then, ashamed of her mirth for which she herself could not account. 'At times, it is best to say no, to stay quietly in one place so that no one notices, so that everyone forgets – till things become better again . . .'

He wagged his finger at her again, the one that wore a blood ruby in a ring. '*Totschweigentaktik,* playing dead, is all very well, in its own time – and place – but not here, not now. You must wake up, you two, and act. You should know when to wake up, and act. Have you not heard of what became of the Nussbaums from the haberdashery? How the police came in the night for him, how he threw himself from the window?' Herr Pfuehl's hands acted out the scene, tumbling through the air like two pouches. 'And how nevertheless they seized and carried away Frau Nussbaum? Yes, she had painted the swastika on her window, she had dyed her hair yellow, but did that help? *Nein, sie war nach dem Osten verschleppt,* deported to the East, you know that.'

'If it did not help her, Herr Pfuehl, then what does it matter what we do? It will not help either.'

Herr Pfuehl gave an exasperated roar. 'You are not illiterate, you Jews, you are not peasants – then why are your minds so closed?' He rolled up the pouch of his hand and squeezed it. He hardly knew why he bothered about this pair stuck in his office room like obstinate mice who turned up their noses at the cheese. Yes, he wanted them out, he wanted to be rid of the past history of the firm and of the Baumgartner name – but it was not only that. He was worried. He was afraid of being accused of harbouring Jews when Hitler was trying to rid the sacred fatherland of them – so his wife had said and she was not so stupid. Nor was Pfuehl entirely in disagreement with the Fuehrer's plans and ambitions, not at all – there were many points on which he agreed with him such as the need for seizing the power of commerce and industry from their unscrupulous hands – but, *Donnerwetter,* there were ways of doing these things. And then, who could consider this miserable pale Jewish boy with his grotesque nose, or his tiny

dark sparrow of a mother, as fit for work in those factories that
the Fuehrer had set up? No, one had to be humane in such
matters and admit that a paint or steel factory or a salt or coal
mine was no place for the late Herr Baumgartner's widow or
son, so delicately brought up in the old Germany with their
piano-playing and singing and reading of the classics. They
were not the Jews of the *Shtetl* after all, of *kosher* and *Hanukkah*
and *Cheder* and God knew what other Galician horrors. 'Think
about it,' he warned, 'and *quick*.'

'It is for your own good, I am telling you,' he pleaded late at
night, returning from a meeting in the Alexanderplatz where
the 'Horst Wessel Lied' had been sung and everyone had
seemed to be wearing a swastika on an armband and his blue
suit had stood out oddly in all that brown. 'I cannot protect
you much longer. You must be gone –' he glared at them, and
at last thought he saw a look of alarm in the boy's eyes. Ah-ha,
so the dim blind worm has let a new idea enter his head at last,
he rejoiced, and pressed his point with renewed vigour.

Finally Hugo came out of the office room to see him in his
own enclosure. He stood there, amongst the pieces of shining
new furniture of the kind his father would never have
tolerated, looking much too big for that absurd corduroy suit
he still wore, his big hands hanging out of the shrunken cuffs,
and saying, 'But what of my mother, sir? She won't come to
India.'

'Won't come to India?'

'No, sir.'

'Have you *talked* to her, tried to persuade her?'

Hugo nodded, slowly, not at all surely. He had not been
certain if his mother took it seriously when he tried clumsily to
paint a picture of their new beginnings in the East – a crude
picture, all tigers and palm trees and sunsets, and perhaps it
was only to be expected that she did not believe in it. 'After all,
they are not so primitive,' he had tried Herr Pfuehl's method
on her. 'You saw that they are educated and have their own
literature. You saw the picture of the great poet in the
Friedmanns' house, Mother,' he reminded her, but she burst

out laughing, in her newly unnatural way, gave him a little push with her hand, now twisted with arthritis, and cried, 'Ach Hugo, don't be ridiculous. Why should your mother read a *bengalische* poet when I can read the beautiful verses of our own dear Friedmanns?' The mention of them gave a twist to her mouth and her eyes turned liquid and threatened to spill over – she had not heard from them since they had left. A little later she returned to her half-jocular, half-petulant manner. 'And what about the snakes and the tigers? How will *mein kleiner Mann* protect me from them? You know how frightened I am even of a little German mouse, Hugo.'

'A German mouse, Mutti? We are not talking of little German *mice*, you know.'

It was no good: she either turned it into a joke, or she turned her back on him, rubbing and rubbing her twisted, purple fingers, and would only grimace at anything that he said.

It was the Gentleman from Hamburg who took everything into his hands, as he explained to everyone, and found Frau Baumgartner a room as a paying guest in the house of some 'influential' people, quite a nice house, on Grenadierstrasse, warm and comfortable even if not in a quarter one would have chosen – but at least it was amongst 'safe' people. It was here that Hugo said goodbye to her, putting his new valise down on the wool rug in the middle of the pine flooring that smelt of disinfectant, and putting out his arms in the sleeves of his new white linen suit to embrace her. His cheek against hers, he said as he had said every night for the last week, 'And when I am in India, I will make a home for us. How will you like that? I will have servants for you and drive away the snakes and bring you gold oranges –'

'What are you talking about, you silly boy?' she rubbed her cheek, like a piece of crumpled velvet, against his. 'What is this fairy story – *diese Märchen* – you are making up for old Mutti?'

'I am not making it up at all, Mü. Don't you remember you sang the song about the country where lemons flower, where oranges glow in the dark foliage? I remember it, see.'

'Silly Hugo, that was written by Goethe, it was about the Mediterranean, not about some dangerous land in the East, *mit den Schwarzen*. I told you I won't live where there are spiders and snakes,' and she pushed him away from her. Her mouth was jerking in all directions, uncontrollably, making her look drunken, or witchlike.

'Mutti,' he pleaded, putting out his arms to touch her, but she held out her hand to keep him at a distance, saying, 'No, you get your work done that Herr Pfuehl has given you, and then come quickly home again.'

So that was what was decided by them when he left her – standing with her hand on the chest of drawers with yellow cut-glass handles on which she had placed her volumes of Goethe, framed by two puce curtains and a pattern of steam-pipes painted to look like bronze. In the midst of all that, her head looked especially small and grey. Out on the landing the landlady, who had undoubtedly been listening to all that was said, assured him she would get Anna the maid to take her a cup of tea. It was not so easy to get tea any more, she said, but she liked to make her guests feel at home. Hugo murmured something about having to go away on business to India and let himself out while the woman went to see about the tea, muttering, 'And a very fine business it is going to be.'

> '*Hopp, hopp, hopp!*
> *Pferdchen lauf galopp!*
> *Über Stock und über Steine,*
> *aber brich dir nicht die Beine!*
> *Hopp, hopp, hopp!*
> *Pferdchen lauf galopp!*'

The boat to the Orient was not due to arrive in Venice for at least another week. Having with the greatest difficulty acquired – and understood – this information from a small window that usually had its shutter pulled down and was scarcely ever known to open, Hugo felt a lurch of fear, found he had to accept it – the prospect of at least seven days in this strange city, not only the first in which he had ever found himself alone but one so palpably foreign as to make him feel he was already transported to the East, it had so little relation to the Europe of the north.

True, the weather was European, it could be nothing else – these lowering clouds of melancholy grey, the fine rain that came down like a soft, clinging net to settle on head and shoulders and dampen them – and yet it was not Europe after all: there was here, a magical, a poetical quality he had never known in Berlin. He walked in the narrow lanes till his shoes were soaked, his feet wet, his new suit drenched, and then entered the nearest *chiesa* to sit in a velvet-covered pew and try and get some warmth from the candles that flickered under a crucified Christ, a weeping Madonna or a gaudily bleeding heart, from lamps of coloured glass in which light glowered like embers from a fire, and breathed in the swirling clouds of smoking incense, watching the candlelight play on a bit of gilt here, a piece of Murano glass there, and asked himself if he was not actually in Tartary or in Persia, in some magical fairyland not only south but far, far east of Germany and everything he had known in his life till then.

Since the most urgent and immediate problem was how to stretch the small amount of money he had been loaned by Herr Pfuehl to cover this unforeseen week in Venice, he found himself a room in a cheap lodging-house – or, rather, half of it, for he shared it with a medical student who was out all night and returned to claim the one bed in the morning, snarling at Hugo to be out and off if he overslept. A maid in the kitchen who wore black and had a moustache gave him coffee in a large bowl before he left the house, washing the tiles of the floor around his feet while he stood drinking it. The door opened on to a courtyard where someone had stacked empty bottles; if he kicked one by accident, the heaps of brown and green and bubbled glass slithered and clattered and made a woman on an upper floor stick her head out of the window and scream at him. She would also come staggering out with buckets of refuse to throw into the canal, scattering bloodied newspapers and chicken feathers across the intervening cobblestones. At all times of the day, the house reeked of frying oil, hissed with the sounds of cooking, and emitted the mutters and grumbles of scores of lodgers hidden up and down the decaying staircases, in stone cells and wooden stalls. Only their groans and their washing gave them away. Parting a wet tablecloth from a dripping apron, Hugo let himself out and remained out all day to let the medical student sleep his share of sleep.

He walked to escape his fear and apprehension. Everywhere the sound of water lapping stone, of footsteps striking stone, so that when he heard a sound that belonged to neither stone nor water, while crossing an empty *campo*, he stopped and searched for its source till his eyes found it – cage upon cage blocking up a tall window above, filled with canaries that trilled and sang because a little light was shining on them from out of all the grey.

At San Marco he paid a coin to see the *Pala d'Oro* and imagine, when close to the gems encrusting the gold sheet, that he was already in an Oriental potentate's palace, for such riches could only belong to the East, could not be of the West with its greyness, its rain, its lodging-houses and black and brown garb. He climbed up in the basilica and walked through the marble maze, the thin soles of his cheap shoes slipping on the glassy mosaic underfoot. The throngs in the chapels below, the incense, the candlewax, the flickers of light and colour in the furry dark, all oppressed him and seemed to repulse him till he was thrust out of the door into the Piazza. Stumbling in its lighted space, he tried to avoid the pigeons and the pigeon-feeders who teemed together, and seemed to him equally gluttonous in their taking and receiving: was this not how beggars were said to behave in the East, beggars and their patrons who gave them alms for their own sakes? Sometimes the easternness of the city disturbed him so much, he wondered if he would be able to face India.

How many feast days could there be in a week? Almost every day shops closed, shutters down, offices shut, while the churches glimmered with candlelight and the bells rang, holiday-makers hurried across the *campi* with festive cakes packed in golden hat-boxes, stopping to buy flowers at the stalls where they bloomed with a tropical luxuriance. Hugo found himself drawing closer, trying to pick out a bunch of violets for his mother, of his mother. Without making any purchase he wandered on to breathe in the odour of newly baked rolls at the baker's and the pastries and the rich dark chocolates he had known only as a small child. Then he felt himself to be inside a chocolate box, surfeited with sweetness and richness, and tore away to breathe freely.

Crossing the wooden Accademia bridge to the news-stand where he might buy a newspaper in a known language, he stopped because the sun was briefly out, and leant over the rail to look down at the Grand Canal, its green glass waves rocking in the wake of a passing vaporetto that broke up the reflections of the pink and yellow palaces into coloured strips and ribbons that shook and shimmered. On the bank a young man, red-haired and fair-skinned as so many were here where Hugo had expected them to be swarthy, sat down in the sun to unpack his sandwiches from a piece of paper and eat them on a patch of wild grass. Hugo would not have stayed to watch if first one head, then another had not arisen out of the coarse, tall grass which then began to stir as if it were a tropical jungle and release the lean, striped, feral bodies of a grey and a black cat, their green eyes watching the man eat from their pointed corners rimmed like actresses' eyes with kohl. The man was looking out over the canal, he did not see them, and they gathered stealthily behind him – slipping closer, their whiskers faintly twitching, and yet alert, ready to leap and vanish like thieves, like the scavengers they were. Hugo, who had owned no animal but a doomed infant hedgehog, hung over the railing and watched as the city cats appeared and took up poses of calm reflection behind the oblivious picnicker – some licking their fur to show their indifference, others waiting to pounce. For a few moments, all held their poses – Hugo on the bridge, the man on the sunny bank with his sandwich, the cats in their attitudes of expectation and alertness. Then a boat passed under a bridge, its bargee wielding his pole and giving a warning cry; the man flung the crusts over his shoulder and rolled up the brown paper into a ball and the cats – in an instant they were at the greasy paper, the limp crusts, growling and spitting over the feast. Hugo walked away.

The ball of fortune shone in a moment of sunlight, and the golden sail that the boy held up for a weathervane seemed to fill with an eastern breeze. Hugo stood at the tip of the Dogana, hands in his pockets, collar turned up so that no one could have told that he was drawing comfort from the light, the warmth. Across the lagoon were the islands and on one the great San Giorgio looked to him like an equation immaculately worked out in stone, a mathematical problem set and solved.

He walked down the Zattere where people had come out to walk in the pale sunlight while the great vaporettos swept by, leaving in their wake a wash of froth and foam. When he was hungry, he began to peer into trattorias he passed and finally found one that did not look too forbiddingly expensive for it had prams with babies and families gathered at the tables. He went and sat down in the thick, heated air that reminded him of the *Bierkeller* at home. The menu posed a problem, every item on it being unfamiliar, and he looked into the waiter's face – for once swarthy and foreign – in despair. The waiter made no response but a young woman at a neighbouring table leant across to recommend the cannelloni. 'Is good, good,' she nodded at him reassuringly from over the top of a newspaper printed in Hebrew. Seeing him stare at it, she smiled, shook the sheets slightly and told him she lived in the Jewish quarter of the city where such papers were available, why did he not come and visit it? A fine place, she had her studio there, was a painter. At that, Hugo began to shift in his chair in unease. She noticed, and shrugged her shoulders, making a moue. 'Staying here long?' she asked, before she returned to her paper.

Hugo burst out, 'I – I am leaving – for India.'

'India!' It had the expected effect. The newspaper was lowered, her face appeared, looking suspicious. 'But whoever goes to India? If you are not a sailor?'

Hugo shook his head, laughing. The cannelloni arrived. Politely she turned her face away so he could eat it. Before he had finished it, she left, squeezing past his table with her thin hips swivelling in the shiny orange material of her dress. 'Good luck!' she murmured, still with a suspicious twist to her lips, and he rose to his feet, dropping his napkin and bumping into the table so that his coffee spilt. He considered leaving his meal and following her, to the Jewish quarter and her studio, but the waiter came up as if he sensed Hugo's intention, and presented the bill. His unfamiliarity with the Italian notes detained Hugo and, when he came out, she was gone.

Thinking to follow her, he ran out on the *fondamenta* but, apart from a small dog on a long leash held by a man in a large coat and a purple muffler, there was no one to be seen. The golden light of an hour ago had thinned to an icy wine-like substance close to freezing. It made the bare trees and the rooftops and walls stand out like a steel engraving. Hugo walked along, thinking he might find the Jewish quarter she had spoken of; if he did not see her there, he might see other Jews. Strange, in Germany he had never wanted to search them out, had been aware of others thinking of him as a Jew but not done so himself. In ejecting him, Germany had taught him to regard himself as one. Perhaps it was important to find what she had called their 'quarter'. Perhaps over here he would find for himself a new identity, one that suited him, one that he enjoyed. The air quivered with possibilities, with the suspense of quest and choice.

For a large part of the afternoon he wandered up one *calle*, down another, crossing slimy black canals by little stone bridges, stopping at corners, crossing courtyards, sidling around the brick sides of a church, stopping in the doorway of a *chiesa* to blow his nose and wonder if he were not hopelessly lost. For a while he even followed a cat on the prowl, a grey cat with a wicked, watching eye, but it leapt over a wall and vanished amidst a clatter of tin cans where Hugo had no wish to follow. He did come across more populated quarters but in the fading light of the late afternoon and the cold crystallising in the air, there were in general not many people about – old ladies in rusty black painfully hobbling home with their market bags, boys in loud boots with books in their bags whistling as they clattered along, but that was all. Overhead washing hung faded and ragged. When Hugo came to a *calle* half-submerged in water and realised the tide was rising, he lost heart and turned around to retrace his steps.

He did so wrongly and found himself in the Rialto with its sudden flurry of sound and activity, crates of oranges standing about, stallholders shouting, women screaming, money ringing, and all around a profusion of design, of arabesques in stone and colour, and for a moment or two he was fooled into believing that his wrong turning had led him straight into the East, into an eastern market, and he stood there, as entranced as he was alarmed. Venice *was* the East, and yet it was Europe too; it was that magic boundary where the two met and blended, and for those seven days Hugo had been a part of their union. He realised it only now: that during his constant wandering, his ceaseless walking, he had been drawing closer and closer to this discovery of that bewitched point where they became one land of which he felt himself the natural citizen.

It made him forget the Jewish woman, the painter, and when it grew dark, he got on to a vaporetto with a crowd of other home-goers. He found himself standing-place and let himself be carried up the canal, believing himself to be on the sea, to be on his way. He had not found the Jewish quarter or the Jewish girl but he had seen another world; perhaps it was where Jewry was located but to him it was the East, and he was both in it and travelling to it, at a distance and yet one with it.

On returning to his lodging-house, he was handed a letter from the shipping company – the boat had arrived, and passengers were requested to embark before midnight.

Packing his valise, he ran out into the moist dark.

THREE

But the light was different here.

His eyes streaming from the glare, Baumgartner stopped to wipe them with his large handkerchief – one of those squares of checked cotton one bought for fifty paise on the pavement – and noticed how far down Colaba Causeway he had come, missing all the cafés and Irani restaurants where he normally stopped for scraps for his *Familie* at home. No tasty Parsi fish in mint sauce, no slops of custard or bits of mutton cutlets for them today. How foolish, how forgetful. How old he was today. Letting out a groan, he was brought up short by the kit and tools of a bicycle repair shop and realised he had only to go down a narrow lane between two buildings and he would be in the courtyard overlooked by Lotte's room. Why not drop in on Lotte and so retrieve something of the day? She was the only one he could tell about the odd encounter with the fair-haired boy, about the flood of memories of old Berlin it had let loose. Not that Lotte knew *his* Berlin. He grinned at the absurdity of the thought, using the handkerchief to mop his neck. It was unthinkable that Lotte had occupied the same Berlin he had, that she could ever have been in the company of his mother, of her friends the Friedmanns, or even the Gentleman from Hamburg. He nearly laughed when he wondered what they would have made of her – disgraceful Lotte with her fat legs that always contrived to show so much of themselves under her skirts, her hair that she dyed a livid, foxy red with henna, her gin-drinking, her dancing, all her disreputable ways. Could she ever have lived in Berlin as she claimed when she was feeling particularly intimate with Baumgartner? Of course at other times she claimed to have been a gypsy who had followed her artiste parents all over the globe. Baumgartner had wondered if they had been circus artistes but there was nothing in Lotte's physique or skills to suggest such an athletic background. She liked to claim that her mother had been a singer of light opera ('I was in her belly, up there on the stage, when she was singing Madame Butterfly – hasn't it had an effect on my eyes?' she would leer, pulling up their corners with her painted nails). But what did it matter – she spoke German, had his language, *nicht wahr?* Putting his handkerchief away in his pocket, he walked up the lane, straddling the drain in which unsightly objects blocked the flow of the soapy slush, causing it to smell unbelievably on this hot morning; he felt drawn to the idea of spending a little time with Lotte, perhaps drinking a cup of coffee with her, listening to a little German, however foul her accent, coarse her expressions and jarring her voice – yes, it had to do with that boy, that boy.

He stopped in the courtyard and looked up to see if her window was open (she always locked it when she went out because 'Everyone is a thief here; we are living in a thieves' den, Hugo, we are surrounded –') and saw that the shutters were, but the curtains were drawn, pink and red and blue flowers stamped all over them. Lotte slept late – he knew that – a habit from her days in cabaret, but it was late enough, and how could she not be awake now when in the garage below her room a mechanic was beating upon the steel rim of a tyre with his hammer – clang, clang, CLANG? And in another room that opened on to the courtyard a man had hung his transistor radio on a nail in the doorway where he sat on a stool, nursing callused feet drawn out of rubber-thonged slippers, a cigarette hanging from his lip – Ramu the bootlegger; Baumgartner recognised him – he supplied Lotte with liquor, country liquor probably brewed from kerosene or insecticide that would one day surely kill her, he had warned her. Suddenly the mechanic flung his hammer into a steel drum and shouted to his assistant for a spanner. An invisible but always audible parrot – perhaps it lived in the room that had a row of money plants growing out of a row of beer bottles on a window-sill – screeched its harsh note over and over again. In the lane, a woman selling bananas tried to raise her voice above that of a woman vending fish with equal ferocity. '*Pomfret, pomfret – jheenga, jheenga!*' screamed the fish-vendor, only to have the banana-seller triumph with the long-drawn screech, '*Ke – laah!*' And out on Colaba Cause-way, the traffic poured relentlessly on, an all-devouring monster on the move.

No, no one could sleep in this hell of noise and glare, Baumgartner decided, not even a drink-sodden Lotte, and began to climb the stairs to the floor above the garage. At the door – he remembered when the paint had been fresh, a fresh fire-engine red, now flaking, peeling brown – he knocked and knocked. The air was suffocating with cooking smells on the closed landing, and he felt the children of the family upstairs staring at him through the banisters, silent except for their noses that ran with clogged, choking sounds; they were the children, he knew, who had thrown fish scales and prawn tails on Lotte's head when she returned drunk one night, setting off fifteen minutes of such hysteria that even the garage hands were impressed and sent for the police; two hours of Konkani and Yiddish abuse later, they had left in helpless defeat. Baumgartner too began to feel defeated and was about to turn and go down the stairs, coffeeless, when he heard Lotte lurching past the furniture inside, then rattling at the chains she had had fixed to her door after Ramu the bootlegger had followed her and attempted to knife her for an unpaid bill. He knew she was staring at him through a spyhole and it made him smile because through the spyhole everyone looked like a burglar, a murderer. He tried to reassure her by winking and thumbing his nose at her.

Finally she opened the door a cautious crack and looked out, suspiciously pinching together her lips, nose and eyes in a tight lock of denial. Then, '*Ach, du lieber Gott,* Hugo,' she said disgustedly, and dropped her hands to her hips, letting the door swing open. The slack flesh hung from her arms like two legs of mutton veined with blue. She was dressed in a slip and stood barefoot.

'Now, Lotte, do you receive guests in this costume?' he chided her, walking in past her, letting his side bump into and press against her as he did so – such clumsiness being permitted the old, surely. If she did not bump back at him, she did not press away from him either.

'Guests are all I need after a night like the last one,' she groaned, following him after locking and bolting the door securely although not before the children on the landing above had screamed several of their names for her, all filthy.

'What kind of night was it then? Up dancing in the Café de Paris till dawn, eh?' he teased, lowering himself on to his favourite chair, a bucket of cane that had over the years sagged to fit his shape. Besides, it had a small flat cushion covered in the same bright material as the curtains. He eased it up against his back, grateful for its support.

Lotte flung herself on to the kitchen chair at the table, spreading out her legs to make a generous meaty triangle, and then flinging up her arms to repeat the attitude over her head on which her hair stood in a reddish frazzle. 'Dancing he talks about,' she groaned. 'In this bloody heat and in this bloody graveyard? What a joke.'

'Come, Lotte, there is enough life in it, you know.'

'Life, what life? Mosquito life, yes, I know – millions and millions of bloody mosquitoes, all coming to nest in my hair, I think –' she ran her fingers through it so that it stood up like orange grass – 'they think I am Mama Mosquito and drink my blood like milk. All night at my ears, crying and crying for more. See how I've scratched myself everywhere –' she leant towards him, exposing the scratches, relishing the harsh gashes she had drawn through her raw skin.

Baumgartner drew back, flinching. One could have too much of Lotte. 'A little coffee may help,' he suggested.

'What, on the skin? Are you *meshuggeh?*'

'Down the throat, Lotte, down the throat,' he waggled a finger, raising and opening his lips to it like a fish on a hook.

But she scowled, clapping her hand to her head and groaning, 'With the sun so hot, it fries you like an egg in a pan? Coffee is not for this land. Better you have a drink with me,' and she gave him a look that was close to a wink, then got to her feet and padded around the table to the kitchen end of her single room.

It was not what Baumgartner wanted at all – he did not care for gin in the morning and with Lotte one could not even be sure it would be that and not the local brew Ramu brought her, a poison called *feni* that stank. He felt despondent as he watched her take a bottle from behind a row of tins in which she kept her rice and sugar, and pick out glasses from the basin in which dirty dishes were heaped. 'So, you want?' she called aggressively and he gave a reluctant, resigned nod, then watched her rinse the glasses perfunctorily under the brass tap that ran into a plastic bucket. 'Ramu brought it up last night,' she told him as she poured out the colourless fluid. 'Real stuff – from the consulates – not that stuff they make of cashew-nuts in the courtyard.'

'Ach, Lotte, how can you trust Ramu?' he sighed, trying to reconcile himself to the fiery drink he did not want. 'You will be lucky if it is cashew-nut. Not so many cashew-nuts in the courtyard – but many dog turds in the drain.'

She splashed some gin on the table, she had set down the bottle so violently. '*Nein, was ist das?* What's that?' she spat at him. 'You need the soap to wash out the mouth. Don't talk dirty about the food – or drink – in my house, *hörst du?* Good food – good drink – don't spit on it, Hugo, *sei dankbar.*' She splashed some water into the glasses from another bottle, then limped across to the small grey refrigerator that stood shuddering and rattling irately in a corner and got out a tray of ice.

Seeing the ice-cubes slither out of it on to a plate, Baumgartner began to feel refreshed, and mopped his neck with his handkerchief, preparing to feel cooler and to rest. 'Of course is good, Lotte,' he pacified her, 'but not Grand Hotel, hah, not Prince's exactly.'

'Prince's!' she snorted, picking up a handful of ice-cubes and throwing them into a glass. 'Grand Hotel!' She tossed some into the other glass. 'So that is what *mein Hugolein* has come to talk about.' She brought his glass across to him, curtseying before him and managing to splash a little on to his knee.

'Careful, careful with the Herr Consul's gin, Lotte,' he warned. 'Too early in the morning for falling down.'

'Early in the morning I know it is,' she snapped, sinking back on the kitchen chair with her glass of gin. 'The crack of dawn, like the English say.'

'And how is it you are being so English today? Some new friend? Last night's party?' Baumgartner laughed, having taken a sip and found the drink both cold and fiery in a pleasurable way he had not anticipated.

'Party, party,' she groaned, wiping her mouth after a long drink. 'Only party I know was going on downstairs in that madman's flat. I tell you, Hugo, is driving me *meshuggeh*, this place. Downstairs, party. Upstairs, puja – priests, bells, hymns all night. Is a madhouse.' She pulled down the corners of her mouth, two deep gashes formed in the soft floury cheeks on each side, and she looked as worn as she claimed to be.

'I told her not to move,' Baumgartner reminded her. 'Such a nice flat she had, that one in Napoli. Free gift, given for life. Some don't know when they are lucky. Just for money, she gave it up.' He shook his head, again regretting the loss of that little flat in which Lotte had once lived, incredibly enough, looking out at the steeple of the Afghan Church and with the smell of fresh fish from the Sassoon docks sweeping in through the window when the catch came in. 'Nice doorman to keep place safe, sweeper to keep all clean, and breeze at the window – but you wanted money.'

'Don't you?' she exploded. 'Without money, one can live?' She slammed down her glass and refilled it immediately. 'You can't be *memsahib* without money. I did try, Hugo, but no, without money, I was only poor old Lotte, not grand *memsahib*.' Unexpectedly she began to laugh, her face turning maroon with each splutter. 'You remember your Lotte in those *memsahib* days, Hugo?' Without waiting for his corroboration, she went on: 'That was when my Kanti was living. Everything had to be nice then – silver dishes for the nuts on the table, plastic lace curtains in the windows, plastic lace for tablecloths – he liked that. And the servant he engaged for me, that useless boy Raju. Raju understood everything. When I was alone, I never saw him – he would sit outside on the landing, playing cards with all the servants in Napoli. So many people lived there, so many servants they had, and all played cards all day on the landings. But once a month we could be sure the telegram would come from Calcutta, a pink telegram with white paper stuck on it – that meant *Sahib* was coming. Then we would both jump – Raju and I,' she laughed to remember, smacking both hands together to denote action. 'Quick, quick, I would shampoo my hair, dress, go out and buy something nice – a piece of pretty cloth – then run to the *durzee* – I had such a clever man then – he could copy from the magazines, so nicely. And I would find shoes to match – or sandals anyway because stockings there were not. And I would get Raju to leave the cards and come away from his friends. He knew when *Sahib* came he had to behave – they all knew that. I would make him clean the whole kitchen, scrub it all with Vim, catch and kill every cockroach. Yes, Hugo, you do it once a month and you can be free of them – even you, in that dump of yours. And I would order soda and put it in the fridge, and beer. Buy stores. Raju would put on a clean shirt. Then he would cook – all Kanti's favourite food he knew how to make. Not mine: never did he learn to make *Kartoffelpuffer* or *Leberknödel*, however much I tried to teach him. But *dal*, *sabzi*, *khichri*, *roti*, all that, Raju could do just the way Kanti liked. And then I would become *memsahib* in his eyes. Perhaps because I went out in a taxi to fetch Kanti from the station. For that, I would put on a dress,' she snickered at Baumgartner, not at all unaware of how his eyes watched her knees, her thighs. 'All those nice dresses fitted me then. *Ja,* Hugo, I had a green silk one, and that yellow print – and my hair was still blonde then – I really must have looked a *memsahib* in the taxi going to the station, going to meet his train. Then he told me not to because sometimes he might travel with his relations, or with other businessmen from Calcutta, and he did not want them to see me.' Her face was still maroon but her eyes and lips had begun to lose their animation and droop so that her voice slurred. 'So after that I stayed in the flat and waited. Not the same thing. Made me sloppy, like this –' she tugged at the frayed strap of her slip. 'But I had the beer cold, the soda and ice ready, and when he came I could give him a little party. He loved it, that old Kanti. Made me sing all my old songs, and tell jokes – he just laughed and laughed. I suppose no one ever sang or laughed in his home, no one made him laugh there. He had daughters, made them take singing lessons like all the daughters in Calcutta take, but he really couldn't stand their singing. "Graveyard music", he called those songs they all sing in Bengal. He liked mine – with a bit of leg, hee hee. Told me that. Old men like it, don't they, Hugo?' She gave him a wink, but with some difficulty; she could not quite control her eyelids. 'Then he became too sick to laugh. It hurt him to laugh. He wanted to go straight to bed and have his drink there. That was all right, I could understand, but he wouldn't get out. Whole weekend spent lying in bed. That was not fun, after all it was what I did all week. Raju would bring a whisky and soda to the bedroom. Always made a face as if he smelt something. Rude boy. Made me so angry, I wanted to kick him, but Kanti would stop me, say I must not shout at Raju, he was looking after me. *He,* looking after me? *Who* looked after me? *Nobody.* Except Kanti.'

Baumgartner watched her slosh more drink, more ice into her glass, tried to remember the nondescript figure of the Marwari businessman from Calcutta. Dry as a twist of tobacco, shrivelled inside the elaborate folds of his white dhoti and coloured turban, the smell of snuff buried inside them, while from his mouth, full of discoloured teeth, the scent of the silver-coated betel nuts he liked to chew made one reel back – it was like a perfumery – how had Lotte stood it? Even then, when they were both young – when they were all young – he had wondered how Lotte stood it.

She extended her arm to him in a royal, languid gesture, her movements slowed by the gin. 'See, each bangle here is from Kanti. Solid gold, twenty-two carats like Indian women wear – no European would believe, heh?' She jingled them on her wrist in a melancholy way, like bells in the wind. 'Now I'm afraid these thieves will murder me for it – like that drunkard Ramu downstairs, or those – those – ' she jabbed with her finger at the ceiling, not able to bring herself to speak the unspeakable name of the neighbours in that region – 'but I can't take them off and put them in the bank. It is like taking off your wedding-ring. Hindu women do it when they become widows but I won't – they are *not* a wedding-ring, after all, only presents. Presents from Kanti.' She turned the bangles round and round on her wrist, making that jangling sound that jarred Baumgartner. This Hindu widow act, couldn't she stop it?

'That ulcer,' she was brooding aloud, 'I told him don't drink, Kanti – just have the soda, no whisky, but he would lie in my bed, his teeth in a glass on the table – and he would say, "What did I come to Bombay for, then? You, and a drink, that is my life, that is what I live for. Give me more whisky," and I knew how he felt, I also would feel the same, would you not, Hugo?' She glared at him sharply till he nodded in assent, not at all agreeing. 'So drink, drink, drink – then one day – phut! The ulcer went, like the doctors said. In Calcutta. I was not even there to hold his hand. His family was already fighting over the property – no one even to hold his hand, there in the hospital. Dogs die like that, in the street. This is how we go, Hugo,' she wagged her head. 'In the end – alone.'

'Oh, Lotte,' Baumgartner protested, but did not elaborate because he could not.

'And then the court cases begin. The long, long court cases. How many years that has taken, and all my savings, all Kanti's gifts. It has ruined my health, Hugo.'

'Yes, yes,' he nodded cynically, 'I see how your health is ruined,' and ogled her fat arms, her solid thighs, her round belly.

'It *is* ruined,' she insisted, 'only this – ' waving her glass at him – 'only this keeps me going. Like Kanti.'

'Be careful,' he warned, suddenly worried. 'Perhaps we should eat, Lotte. A sandwich maybe.'

'Oh, I never eat *Mittagessen*.' She made a face at the suggestion, and lit a cigarette instead. 'No breakfast, no lunch. At night, perhaps, a little, if I can force myself to go and shop – ' she walked her fingers across the table – 'downstairs.'

Baumgartner became alarmed. That was not how he lived, and his stomach was demanding what it was used to, quite vociferously. 'Just some bread and cheese, Lotte,' he pleaded, for his own sake more than hers.

'Bread and cheese?' she screamed. 'He thinks he is in *Deutschland,* hah? Or in *der Schweiz?* Choice between Roquefort, Camembert, and Brie perhaps? And bread – *Weissbrot, Schwarzbrot, Pumpernickel* maybe?' She became red in the face with indignation.

Baumgartner withdrew, ashamed. 'I only thought – it is so late – too much gin is not good, Lotte. Why not beer instead – in the daytime?'

'Hah!' she snorted. 'Better than the beer in *this* country. Beer only gives the germs food to grow. You need something strong to kill them – like gin.'

'Ach, *Lottchen,* you have lived here fifty years and no germ has got you yet. Just think how many germs – and mosquitoes, and bugs and lice *you* have murdered in this time, hah?'

'You remember that family that lived in Napoli, at the top of the house? How they used to send me, sometimes, a tray with food when they had a special puja for a grandchild or a wedding or whatever it was? I always gave it to Raju, I knew it was full of germs. Funny,' she added in an afterthought, 'that they sent it to me, no? They must have thought – they must have thought Kanti and I – that it was all right. But when he died, all that stopped. Then they sided with his sons, then they too said I was not married, could not keep the flat. So what could I do, Hugo, but give up my beautiful flat in Napoli? They offered to settle out of court – quite a lot of money it seemed to me – so I took it. After all, I had this place; it used to be my shop, my little factory – '

Baumgartner stared at her as if he suspected her of having gone soft in the head with all that gin. What was she talking about now?

Seeing his disbelief she grew shrill. 'You don't remember? My hat business that Kanti set up for me? Just after the war? You don't remember he bought this room for me – for making hats?' She reached out to give him a push with her hand, forcing him back into his cane bucket. 'Hugo, *du bist ja so dumm,* so silly – can't remember Mother Braganza and the two daughters, they used to sit here and make the hats I would design – just after the war?'

He swung his head slowly in a way that could mean yes or no – whatever she wanted of him; a tactic which had often proved useful in his long life with its complicated demands. Staring down at Lotte's feet which were surprisingly pale and narrow on the stained and discoloured floor, he was seeing again his mother's cheek white under the black netting of the veil and the fresh violets pinned to her little black cape for a Sunday morning walk on the Kurfürstendamm. He could not say this to Lotte, who was unlikely to have come across such an apparition in her life on the stage or in a circus tent, and so for a moment they stared at each other in angry incomprehension.

Then Lotte decided to spell it all out for her poor, fuddled, senile old friend. Swinging one leg over the other so as to give her loose flesh a more closely packed arrangement, bulging with maturity, with experience, she drew on her foul-smelling cigarette and reminded Baumgartner, 'I had told Kanti I wanted to do something – to be busy, not to be always waiting for him in the flat – and that I could make a business out of hats, European hats. So he bought me these magazines – European magazines, I *loved* them, looking at all those elegant clothes, like one sees in Europe – '

Baumgartner gave a small snort, wanting to ask her if she expected him to believe that she came from a world of *haute couture,* from Paris, but Lotte refused to listen, or to be stopped.

'And I found Mother Braganza and her two daughters. I found they could copy very well. I would show them a hat with feathers, a hat with beads, a hat with a veil. Once I had them make a little one like a Chinese coolie hat, and under it this veil, black net, and on that little-little beads, Hugo – *ach,* it was *élégante.'*

She uncrossed her thighs and her eyes looked glassy, either with gin or the glare from a crack between the coloured curtains at the window. 'But what was the use of all that fashion here?' she cried, throwing down her cigarette. 'I had forgotten I was living in India!' she laughed. 'India – the land of the sari – of veiled women – what did they know about *hats?* Such an idiot I was, I really thought they would wear my hats. Hats – on top of a sari?' she spluttered. 'And all the time Mother Braganza was telling me, "Madam, no one wear this kind hat. No make this hat, madam. Make for church, for wedding, confirmation, funeral, then you sell. Make with orange blossom, white net, paper flower, my girls will make, Cecilia and Rosalie will make." But did I listen? Of course not! I, make little girls' veils to wear at confirmation?' She shook with laughter, splashing gin and water all over her lap as she refilled her glass, quite ignoring Baumgartner who held out his towards her. 'How could I do that, coming from a Europe where people knew about fashion and elegance? I couldn't make church outfits for the Braganzas and the Lobos and the Lopezes of Bombay, it was too much. And so I kept on with feathers and beads – and all those hats just lay there in this room, rotting. You know how this climate rots everything – the damp, the dust, the insects. When I moved out of Napoli and came here to live, no more the *memsahib,* no more the designer, just poor old woman, me, I had to sweep out all the feathers and the dead moths and the silverfish. So much rubbish. *Ach,* it made me sad,' she ended with a scream of laughter, and actually let Baumgartner have a bit of gin in his glass. 'And Mother Braganza put her daughters on the street. From making hats, they became prostitutes,' Lotte sighed, plucking at the tattered lace on her slip. 'And now they and their clients and their children – all living up on the roof – they abuse me. They throw rotten fish at me. They call the police – the police – ' Lotte's lip began to shake.

'Not a good idea, the hats,' Baumgartner summed up, sinking back with his glass.

'No,' she agreed, 'much better to stay in bed, drink gin and forget all this – this banging, this shouting, this madhouse – ' she pressed her hand to her head because down in the courtyard the mechanics were guiding a lorry down the lane on to their premises, bellowing orders and racing the engine as they did so. 'At least I had this place to come to – when they took Napoli away from me, Kanti's sons. Those boys – I knew them when they were little. If they were sick, I made them porridge. At night I sat holding ice to their foreheads. I kept away the priest, called the doctor. Not even a thermometer they had in the house till I went and got one. If they wanted to dress smart, I went and chose their clothes. But when Kanti was dead, then they said, "Who is this woman? We don't know this woman. Throw her out." Gave me my money and put me out on the street. *Ja,* Hugo, that's how it was.'

She leant forward, tilting out of her chair at the table, her tangled hair falling on her freckled shoulders that were cut by the dirty satin straps of her slip. For a while she brooded, then poured out some more gin, lit another cigarette and threw herself back, facing the silent man in the cane bucket chair. '*Ja,*' she said in her brassiest voice, 'that is the sad story of Lola of Prince's, eh, Hugo, *mein Liebchen?*' She gave him a wink, remembering that shared experience – surely he remembered *that?* 'You remember the old Lola, don't you, Hugo?' To refresh his failing memory, she stretched out her leg, pointing her toes, trying to flex the calf muscle and tighten it into an elegant line. 'Lola, sweet Lola, of Prince's, ah-ha,' she sang.

Baumgartner found himself smiling too. That was a period of Lotte's multicoloured history that he had known more intimately than her later incarnation as a *memsahib*. Nor was he averse to being reminded of Calcutta, of Prince's, his own youth, the days of cabaret and Scotch, of Tommies and GIs, profiteering and wealth, the guns of war at a safe distance and yet close enough to edge the scene with a certain hysteria, the unforgettable hysteria like a drunkenness, a fever bordering on delirium.

'And can Lola still do the can-can?' he teased her.

She stretched out her leg again and jabbed him with her toe. 'To which era you think I belong, eh? To your grand-mother's?' Banging down her glass, she heaved herself to her feet. 'Can you remember nothing?' Putting out her arm, she bent her back and swung around with an unexpected agility. 'Can't you remember Gisela and I in our blue satin gowns with red bows – like this?' She pranced about in her slip, holding up one tattered corner of it as she did so, the other hand on her hip, humming:

'Tea for two and two for tea,
Me for you and you for me . . .'

Baumgartner leant back in his chair, clapping. 'Bravo! *Ja*, I remember it, Lotte. And Gisela with her hair just out of those curlers – she always had a shampoo before a performance – and then each of you did a piece separately – what was it?'

Lotte pulled away the chair from the table, lifted one leg and rested her foot on it. One hand on her hip, with the other she held an imaginary cigarette to her lips. Then, flinging her hair out of her eyes with an equine gesture, she sang out of the corner of her mouth, down-turned:

'Underneath the lantern by the barrack gate,
Darling, I remember the way you used to wait . . .'

'"Lilli Marlene",' shouted Baumgartner, clapping his hands. 'Bravo, "Lilli Marlene"!'

She bowed with a great grandeur of manner but it made her lose her balance and with it her flair for impersonation. Throwing herself on to the chair, she planted her hands on her knees, looking both pleased and ruffled. 'But that Gisela,' she said when she got back her breath, 'that Gisela, she went to that fat little manager – Om Sahni, you remember him, Hugo – and told him, "I come from Russia. I am from the Ballet Russe. I was prima ballerina. I danced Odette, Odile, Giselle . . ." What was she not star of, that Gisela? Never *corps de ballet,* always from birth prima ballerina! And Om Sahni who had been making soda water and bottling it in the shed behind the hotel before he became manager, he believed every word she said. How could a *memsahib,* a blonde lady with a white skin, tell a lie? And he would put on a shiny satiny suit and wear a tie made of sofa material, you know, and sit very close to the dance floor and watch her leaping around in satin slippers with chicken feathers coming down over her ears with tears in his eyes. *Ach,* if Pavlova could have seen Gisela dance the Dying Swan in the Grand Hotel in Calcutta, she would have risen out of her grave and hit her on the head with hammer and sickle, I think – a Bolshevist it would have made of her.'

'Show how Gisela did the Dying Swan, Lotte,' Baumgartner encouraged her but Lotte would not. It was not that Lotte admitted to any limitations of her own but it was now the stifling peak of noon, she had already drunk enough gin to feel waterlogged, and talking made for less perspiration than dancing.

'Clever she was, Gisela, and Om Sahni was not the first man she made a fool of – there had been enough in Shanghai. That was where I first heard of her – never met her of course, my family moved in different circles, had nothing to do with cabaret – but there used to be these posters, I saw them myself, of The Lily of Shanghai. And before that Singapore, before that Macao, before that – she *said* Russia.' Lotte sputtered with laughter. 'Grew her hair long, dyed it dark red like a beetroot, painted her cheeks blue to look hollow, and began to speak like a Russian. Quite an actress, that one,' Lotte chuckled admiringly. 'She even said she was a refugee, a czarina I suppose, fled from the Reds. Where were her jewels, her furs? One day I called that Russian I knew – that Besauloff who used to travel in the Himalayas, you remember? He was from a good family in Russia – his mother came to see him once and she was a countess, I think. So I asked him to come and meet Gisela, ask her some questions, but when she heard – she ran away! She had appointments – doctors, dentists, everybody was waiting for her – and she could not stay to lunch and she could not meet him. Of course not!' Lotte laughed and laughed, so that Baumgartner had to join in although he had heard the story often enough. 'But it did not matter to Gisela. If she had not brought her Russian furs and jewels with her, she found people like Om Sahni to buy them for her in Calcutta, temperature fifty degrees Celsius, and he bought furs from Kashmir that he said were beaver and fox but I think just jackal. Yes, yes, jackal – that piece she wore round her neck with two eyes and four paws and a little tail hanging down. But that was only the beginning for our Gisela, wasn't it? After that, that Raja of – of what, Hugo? – he came to Prince's, saw her in her ballet slippers, asked her to teach his wives and daughters ballet and off she went to the jungles with him. To collect some real furs and diamonds, she said, and you know how her eyes gleamed to think of that.' Lotte laughed raucously, as if in approval of her friend's greed and cunning and success. 'Everyone was like that in the war, was it not so, Hugo? People made money, made fortunes – then vanished – phut – like that. Only we stayed, like fools. Here, amongst the thieves, the cholera, the mosquitoes – ' she slapped her arms in rage.

'Where could we go, Lotte? Where could you and I have gone?' Baumgartner had taken out his handkerchief again and sat twisting and crumpling it.

'Hmm,' she muttered, scratching her arms thoughtfully, brooding. 'Yes, there was nowhere to go. Germany was gone

– phut. Europe was gone, all of it. Let us face it, *Liebchen*, there is no home for us. So where can we go? Hah? Tell me.'

'Venice,' said Hugo unexpectedly, wiping his face and then raising it so that it shone above the soiled rag. 'If I could go, if I could leave, then I would go to Venice.'

Her jaw dropped. For a while it attempted to utter some sound, but hung emptily. 'Venice, he says,' she said at last. 'Venezia – no less. As if he were a duke, or a count. You a millionaire, maybe, in your dreams?'

Baumgartner laughed, shamefacedly. 'Only an idea, Lotte,' he apologised. 'Once I was there – for seven days. I caught the boat to India from there. It was so strange – it was both East and West, both Europe and Asia. I thought – maybe, in such a place, I could be at home.'

'At home – in Venice?' she screamed, beginning to shake with volcanic laughter.

Hurt, he retreated. 'Let me be, Lotte,' he muttered, and struggled out of the chair. He blundered about the room, bumping into furniture till he found the kitchen shelves and there he clattered about amongst the pots and pans, hoping vaguely to find a piece of bread or some fruit or cheese, anything that would give his stomach a little comfort, a little solidity so it would not ache from emptiness or slosh with fluids. In one pot he found a coating of cooked, yellow food and turned away in disgust: he was not hungry enough for that. Dropping it, he blundered his way to the divan and sank down on it like a large bag dropping and settling. 'Is so late, Lotte,' he complained, not quite knowing what he meant, and then pulled off his shoes and lay down, rolled over to face the wall, shut his eyes and after an initial swirl of giddiness, felt himself falling through layers of oblivion, grey upon grey, each darker than the last, thicker, blocking out colour and sound. ' "Lilli Marlene",' he muttered, 'I remember that, Lotte – "Lille Marlene",' but was too deeply embedded in grey felt to hear her reply.

Eventually he felt something press against his back. He thought with sleepy affection that it was his cats who had come to lie on his chest or beside his pillow, and purr. He put out his arm to enfold Fritzi and Mimi, Miese and Lulu. Instead of their stifling, adhesive fur, he met only Lotte's hairless smoothness and bareness. The human, womanly quality of her slack old skin, soft as flour, drew a groan of pleasure out of his empty stomach – it was good, like bread. He turned and put his arms around her, rubbing her back, again forgetting she was not a cat, murmuring '*Wie geht's dann,* Lulu, eh? What is it you want?' Like a cat she pressed upon him, nuzzling, nibbling, without speech. With small groans they made themselves comfortable against each other, finding concavities into which to press their convexities, and convexities into which to fit concavities, till at last they made one comfortable whole, two halves of a large misshapen bag of flesh, and then they were still and slept the heavy noontime sleep of the tropics, sighing and snoring less and less till they became totally immobile, silent.

FOUR

It had seemed bedlam when he disembarked and walked on to what he was assured was Indian soil – the crowds, of Indians, Britons, Americans, Gurkhas – coolies carrying their luggage – cabin trunks and bed-rolls – officers stiff with laundry starch and gleaming with Brasso and boot polish – hawkers and traders scurrying around with baskets and trays – *memsahibs* and blonde children with lopsided basin-shaped topis on their bleached hair – Indian women in shapeless garments squatting passively with their baskets or babies – and over it all, congealing them into one restless, heaving mass, the light from the sky and the sea, an invasion of light such as he had never known could exist – and heat like boiling oil tipped out of a cauldron on to their heads, running down their necks and into their collars and shirts.

He stood for a long time, unsteady on his legs, so long used to the pitching of the ship, trying to find the courage to make his way through this tumult, find a hotel, the address he had in his pocket. The coolies did not trouble him – he had no luggage they could carry – he was left to himself. On that first day as on every other day, left to himself.

He would have wanted, on that day, to have a hand settle on his wrist, lead him. Or at least a signboard. In a familiar language. A face with a familiar expression. He could not read these faces, or their expressions – joy? agony? panic? He felt his own panic going out, mingling with theirs. Then his paralysis gave way, he made a move – when the crowds stopped swirling and began to drain through the gates to the city. The crowd had thinned so there were empty spaces between the people through which he could see a way, so he picked up his duffel bag and moved at last.

This was his entry into India.

To the tonga-wallah, on climbing into the creaking carriage that stank of horsedung, he said, 'To the Taj Hotel, pliss,' because it had been described to him as an eastern palace. Having also been told that the engineers had mistakenly built it with its entrance to the city bazaar, its back to the ravishing sea-front, thus driving the architect, an Italian, to suicide, he was not perturbed when the tonga ambled through the bazaar, its horse narrowly escaping death a hundred times, its driver screaming abuse and directions till blood ran from his mouth – Baumgartner took it to be blood, but in the East colours were not, he knew, the colours they were in the West – and deposited him on the steps of the dingy green front of a multi-storeyed but narrow house of rusty iron and stucco in a lane filled with vehicles of a greater variety than Baumgartner had imagined were possible. This was the famous, or infamous, back-to-front, he told himself and climbed out. He carried in his own bag since there was no porter at the door as might have been expected from the lyrical descriptions of Eastern luxury he had heard from his fellow voyagers. On entering the lobby that was just a narrow passage, reeking of food and streaked with the red that the alarmed Baumgartner took to be blood from a gun battle, he found himself in a seedy house with no lighting and was shaken by grave doubt. He would have fled if it had not occurred to him that this was a place he could better afford than a suite in a luxury hotel. After standing around helplessly, he finally cleared his throat – and found it hurt. A germ? A deadly illness? All seemed possible, too possible, in this setting. Eventually a woman appeared, seemingly from the cracks of the floor above, sidling down the staircase,

adjusting her hair and her cotton garments as she did so, with a
wet, dripping hand.

'Wanting room?' she screamed at Baumgartner, aggressively
thrusting out her chin in a challenge. 'One upstairs – room
fourteen free.'

Following her up the wooden stairs, Baumgartner cleared
his throat again, this time to ask, hesitantly, 'This Taj Hotel?'

She turned upon him like a jungle cat, spitting. 'Yaiss,' she
screamed, 'this Taj Hotel. Why not Taj Hotel, heh? Only one
can be Taj Hotel? Ten, twenty Taj Hotels in Bombay – no one
can tell me this no Taj Hotel, this Bombay Hotel, Goa Hotel,
Hindu Hotel, I no listen!' she screamed. 'I say Taj Hotel, then
this Taj Hotel,' and she marched on down the dark passage to a
door at the end that she flung open. 'Wanting?' she challenged
him, crossing her arms to wait for an answer.

Baumgartner meekly bent his head and walked in past her,
too exhausted and too nervous to argue. He had had trouble
recognising her language as English; it had seemed to him
more like the seeds of a red hot chilli exploding out of its
pod into his face. He mopped his face and turned to ask her
some necessary questions but she disappeared, banging the
door shut. It took him a while to get used to the dark. Not
only did the single window look out on a concrete wall some
six feet away, preventing all light and air from entering, but
the excessive dirt that coated every surface from the light
bulb to the cotton mattress and the floor added to the
gloom.

He stood by the window, studying the scene with great
seriousness, knowing himself to be tricked. It was the first of
India's tricks. But was it a trick?

Was it not India's way of revealing the world that lay on the
other side of the mirror? India flashed the mirror in your face,
with a brightness and laughter as raucous as a street band. You
could be blinded by it. But if you refused to look into it, if
you insisted on walking around to the back, then India stood
aside, admitting you where you had not thought you could
go. India was two worlds, or ten. She stood before him, hands

on her hips, laughing that blood-stained laugh: Choose! Choose!

The man behind the office desk, fanning his face with a folded newspaper, was not what Baumgartner had been told to expect. At least, he declared he was not. 'No, no, quite wrong, quite wrong,' he kept repeating, as Baumgartner tried to question him, in his new and hesitant English, about the business the Gentleman from Hamburg had assured him existed in Bombay. The man behind the desk seemed puzzled at the mention of Hamburg, timber, shipping . . . every word that Baumgartner managed to summon out of his new language, dragging it off his tongue with a reluctance bordering on paralysis, the bald, dark man in the long white cotton shirt with small gold buttons shook his head at in mystified denial. On the wall behind him hung a picture of an eleven-armed goddess, and over its frame was draped a garland of tinsel. Baumgartner found himself staring at it in his frustration – it drew and held his attention and seemed increasingly weird, foreign, exotic and inscrutable to him.

Then he chanced to find the word 'Ex – port'. 'Ex-phott,' he said, and the fat, puzzled, perspiring man seemed to roll himself up into a ball, tight with excitement, and then explode out of his seat.

'Ex-pawt!' he gasped, clutching the side of his head. 'Ex-pawt. *Of course*, ex-pawt. Germany, Europe. Shipping, timber – I know, I know.' He charged around the desk, grasped Baumgartner by the hand and pumped it up and down, then slapped his shoulder for good measure, and began to babble at such speed that Baumgartner gave up even trying to follow. Instead he gazed at the eleven-armed goddess for an explanation – perhaps she had brought about this flood of communication, perhaps she was the goddess of good fortune. Certainly the tinsel draped around her winked and gleamed as it turned and susurrated lightly in the breeze from the electric fan.

He waited till the man had run through all the gestures and

tones of excitement and sat down to mop himself with his large bandanna. Then he took from his pocket the letter from Herr Pfuehl and handed it over.

'Letter from Foo-ol? You have?' The bald man's face emerged from behind the bandanna, beaming, but it was clearly no longer necessary. 'Please have lunch with me. We will go out, and eat, and talk.'

On their way to a restaurant, bowling along the sea-front in a horse carriage, Chimanlal waved an arm at an imposing pile of stone that lined and overlooked the bay. 'The Taj Hotel,' he said, proudly showing off the sight, and seemed gratified when Baumgartner swung around in his seat and stared as though he had seen something he never expected to see in all his life.

'*That* – Taj Hotel?' Baumgartner wonderingly enquired.

Chimanlal nodded, pleased to see him so impressed, but instructed the carriage driver to go a little further. 'Vegetarian restaurant, vegetarian food,' he explained, on dismounting, 'is famous for. You are liking vegetarian?'

Actually Baumgartner could not have told if what he put in his mouth was fish, flesh, fowl or foliage – the sauce in which all the bits and pieces floated was so fiery it scalded the coating of his tongue and made him burst like a fountain into perspiration.

His host seemed pleased at that too, as though it were a special act of politeness on Baumgartner's part. He laughed and shovelled more rice on to Baumgartner's shining tin tray. The rice steamed, the sauces sputtered, Baumgartner perspired and fished around in it all with a large tin spoon, admiringly watching his host manage all the complicated exercises involved with just his fingers. Finally the heat of the food and the heat of the time of day overcame them both; no more eating was possible. The trays were taken away by the boy-waiter who wore an amulet on a cord round his neck, and little plates were brought of condiments Baumgartner felt compelled to sample; the flavours proved such as he could not have imagined. The sweet, the astringent and the perfumed swirled around in his mouth; he kept his lips tightly together so none of this lethal mixture could escape. Chimanlal tossed handfuls into his own mouth, crushed the scented seeds casually, leant back in his chair, picked his teeth, and began to talk of business, of exports, of shipping, of trade in what seemed to Baumgartner a bewildering combination of two or three languages. He replied in his own selection of two or three. It seemed Chimanlal could give him a valuable introduction to an associate in Calcutta; it seemed there were all kinds of possibilities in the business world of India. Miraculously, Baumgartner could play a role in it that might turn out quite profitable.

Out on the latticed veranda the light from the afternoon sky fell in great blocks of white heat. Somewhere beyond that veranda was the street, the traffic, the noise, and beyond that the sea, the ships, the rose-red arc of the Gateway of India. Baumgartner felt his world not merely opening up but torn open, hacked open, to the Eastern light.

'What, on your very first day you ate curry? And you did not get food poisoning? Dysentery? Not even diarrhoea?' Lotte had been outraged when he told her, years later. '*Mensch*, it must be like a rubber tyre, your belly.' Baumgartner laughed, rather proudly. It set him apart from his fellow countrymen, from others as pale as he in this foreign land. It was one more thing, he eventually realised, that set him apart from them.

Then the two days and two nights on the train, rattling and rolling along the rails laid on the dryest earth that was imaginable. He sat at the window, staring at that hard, flat earth – at first a friable red, then a crumbling black, and finally mile upon mile of dun colourlessness till the sun made him feverish, and the sameness of the scene shiver. He pulled down the wooden shutter in a cloud of dust and soot and settled back with his head against the bunk, rolling. Even boxed in, shuttered, he could still see the flatness and dryness and the unvarying colourlessness of the land thundering by, hundreds upon hundreds of miles. The coconut trees that stood out like blackened spokes and bore no fruit, nothing, just some dead, dry leaves, fan-shaped, like broken umbrellas. The villages or townships that seemed too meagre, too like the flat pale earth itself to be differentiated from it as human habitations – shelters that were no shelters but merely a part of the featureless land. The cattle that wore their hides draped in loose folds on their skeletons, roaming aimlessly in search of non-existent grass. Birds like clouds of mosquitoes hanging upon the air in the distance. Only the sudden leap of a boy, a goatherd, in jubilation at the sight of this vehicle in thundering motion along the rails, waving to Baumgartner when he pulled up the shutter and leant out in the grey of the evening. Baumgartner waved back, his heart suddenly pounding with joy, with fear.

Because alongside the train was always the shadow of the past, of elsewhere, of what had been and could never be abandoned – an animal in its grey pelt, keeping pace, clinging, refusing to part. An animal like a jackal in the day, a hyena in the night. In the darkness, it continued to chase the train, chase Baumgartner.

The passengers. A Jesuit father on his way to the seminary in Chanderanagore. Returning after sick-leave. Dressed in black. His face haggard and green with many seasons of malaria and dysentery. Reading the Bible, also in black. His lips moving, eating the words. Then eating a banana. Looking across at Baumgartner and saying, 'The only thing you can eat on a journey in this country. It is not touched by their hands, you see, it is protected by its skin. The skin – it is thicker than ours, see.' Peeling it delicately, precisely, then flinging the skin out on to the station platform where a cow, foraging amidst the empty cigarette packets and paper bags, swung its face low and snatched it up with its long black tongue and munched it lugubriously. 'And peanuts, in their shells,' he added, as though inspired. As if he had conjured them, children appeared from behind the cow, children without a stitch of clothing on them except for those amulets on black cords he had seen before, holding out paper cones filled with peanuts. They were no apparitions – their voices rang ear-splittingly: they might have been made of tin, or saws.

Two British soldiers in khaki. Their voices too loud, rasping. Yet Baumgartner could not understand a word, was not certain even that it was English. They rolled their words in their mouths, like potatoes. They were as foreign as those children on the platform – black, naked, raucous.

A block of ice was brought in and placed in the middle of the compartment in a tin tub. The ice melted and dripped and leaked through the day, smelling of damp straw and mud. The British soldiers kept their brown beer bottles lying alongside it in the tub. They turned the bottles over as gently as if they were babies. They opened one and offered it to the priest who refused, curtly, then to Baumgartner who felt he had to refuse also lest they discover his nationality. They looked at him as if their worst suspicions were confirmed.

In Calcutta, the tropical green. After all that dun dust, that bone-meal grey, suddenly, out of the night, this sprouting green, this fountain of green vegetation, as overwhelming as the aridity had been before. Like the desert, washed by white-hot light so that the green glinted as fiercely as metal or glass. But pools of dense shade, still, stagnant water. Even the people were damp – moisture seeped from under their hair and ran in rivulets, drenching their clothes. Baumgartner, struggling yet static in the crowd at the station, was soon damp and streaming, too. But he made his way, with the last reserves of his quickly melting energy, to the address he had been given by Chimanlal. Here under the indolently turning electric fan with its broad wooden blades edged with grime, the man at the desk flattened out Baumgartner's letter of introduction under his brown fingers with their brown nails. Looking up across it, he smiled, as if offering a slice of fresh coconut. He knew the Man from Hamburg. Also Chimanlal from Bombay. He knew the timber trade. Also the shipping industry.

Everything was possible, available. He would give Baumgartner a place – he waved an arm in a fine, delicately ruffled, white
muslin sleeve – here, in his office, to go through the files,
study the market, make plans. With his, Habibullah's, help
and instruction, he could begin at last.

He stayed in a hotel on Middleton Row that looked like a
substantial villa. The expense worried him – Herr Pfuehl's
kind loan was dwindling – but, with the help of Chimanlal's
introduction, he would soon be earning and then a good
address would be a necessity, not an indulgence. His room,
high-ceilinged, had french windows with green shutters.
Baumgartner had imagined such shuttered windows were to
be found only in the South of France, along the Mediterranean. He stayed gratefully behind them all afternoon. In the
evening he opened them and looked into a garden where
strings of electric lights were lit in the trees and waiters idled
with trays of glasses and ice, cold drinks, iced beer. Later, a
band played. Ravished by the sights, the sounds, Baumgartner went out, ordered beer, sat in the dark, listening, drinking.
He had bathed and wore his lightest clothes; in abandoning the
thick, heavy clothing of Europe, he felt lighter than he had
ever been, physically unburdened. The air – so warm, so
humid, so languid – made him drowsy, relaxed. He felt he was
in paradise – or would have, had it not been for the immense,
ferocious mosquitoes.

Driven indoors by their assault, he took off his shoes, felt his
feet bare on the cool marble. He had never in his life done such
a thing: what would Mutti have said? He found some fine
letter-paper and under a lamp around which moths lurched
and flapped, he began a letter: 'Liebste Mutti . . .' His hand
became damp and stuck to the sheet of paper, blurring the ink.
He perspired as though he were doing heavy labour. But he
wrote, putting in all the things he thought she would like to
read – about a snake-charmer he had seen on the Bombay
streets, about the bananas and papayas he had had to eat – and
left out the raucous, naked children at the station, the cow that

ate cigarette packets, the land that bore no fruit. Also the British soldiers, and the Catholic priest. She would not understand, it was too bewildering. To reassure her, he added, 'Soon I will be earning. Tell me if you have enough or I will send you what you need; also, repay the loan to Herr Pfuehl.'

Going out for a packet of cigarettes from a stall he had noticed at the corner, late at night when the shops were shut, he was hailed by two women who stood by a high wall that stank of urine and garbage. They wore white frocks, like nurses, and jewellery of glass, and tin. When they smiled at him, waving 'Hoo-hoo, To-mmy,' he saw that their teeth were stained red. When he had bought his cigarettes and turned away, they grabbed him by an arm each, crying, 'Less have drink, Tommy, come *awn*.' They told him their names were Rosie and Violet, but they smelt of Eastern flowers – jasmine, or lotus, as well as perspiration, cheap cigarettes, alcohol and the stuff they chewed with their strong, flashing teeth, spitting frequently to rid their mouths of its crimson juice.

He found he had to build a new language to suit these new conditions – German no longer sufficed, and English was elusive. Languages sprouted around him like tropical foliage and he picked words from it without knowing if they were English or Hindi or Bengali – they were simply words he needed: *chai, khana, baraf, lao, jaldi, joota, chota peg, pani, kamra, soda, garee* . . . what was this language he was wrestling out of the air, wrenching around to his own purposes? He suspected it was not Indian, but India's, the India he was marking out for himself.

Baumgartner on the steamship, travelling to Dacca. Baumgartner with his feet sweating in white canvas shoes, propped up on the rail, sitting in the shade of a straw hat and studying the bank in an attempt at separating the animate from the inanimate. The forest that was like a shroud on the bank, ghostly and impenetrable. Crocodiles that slept like whitened stones, spattered by the excrement of the egrets that rode them delicately. Bamboos that stirred, women who lowered brass pots into the muddy swirl from which a fish leapt suddenly – but when he remembered them later, in a hotel room in a steaming city that rang with rickshaw bells, he wondered if it had not all been a mirage, a dream. If it had been a real scene, in a real land, then Baumgartner with his hat and shoes would have been too unlikely a visitor to be possible, a hallucination for those who watched from the shore. If he were real, then surely the scene, the setting was not. How could the two exist together in one land? The match was improbable beyond belief.

Baumgartner with fever. Fever filling his limbs, and belly, with lead. Making the surface of his skin crisp, delicate, sensitive. The head cracking, at the temples. The mosquito-net parcelling him up and hanging limp because there was no air. The medicine carmine and bitter, so bitter he could not have believed such bitterness possible, in a bottle marked with a notched strip of white paper. A glass, a long-handled spoon. 'Malaria one does get here, Mutti, but quinine grows here too and puts it right,' he wrote on fine blue paper. 'So many mosquitoes in this land,' whirring in his ear like electric fans, stinging him all over with their nettles. How did they enter the mosquito net? He tried to hunt them by the beam of his electric torch but the fever and the quinine made him giddy; he fell over, exhausted.

In the South, the heat of the sun was an assault, a violence. Amongst the slimness and darkness of the men and women in their white loose garments, he felt himself a great hunk of red meat, cooking in his own juices. They gave him coffee in a metal tumbler that nearly fell from his blistered fingers. When he ate, it was his tongue that was blistered and peeled. Daily he grew redder. Would he one day be darker? It seemed desperately important to belong and make a place for himself. He had to succeed in that if the dream of bringing his mother to India and making a home for her was to be turned into a reality. The news that came from Europe became rapidly more alarming; it was as if she, and therefore he, Baumgartner, were being pursued, run down to earth. She had to be made to leave, she had to be brought away, and then somehow he would have to make her accept India as her home. It was becoming clear to him that this was the only possibility, there was no other. It was why he plunged into it with such urgency.

At the auction he stood amongst small men who seemed to gibber with the excitement of seeing the giant teak trees, the great monuments of timber cut and piled in the yard. Elephants had dragged them from the forest, men could not have. He bought teak in the North, mahogany and rosewood in the South. He stood in the docks in Calcutta, despatching it. Then wondered if it would reach its destination. War was imminent, war loomed behind every lamppost and bush in the form of soldiers, stinking with fear and unwashed clothes.

He stood in the middle of his room in the hotel on Middleton Row, holding the fine sheets of paper across which her writing slanted, and stood reading them, before going in to bathe or change although he had just returned from a journey through Assam. He devoured the writing, then the spaces between the writing, hunting for the reassurance that the words so lacked. It was a cold winter and there was no coal but . . . there was of course no butter to be had but the neighbours were kind, they looked to her needs . . . he must not worry . . . there was no need to worry . . . the oftener she repeated the phrase, the more agitated he grew. The gin and tonic he had ordered to drink while reading the news from home stood untouched beside the *chaise-longue* on which he could not now sink down and rest.

The unease only increased, till one day the letter he was handed at the desk on his return from yet another journey, turned out to be his own stamped *'Adresse Unbekannt'*.

Address Unknown? Now what was this? Had she moved? Where to? Why? He must send a cable, to Herr Pfuehl, to the landlady of the boarding-house on Grenadierstrasse, to his mother. Rushing out of the hotel, he ordered the taxi-driver to take him to the nearest post office. It was shut. They dashed to the main post office on Dalhousie Square. At a grimy counter, watched by a betel-chewing clerk, he filled in one telegraph form after another, perspiring profusely.

Gratefully he let himself be taken to a club that night by some of the other inhabitants of the hotel. At the round table in a room almost pitch-dark but brilliant with the noise of the band, he drank gin, not beer. Someone brought a big blonde woman in a white dress to the table. 'Here, someone from your own country,' was the introduction and they looked at each other warily. 'Lola, from Prince's,' laughed the young men who jumped to their feet in excitement. She raised a round, plump arm and patted her hair which was thick, frizzy and yellow, a straw mat on her red, ringed neck. In those raw, sore rings of her neck, so like his own, he saw their kinship. When they put her on a chair next to his, he stammered, 'How came you here?' in the German to which he was no longer accustomed. But hers was worse.

Prince's. The band played music that was like treacle, or tinsel. It filled the eyes and ears and suffocated. In that drowning well of sly, subdued light and raucous, unmodulated music, Lola danced, blonde and pink and white like a tattered doll. She danced with a trim bony woman who had orange hair, violet eyelids and purple nails. Together they danced and made eyes at the men who crowded around the dance floor as if it were a circus ring. The men climbed on to the tables, on to each other's shoulders, whistled and clapped till they fell over. Like possessed marionettes the girls struck the floor with their heels, swung their hips and gestured with their hands, the one with yellow hair and the one with orange, singing together:

'Lola and Lily
are fifteen and free,
Lola and Lily – '
and, together with the bandleader, all the men in the audience roared:
'O give them to me!'

The first time she visited him in his hotel room, she flung herself on to his bed, kicked off her red sandals, twiddled her brightly painted toes, and laughed, 'Lola! They call me that, those *Dummkopf* people – don't even know a Lola has to have black hair, black eyes, skin like a magnolia flower. To them, you can have blonde hair, blue eyes, pink cheeks and still be Lola.'

'What were you at home then?' he smiled from the chair by the window where he sat smoking, both pleased and uneasy at her intrusion, ushered in by the smirking waiter from downstairs. He found himself enjoying the feel of German in his mouth, as familiar a taste as brown bread or beer, but puzzled by her accent, to his Berliner ear slurred and rasping.

'What was I at home?' she laughed, lifting up the mat of strawy hair from her neck in that characteristic gesture which he now saw she made to show off her plump arms and the line of her breasts, raised under the cotton material printed with red flowers and green parrots. 'Lulu – in Germany, I was Lulu.'

He gave her a wink. 'Lulu is not German.'

She turned on him angrily. 'What Germany are you speaking of, you turnip-nosed *Jude*? My mother might have named me Lotte, but once I became a dancer I was Lulu.'

'And when was that?' he asked, willing to forgive her her little outburst for the sake of her friendliness, her German tongue.

'*Ach*, I was ten, twelve, daughter of show people, part of a show team.' She pointed her toes, showed him the arc of her foot, with a kind of professional pride. 'My mother sang opera – she was Madam Butterfly when I was in her womb. Can you not guess? Of course I wanted to be someone in my own right, wanted to act. In a theatre. But once any director saw me dance, he forgot about my acting. I could have played any role – always was a monkey, *ein Affe* – Sarah Bernhardt was my goddess, but my parents had taught me to dance and dance I had to. So Lulu I remained. A good name for a dancer, *nicht wahr?*'

He smiled in agreement, and got up to pour her a glass of gin from a bottle on his dressing-table: it was too early to go down for a beer, the waiters in the garden below were dragging the chairs off the tables with loud crashes, laughing and abusing each other in a friendly way, like noisy birds. Handing the drink to her he asked, 'And the other – who is your partner? What is *her* real name?'

'My partner? Who – that Lily-of-the-valley?' Lotte made a grotesque face, then drank a gulp of gin that made her smile again. 'Lily-of-Shanghai she was in the past. And before that, at home, she was – she confessed to me when I saw it on a letter that came for her – just Gisela. Gisela the Goose Girl, I teased her when I handed her the letter. She was *furious*, I can tell you. She had told everyone in Calcutta she was Giselle from Russia, but then I popped up and told everyone I had seen her show advertised on street posters in Shanghai where she was Lily, one more Lily amongst hundreds of Lilies in hundreds of cabarets and bars, ha-ha!' Lotte flung her legs up in the air and did a little flutter of her feet in mid-air. 'But when I went to the Grand Hotel for a job – '

'How? What brought you here, to Calcutta?' Baumgartner could not help interrupting.

'*Ach*, don't ask me that – if I start telling you we will be sitting here all night, all day. I was on a boat, it brought me up that drain they call the Hooghly and it dumped me here in the mud of Calcutta. I had to earn a living, *nicht wahr*? How? By dancing, as I had done since I was ten, twelve. Some sailors I met in a bar took me to the Grand. There was Gisela. She didn't like me barging in, I can tell you, but the proprietor, he was getting a little bored with the Dying Swan, he wanted something new. What is better than one girl?' She poked Baumgartner's leg with her toe, playfully. 'Huh? Tell me. You don't know? *Ach, du* poor *Dummkopf* – *two* girls, of course. Even that idiot proprietor knew that. He thought at once: ah-ha, now I will have two dancers, twins, one in pink, one in blue, like that, and everyone will love it of course. And poor Gisela, she had to put up with me if she wanted to keep her job. She wanted it all right – a good job to have in this city.' She closed one eye in a wink as loud as a smack. 'Give me a cigarette, Hugo.'

Baumgartner ordered cakes for both of them, at a table in Flury's. The proprietor was Swiss, they said, and the pastries were very fine. The girls wolfed down one after the other, licking cream off their fingers, quarrelling over the cherries, rolling their eyes at the chocolates. Baumgartner watched, over a cigarette, pleased even if they paid him no attention, eating and talking only to each other, almost incomprehensibly.

No sooner were the pastries gone than Gisela started to hum in a bored way and look around the restaurant for some more interesting patron. (In the ladies' room at the back, adjusting her garters, she had said, 'Now, really, Lotte – this is going too far. German he may be but who wants a German just when war is going to break out? And such a turnip, Lotte – a *Jiddischer* turnip too.') Even at that hour of the morning, she had painted her eyelids violet, her cheeks carmine, her lips purple and wore on her wrists and fingers a collection of intricately cut glass – yellow, blue, green. Baumgartner, stealing glances at her, felt she could not possibly be from Germany, she was altogether a product of the tropics, the overheated East, a parakeet or macaw. But when she glanced across at an immense Russian at the next table and said, '*Wo kauft sie dann ihr Brot* – I wonder where she buys her bread?' he had to laugh, it was a remark straight off the Berlin streets.

In no time she had spotted an acquaintance from the night before, a wealthy race-going Marwari businessman. '*Excusez-moi, mes amis,*' she hissed at Lotte and Baumgartner, 'but he gave me a pearl once – this size – and has the best tips for the races,' and sliding away from their table, she flew across the restaurant to join more promising company.

'That Gisi – Goose Girl she may have been but now she is Gisi the Gold-digger,' Lotte remarked wryly, with both envy and rancour.

That was the crowd the girls gathered around them – meeting them at the Three Hundred in the evening before they moved on to Prince's for the cabaret, or else reversing the order and going to the Three Hundred after the cabaret. The place – a mouldering villa with porches, shuttered windows, night-flowering creepers, malevolent-looking watchmen – was kept in pitch-darkness, only cigarette lighters and diamond rings flared, briefly. In the murk swirled the lucrative aura of bankers, traders, racehorse owners, landowners from small northern states who were not quite rajas although occasionally the Maharaja of Burdwan or the Maharani of Cooch Behar were excitedly pointed out to Baumgartner, and stories of elephant hunts, tiger shoots and fabulous banquets were told over the gins and whiskies in the secretive dark. There were also some more daylit characters – young men from the mercantile firms, mostly Englishmen, who dealt in jute, tea or coal and talked of rugby and squash, a few Indians amongst them. There was a Russian adventurer, a great tall man with a face like a sledge who told laughingly of all the hotels he had bought and run, only to lose them to pay the debts he ran up at gambling tables, and – less plausibly but more entertainingly – the errands he had run for czars, Mongol chieftains, Chinese drug-peddlers and wealth-crazed rajas, while the crowds at his table plied him with more and more drink so that he should embroider his stories still more lavishly than the time before. Always there was a point in the evening when he would go down on the floor, strike out with his legs and sing 'Galinka' till he fell over, dead drunk, too large and too heavy to be lifted and carried out; then he became a kind of ceremonial altar for the night's celebrations, which only came to an end when he woke and called for a pink gin. There was an Italian traveller who had been to more wonderful places – the Himalayan passes, Tibet, Bhutan, Ceylon, the Andaman, Laccadive and Nicobar islands – but he told less, held back more so that rumours surrounded him like a black net. There were game hunters resting after the ardours of *shikar* in the forests of Cooch Behar and the Sunderbans. There were also, less colourfully but more ominously, an increasing number of soldiers, in khaki, much more dour and subdued than the others till it was time for the sundowner and after that they were the most uncontrolled and the most alarming of all.

Baumgartner had very little to contribute to the conversation in those gatherings – trade and business practices were too commonplace to flaunt – but in the company of the men in khaki he found himself going absolutely silent, listening in a strained way, losing his smile. Even if they were not responsible for the silence from Germany, the complete absence of any response to his telegrams, of the news of his mother for which he was still waiting, he knew they were caught up in the same blind chaos, an active part of it, and he feared them instinctively. At times he caught a reflection of his own attitude in Lotte and Gisela, even though they disguised their disquiet with laughter and foul language. They would leave early, pleading a headache or work at Prince's. Sometimes one or two of the soldiers would accompany them. Then Baumgartner would leave alone, stopping under the dim streetlamp to pour some coins into the bandaged stump proffered by the leper who waited legless on his little cart for the generosity of the drunks. As he strolled back to his hotel in the liquified heat of the August night, Violet and Rosie would detach themselves from the urine and betel-stained wall and pout, 'Very big *sahib* you have become. No more time for old friends, eh?' and pull at his sleeves, demand money, demand cigarettes.

'Lotte, is not good, to be with these British soldiers,' he protested one morning when she came into his room to show him an armful of shopping she had done on Park Street. She had not told him who had paid for the gold sandals, the silk scarf or the sequinned bag that she flaunted before him, but he guessed.

'Poof, what does it matter? Is a British soldier worse than a German soldier or an American soldier? Soldiers are everywhere the same, *mein* Hugo – free with money when they are in port!' She did a few dance steps to make the gold heels flash and click. '*Ach*, what a port is Calcutta! Could Shanghai be better, or Hamburg even?' The shopping had gone to her head, Baumgartner thought, that was what the feel of money did. While he fumed, she swung the sequinned bag on her wrist and laughed to see it glint in the heavy morning light that poured in through the open window. Outside were red and yellow canna lilies, loudly chattering mynah birds, a flowering tree. She seemed delighted to take her part in these cockatoo colours, this macaw setting.

'Will soon be war between our countries,' he warned.

'You still read newspapers?' she pouted at him. 'As if war in Europe will have anything to do with us here in Calcutta. Hugo, how silly you are. *Sei doch nicht so blöd.*'

'How will it not?' he argued. 'We are in British territory, and we are German nationals – '

'You are, but I am not,' she interrupted.

'No? What do you mean? What nationality have you?'

'*Ach*, what does it matter? I can change any day that I want. Many men are wanting to marry me – that Kanti Sethia, he is always asking and asking.' She was standing still now, at the window, looking out, swinging the little bag on her wrist; it flew round and round her like a bright bird.

'Kanti Sethia?' Baumgartner was speechless for a few minutes, his lips moving soundlessly. The faces of Lotte's admirers passed before him in rapid succession, so rapid that they blurred. The handsome tea-planter with the small moustache over his big, square teeth who came from his tea-garden in Assam once a month to see her dance? The dashing attaché of the Maharaja of Burdwan? Or the jeweller who took her and Gisela to the races? Could it be the jeweller – the small brown monkey of a man who took snuff and blew it into a bandanna, carried a walking-stick, wore a white dhoti and a small black cap and became insensible after drinking two whiskies? 'Ach, Lotte, who?' he cried in pain. 'The jeweller? Fifty years old or perhaps more?'

'Hunf, what does it matter?' Lotte shrugged. 'If I have to change my nationality I can marry him and change at once. Don't you see me as an Indian bride, Hugo?' She left the window and came towards him, prancing. 'In a gold sari, with a red dot here in the middle of my forehead, and a diamond nose-ring?' She began to leap around the room with laughter and excitement.

'Du bist verrückt, you're mad, Lotte. He must be married and have a family – how could he not? Here they marry at fourteen, fifteen – '

'Then he should have a change – to Lola, whoopee!' she screamed, flinging the sequinned bag clear across the room.

It was in Prince's, at a table where Baumgartner alone of the men was not dressed in khaki and where Lotte and Gisela alone provided colour by their costumes, that Baumgartner raised his glass to the two of them when they came up after their performance and said, 'Prosit!' The next instant there was a hand on his shoulder, a khaki cuff before his eyes. 'Jerry, eh? Jerries, you all?'

Someone shouted, 'Don't be a bloody fool. These are the dancers. You want to stop the show?'

But the hand did not let go, it held harder. Baumgartner tried to shake free. Commotion broke out. In the uproar, Baumgartner lost Lotte, lost Gisela. He kept looking over his shoulder, searching the heaving mass for a glimpse of pink or blue silk, saw them just as they were whisked away by the hotel manager. He tried to follow but was held fast. He heard his sleeve rip. 'Now look,' he began to protest when someone hit him on the back of the neck. For a few moments he could not see clearly, everything became a squirming mess of red before him, then he struck out with his fists and heels as he had not done since he was a schoolboy, trapped in a corner of the schoolyard while everyone chanted:

'Baumgartner, Baum,
Hat ein Nase
Wie ein Daum!'

He even found himself so far back in infancy that he actually bit into a hand that was clapped over his mouth. He tasted blood – warm, sweet, disgusting. Three men jumped on top of him, feet first. When he came out from under them, he found a policeman bending over him – just in time, for someone had broken a bottle and was flashing that at him. All around them, skulls were cracking under batons, crisply. He covered his own head with his hands, defensively. But the policeman lifted him up by his elbow and called him '*Sahib*'.

In the police station a man with great rings of tiredness under his eyes, and stains of perspiration on his back, apologised, 'I have to arrest you, sir. War is declared and we must take you into detention camp. Very bad, sir, very bad.' Looking abject, he added, 'British make rules here, sir, not Indians.' Baumgartner, feeling the salt of blood on his lips with his tongue, smiled in relief at being in his hands, not a white man's. 'Will my letters be forwarded?' he asked. 'Will you deliver mail at the camp? Can I write a letter before I go?'

He was still asking the same question of everyone he met in the improvised camp in Fort William to which he was taken with the other 'enemy aliens'. They threw him uncomprehending looks but one man put his index finger to his temple and turned it like a screw. '*Mensch*,' he said, 'here we are in a military prison – and you are wanting to know when the postman will come?' Some blurted into laughter, but were quickly silenced by a shouted order from a camp guard.

This shout woke them next morning in their tents. 'Here, what's this? Get up and make your beds, will yer?' The red face at the opening roared. Falling off his canvas cot in fright, Baumgartner – like his fellow inmates – tried hastily to pull the blankets across the tumbled, tossed sheets, feeling exposed and ridiculous in the underwear in which he had slept, not having brought pyjamas, and which was being regarded with such a ferocious sneer. Every stain, every hole seemed to be studied and noted as he bent and bowed and performed all the actions expected of him before the guard moved on from his cot to the next. There, instead of roaring, he stood with his chest and stomach protruding in an attitude of satisfaction, because Baumgartner's neighbour was performing a miracle, turning that camp cot into an envelope, neatly turned and finished so that it hardly looked made by the hand of man. 'Hmm,' said the guard, sticking out his baton to tap the unwrinkled surface of this model of competence, 'this – *this* is how I want the beds to be made.' He stalked out, very much the cock of the coop, but only after a glance at the maker of that model, a blond and silent man called Schmidt, who then turned to Baumgartner, passing on to him his own version of the guard's sneer, making Baumgartner see that they were of a kind – the ruling kind.

Every morning their tents and beds were examined; even after Baumgartner learnt to get up and prepare for *Appel* on time, he could never master the technique required of him even if the guard roared, 'Can't you see how Schmidt does it? Can't you try and be like him? Eh?' and that glance would pass between the two men, the rulers, and in passing it on to Baumgartner it would undergo that same shift, that same change.

Yet the exasperated man at the folding table in another, larger tent, refused absolutely to see them as different, separate individuals. In reply to Baumgartner's mumble about his name, his Jewishness, he snapped, 'Stop that whining and show me your passport, will you? That's all yer asked for – yer passport, hear?' Baumgartner, sweating profusely, managed to find it and hand it over with slipping, slippery fingers; he stood waiting while it was studied, page by page, thumbed through with the new ferocity that had been let loose and become the new regime. It did not take long before it was thrown back at him with a snap: 'German, born in Germany,' and Baumgartner was still trying to form the English words in his mouth, 'Yes, but of Jewish origin, therefore a refugee – ' when he was caught by his sleeve and propelled out of the tent into a queue waiting to be handed into a truck stalled in the mud of the churned football field. Heaved into it, he found himself pressed against Schmidt who drew himself away to the extent he could in that overcrowded vehicle, but by his silence conveyed to Baumgartner the utter disgust he felt at being placed in the same category as him. Baumgartner felt only fear.

The railway station swarmed with soldiers, and with coolies bent under tin trunks and olive-green bed-rolls. The clink of army boots, the snap and slither of leather and khaki cotton. The clipped British voices giving commands, the snapping salutes and whistles being blown. The cat-faces of the Gurkhas inscrutable under their floppy hats, holding on to their fixed bayonets. Incongruously, the *chai*-wallah wandering through the crowds with his kettle of sweet, smoky tea and a milky glass at the end of each finger, '*Chai, garam chai*' his lugubrious cry. Indians peering through the dark at the foreigners with curiosity. Refusing to accept the prospect of spending years together in captivity, they would not look at each other except when the need for a cigarette or a match overcame their reluctance.

It was while Baumgartner was lighting a cigarette for one of his fellow prisoners that the man, a thin and evidently ill fellow with a beard, said to him under his breath, 'That Schmidt – you need to keep away from him.' Baumgartner looked at him questioningly and was told, 'A Nazi.'

'How do you mean?' Baumgartner asked, also in an undertone. 'Party member?'

'Of course. There are many. Those are the ones we'll have to watch out for. They're keeping their eyes on *us*, you may be sure.'

Baumgartner shifted uneasily, as if he felt the impulse to break and run, but a Gurkha stepped forward and pressed him back with the tip of his bayonet.

In the central internment camp in Ahmednagar where the 'hostile aliens' from all over the country were poured like ants from a closed fist into a bowl of dust, and swarmed there in a kind of frenzy, it became daily more clear that a system was being devised to screen them and find reasons and ways to keep them in captivity. Baumgartner had more than one interview: he spent many hours waiting in a line outside a hut, slowly moving up, clutching whatever papers he had with him – his passport, visiting-cards of business associates, a few letters from his mother that he had folded and slipped into his wallet – placing them before the officer at his camp table, certain they would see he had been arrested for no reason, being harmless, no enemy, merely a refugee from Nazi Germany who wished only to pursue his business interests in India. The papers were thumbed with expressions and gestures of rage and exasperation. 'What am I to do then?' the man bawled when Baumgartner again protested at being labelled a German and 'hostile'. 'Got a German passport, says you were born there – then what am I supposed to take you for, a bloomin' Indian?' The papers were flung at him, and he retreated, baffled, wondering what magic word he might find that would release him from what was a monstrous mistake, or madness.

'They don't understand a thing,' the small, sick-looking man with a beard told him, with bitter sympathy. 'They don't even know there are German Jews and there are Nazi Germans and they are not exactly the same. All you can do is hope to get a chance to speak to someone who does know – some Englishman.'

A few did – appeals to the Jewish Relief Association in Bombay, and to British civil servants who were more humane and informed than the guards at the camp, seemed to be of use to them and they walked out of the camp with expressions of disbelief and incomprehension, but others, like Baumgartner, who had no one to appeal to or on their behalf, were left to feel the net tightening over them. They were to remain in captivity for six years.

It was at the final internment camp, to which they were taken after passing through the initial and the intermediate ones, that Baumgartner had his first glimpse of the Himalayas. There they were – an uneven line of smoke wavering against the pale glass of the sky, leaving upon it a faint smudge. The Himalayas. He thought he could smell them: sap, resin, wood-smoke, a tingling freshness, from that immense distance and height sending down some hint of ice and snow and streams.

He became aware that others were standing and staring, too, when he heard a mixture of German and Italian voices and turned to see two or three men in lederhosen, thick boots and woollen stockings, standing in a group and talking of the mountains – Nanga Parbat, Nanda Devi, Kanchenjunga – in strangely technical terms, and he gathered they were actually mountaineers who had climbed some of those peaks before being arrested in Karachi where they had been waiting for a boat back to Europe. They talked as if they would be setting off for the mountains as soon as they had laid their strategy and completed the preparations which they had already begun to make.

Baffled by the mountaineers' terminology, Baumgartner withdrew and from a distance eyed their hefty shoulders and muscled legs, feeling himself by comparison soft and feeble. But he wondered at their naïveté, their unshaken belief that they would climb the mountains again. Baumgartner, looking about him, seeing the barbed wire fencing, the gates guarded by guardhouses on stilts, the barracks and the cinder paths and water tanks, knew that no one would leave, that they would all be staying.

During the first few days while everyone milled around like a herd of cattle in a cloud of dust that would not settle but got into their eyes, hair, mouths, throats and lungs, making itself the basic component of their camp lives, Baumgartner saw efforts being made at imposing some order, some kind of discipline. Timetables were pinned to the notice-boards, whistles were blown and sirens sounded. The men queued up in order to collect blankets, tin spoons and plates, work tools. They queued up again to have their tin plates heaped with coarse rice and lentils ladled out of buckets; then they lined up on benches in a great draughty hall to eat the stuff. At the sound of another whistle, they were all in the bathhouse, washing themselves with cold water. Another whistle and they sank into their bunks, expected to sleep, like schoolboys. In different circumstances, it might have seemed an insane but all the same highly comical dream – grown men finding themselves returned to their school, a rigorous and not uncharacteristically vicious one.

But in between the whistles and the sirens and the flurried activity that they set into motion, there were too many empty spaces and these proved the more difficult to accept. The British commandant who faced them across the parade-ground every morning, stared at them as if in despair. He seemed to flinch from giving orders and to hurry away as soon as he had done so, as from something distasteful. Baumgartner ought to have felt reassured, to have sensed that no severe hardships were in store, no excessive or unreasonable demands were to be made of them, but unfortunately the looseness, the laxness of the regime really meant that empty spaces were allowed into which others could step.

There were of course the lesser functionaries of the camp to whom the commandant left the daily routine. It was these who made their presence felt, strongly and unpleasantly. They took a particular pleasure in rounding up the men and undressing them, then separating them according to size and appearance, like cattle, making jeering remarks as they did so. Baumgartner found himself standing with his hands dangling, his knees buckling, while they looked him over and joked; he found himself trying to join in the laughter, uncertain whether to do so would help or worsen matters. It turned out that this marked him something of an idiot. The stick jabbed into his ribs meant further laughter but ended in relief – he was not to join the ones who were to carry bricks, from one end of the camp to the other, solely for the sake of carrying bricks, but those who were to labour in the fields, which at least had some point.

Besides, this had for Baumgartner a certain romance. Why? He could not have said. His childhood in Berlin and youth spent keeping accounts at his father's desk had certainly given him no introduction to the soil, to Mother Earth, or even a facility for handling tools. To himself he admitted the need to escape from the constant and oppressive company of his compatriots, the chance it offered to be in the open, forget for a while what captivity meant, and have no one to ask how he came to be there, where he had been and what he had been doing before his arrest, what he would do after his release . . . One could only answer such questions so often, and although for others this initial interrogation often led to friendship, in his case it never did. The habits of an only child, of an isolated youth in an increasingly unsafe and threatening land and then of a solitary foreigner in India had made Baumgartner hold to himself the fears he had about his mother, about what was happening in Germany, allowing it to become a dark, monstrous block. Of course the same fears were known to the other internees but on them it had the effect of making them seek company, pour out their anxieties and obsessions into willing ears, and then even forget them in the pleasure of society, while Baumgartner watched and marvelled at this gift for passing on or even shedding whatever was burdensome: it seemed to him he shed nothing, that – like a mournful turtle – he carried everything with him; perhaps it was the only way he knew to remain himself.

Joining the land labour crew, he found that once released into the fields of tall, susurrating sugar-cane, the internees would fan out with their hoes and, as long as they gave the impression of being at work, the guards did not supervise too vigorously. It was the work that was much harder than he had expected, especially in the damp, steaming heat that followed the monsoon, and the sugar-cane was a sharp-bladed, rough-surfaced plant that made its hostility felt so that dealing with it was no green idyll. But there were breaks, there were moments when he could break through the smothering wall of green, find a flat stone and sink down to smoke a cigarette under the colourless sky where a fishing eagle circled vigilantly, watching him without losing a single turn of the spiral for his sake.

He found he was sitting beside a ditch in which weeds stood dejectedly in mud and scum, the area being too poor for there to be any garbage that could be thrown in to enrich it, and a stretch of unpaved road leading to a village that sat low in the fields. Even though his cigarette stank – it was a local one, wrapped in a *tendu* leaf, fierce enough to make his head swim – he could smell the distinctive Indian odour – of dung, both of cattle and men, of smoke from the village hearths, of cattle food and cattle urine, of dust, of pungent food cooking, of old ragged clothes washed without soap and put out to dry, the aroma of poverty.

Sometimes when he sat there, women would come out of the village, flat baskets on their heads, and seeing them approach Baumgartner would tremble slightly with the sensation of communicating with the outside world even if only by sight. The women themselves never gave away their consciousness of his presence by so much as a glance or a giggle. Talking to each other, they swayed past him on their way to an enclosure where they squatted on their heels and began to make pats out of the dung they had brought from their cowsheds in the village.

Baumgartner had watched at first disbelievingly when he saw their long nimble brown fingers dig casually into the wet, gleaming stuff, patting and rolling the handfuls into balls, then flattening them out on the dry sand or on the red rocks, pressing their fingers into the cakes so their impression would be left behind. Then they would drift back to the village, empty baskets hanging from their hands on which heavy silver bracelets and thin glass bangles slipped and clinked pleasantly while they talked to each other with an absorption that excluded Baumgartner – a mere foreigner, a *firanghi*.

If he returned to the spot in the evening, he would see them again, squatting to turn over the cakes, test them by breaking off bits to see which were the driest and could be collected and carried back to the village in their flat baskets. It was these dung cakes that accounted for the pungency and pervasiveness of the smoke that rose through the old, mouldy thatch of their roofs. It was this matter of feeding the cows, collecting their dung, turning it into fuel and using it to cook their meals that seemed to rule their lives – at least that part Baumgartner watched with such bewilderment and fascination.

When he overcame and left behind his initial horror at the sight of women carrying excreta on their heads, and digging their hands into it as they might into wet dough or laundry, and his initial bewilderment at lives so primitive, so basic and unchanging, he began to envy them that simplicity, the absence of choice and history. By comparison, his own life seemed hopelessly tangled and unsightly, symbolised aptly by the strands of barbed wire wrapped around the wooden posts and travelling in circles and double circles around the camp.

Trailing back past the barracks with his hoe, he heard a violin playing with too much quivering emotion. '*Guten Abend, Gute Nacht*'. In that unusual and unnatural stillness when the day paused before it fell headlong into the night, the violin string struck his ear and vibrated as his mother's singing had, making him shiver and long for her to stop. What he had wanted was her voice – normal, sensible, everyday, just as now he wanted news that was believable, acceptable. He got none, nothing. Letters came to the camp and were distributed on certain gala days – they were rationed, of course – but there were none with German stamps. He had never received any replies to the cables he had sent to Berlin; Herr

Pfuehl had remained silent, so had the boarding-house landlady. Now he wrote letter after letter to Habibullah, to Lotte, asking for his mail to be forwarded, but since he heard nothing from them he wondered if these letters ever left the camp. He could not help studying the 'Hut-father', who collected the mail, with suspicion, and discovered that the other Jews, too, wondered if their letters were censored or destroyed by this grim and powerful character even before they reached the British censors. Their complaints were given the terse reply that no internee could address the commandant directly; if they had any complaints, these must be made through the Hut-father. The attempts to do so only led to some severe punishments and Baumgartner was left listening, intently, trying to catch sounds in the air, receive answers. Anything, but not this silence – this whining, humming silence that seemed to come from the sky that had no colour, and the dust of the earth, its particles grating upon each other, torturedly.

Winter came, and should have been a season of health and vigour for this European community: the air became dry; from the mountains an ice-tinged wind blew down. The barracks had no insulation and draughts blew through them, along with the choking dust from the trampled, grassless grounds. With no insulation and no fuel for heating, the cold weather was not the delight it might otherwise have been. In their thin, inadequate clothing, and with the insufficient and monotonous food in them – only those who had managed to get work in the canteen, serving the officers, had anything like good, adequate food – they found themselves shivering, hating the cold water with which they washed, the damp sweat of the cement floors, the dusty winds that swept over the parade-grounds, the total lack of *Gemütlichkeit* of which fond memories insisted on staying alive to torment them.

Huddled under their blankets by night, they listened to the voices raving on the radios they hid there.

The *Athenia*, bound for Canada with 400 passengers and crew, torpedoed by German submarines, sank 250 miles west of the Hebrides: 112 lives lost.

'Where is that wine you made, Finckel? Come on, out with it! No, tonight!'

Brest-Litovsk overtaken on 18 September by German forces from the west, Russian forces from the east. A German–Soviet pact.

'Come on, bring out the *Zigarren*, *Zigaretten*, folks!'

The HMS *Courageous* torpedoed and sunk in the British Channel on 17 September – 500 men lost.

'*Knorke!* Splendid!'

24 October. Danzig. Von Ribbentrop's diatribe, like thunder, like battle fire.

'Listen to him! *Mensch!* Did you hear? Have you heard? *Ach, er sprach prima, nicht wahr?* Wonderful speech!'

7 November, in Munich, and Hitler this time, his voice even more stratospheric. No one could understand, but never mind, the secretly brewed liquor and the secretly rolled cigarettes were passed around by the Nazis in the group with such vigour that even the guards took notice and confiscated the radio. Another was made. The Jews watched and listened in silence.

30 November, and the Soviets attacked Finland.

'*Allerhand! Ganz allerhand!* Fine show!'

14 December, and the *Graf Spee* tackled the British warships in the South Atlantic. On 17 December she steamed into the sunset off Montevideo and went up in a bomb blast.

'*Deutschland, Deutschland über alles!*'

12 March, Finland capitulated and ceded territory and independence to the Soviet Union.

19 March. The RAF raided the German air base on the Isle of Sylt.

'What do they think they can do, the *Schweinhunde*? We will show them.'

9 April – yes, Germany showed them. Germany invaded Denmark and Norway.

11 April. Churchill on the air. Churchill in the House of Commons. Churchill at 'the first clinch of war'.

'Shut him up with a cigar.'

'*Ja*, the biggest cigar you can find.'

Allied troops in Norway, out by May.

'*Deutschland, Deutschland über alles!*'

10 May. The invasion of Holland, Belgium and Luxembourg. Britain on her knees. Churchill on his knees. 'I have nothing to offer but blood, toil, tears and sweat.'

'*Hörst du?* D'you hear? *Ist das nicht prima?*' The Nazis in the gathering slapped each other on the back till the guards threatened to invade the barracks again. The Jews exchanged looks and dispersed silently.

15 May. The German advance upon the Channel, upon France.

21 May. The British attacked at Arras, driven back through the Somme.

28 May. Belgium surrenders to Germany.

'*Allerhand! Knorke!*' The Jews kept to themselves, in a herd, the need to defend having arisen. Some spoke of suicide, others hissed 'Ssh!' The wine and the liquor, the subdued splendour under the blankets.

4 June. The fall of Paris. The French Government's retreat to Bordeaux.

10 June. Pétain in power, applying to Germany for a truce.

22 June. The truce is signed.

'Ah-ha! Ah-ha! *Nun wer ist der Kraut*, now who's the Jerry? Ah-ha' sang the Nazis, and the Jews watched and listened and were silent.

17 June. *Der verfluchter Hund* Churchill raving and appealing to the French, to the British. 'Upon all the long night of barbarism will descend . . . unless we conquer, as conquer we must, as conquer we shall.' What hope had he of that now?

3 July. None. So he blows up the whole French fleet, the madman. The whole bloody fleet.

August, and the Battle of Britain.

The Luftwaffe and yes, casualties. Of course, casualties. What could one expect? It was a war.

It was summer again. The parade-ground was an inferno of sun, heat, dust, glare. The camp commandant was seen to wilt. Drooping on his dais, he faded before their eyes. Retreating more and more into his own company – perhaps somewhere in the bowels of the comfortless prison he had a cool den, shaded, watery, where he went to revive – he had allowed the Hut-fathers and the Camp-father to take over the camp. Baumgartner watched how a certain group, a certain kind of German took over – and ran it efficiently, ruthlessly. Perhaps he had 'gone native' in his brief time in India, perhaps that was what made him aware for the first time of what was meant by 'German efficiency', '*Gründlichkeit*'. One had to admire it – the way everyone was kept occupied, how everyone and everything was put to use. The utilitarianism of the system – yes, admirable. But with it went an authoritarianism that really came into its own, really triumphed on that hellish parade-ground under the summer sun. Whereas the British commandant had only half-heartedly carried out what was a mere formality, almost a mockery of a true ceremony, the Nazis seized upon it with an authority that was awesome. To Baumgartner, at least, awesome. In no time, the men were lined up, the lines straightened, the men straightened, mouths opened, and a sound drawn out of them that seemed to answer the force of the summer sun, the force of the dust winds, with an equal force.

> 'Then comes a call like thunder's peal,
> Like billows' roar and clash of steel
> The Rhine, the German Rhine so free,
> Yes, we will all thy guardians be,
> Dear Fatherland, sweet peace be thine,
> Dear Fatherland, sweet peace be thine.
>
> Firm stands the Watch and free,
> The Watch on the Rhine . . .'

Before this onslaught, the British quailed. When winter came round again, they were running – running from Malaya, from Singapore, from Burma, and it was not only the Japanese who were after them, it was the Germans in the camp. Singapore fell on 15 February, Rangoon on 8 March, the Andaman Islands on 23 March. The eagles that glided in the air above the camp flapped in astonishment at the volume of sound that rose from the flattened earth:

> *'Heute gehört uns Deutschland,*
> *Morgen gehört uns die ganze Welt.'*

But the Russians did not flee. They stood firm too. At Stalingrad.

The secret radio seemed to have suffered a blow, dealt all the way from Stalingrad. It grew fainter, grew garbled, died. It was confiscated. Another appeared, but this one had a demon in it: it gave only the English news, the English version. This was disturbing. To the Nazis in the camp in one way, to the Jews in another. Looking at the faces of the latter in the dark, Baumgartner saw how they caught each other's eyes, then glanced quickly away. Could the war possibly be ending now? Could it end in defeat? What would the defeat of the Nazis mean for them – and for those at home? The others began to keep them out, push them roughly out of the ring, muttering words that sounded like *'Jude, hin!'* although that might have been the imagination. Baumgartner was willing, even eager, to give them the benefit of the doubt. If there was doubt, then there was hope – a little.

On the parade-ground, it was not enough that they had to stand in a line, stand straight and sing *'Deutschland, Deutschland über alles.'* Now the German flag was being flown, and now the order rang out: Raise your right arm, say 'Heil Hitler!'

Baumgartner was willing to go along with all these absurdities in the resigned, half-hearted way taught him by years of helpless submission to bullying, first in Germany, then in the camp, which was an extension of the former. But there were others who were not willing to submit. Kept out of the ring that gathered around the radio at night, they muttered, 'Didn't you hear? Didn't you hear what is happening to the Jews in Germany, in Europe?' They made a ring of their own, run by the younger, more volatile and impassioned members of their community, of whom the faded, disheartened, fear-engulfed Baumgartner was not one. One day this group of the excluded ones would not line up on the parade-ground, or straighten up. When they were ordered to raise their arms in salute to the flag, they put their hands behind their backs. When the others roared, 'Heil Hitler!' they were silent. Baumgartner gratefully joined their silence. He realised at that instant that silence was his natural condition.

At once other men broke out of the ranks and came up behind them to manhandle them, wrench their arms, give a few kicks and blows 'to bring them to their senses'. The younger and abler of the dissenters hit back – they had taken the vow of silence but not inaction. The roughness grew rougher. Baumgartner felt himself being dragged one way, kicked another. He was on his knees, his mouth full of dust, perhaps also blood from a cut lip, when the whistles began to blow and the guards to come rushing up with their batons.

The next day the scenario was repeated.

It took the reluctant commandant several days before he admitted action had to be taken. It was no longer enough to say, as he was reported to have said when first informed, 'Why is everyone so excited? This happens all the time in our public schools – it doesn't mean much, just a thrashing.' The Jews were now separated from the Nazis, in barracks at another end of the camp. There they sat on their new bunks, hands hanging between their knees, and looked at their camp-mates with bemused looks.

'And what shall we call our new home?' one said finally, stroking his beard. 'Auschwitz or Theresienstadt?'

Excluded from the morning assembly, they were excluded from most camp duties as well. The Nazis amongst the

Germans, who seemed to be running the camp – on behalf of or in collaboration with the British – said they were willing to have the Jews do the menial work for them, but the Jews declined. Now they were idle and sat or lay on their bunks, staring up at the pinholes in the corrugated iron sheets of the roof through which the sun drilled white-hot needles of light. There was too much time and emptiness now, and into that vacuum thoughts flooded in that it would have been better not to have – the roughest labour, the worst manhandling would have been preferable.

Baumgartner lay with his arms across his eyes, shutting out the probing needles of sun and heat, wishing there were some way of shutting out the voices as well. How, why were the others so much better informed than he? Although a part of him greedily, hungrily took in every morsel of information that came his way of the situation of the Jews in Germany, of their disappearance, of the labour camps, of Nazi propaganda, another part frantically built a defensive barrier against it. It was as if his mind were trying to construct a wall against history, a wall behind which he could crouch and hide, holding him to a desperate wish that Germany were still what he had known as a child and that in that dream-country his mother continued to live the life they had lived there together.

He was able to live, ostrich-like, under the sands of this illusion, because although the letters written by the Jews were now taken in and posted – so they were assured – there was still no word in reply. He wrote again to Mr Lobo, the hotel manager with whom he had left his few belongings and whom he had asked to keep his things till he returned to Calcutta and collected them. He asked once more for his mail to be forwarded – but received nothing. What could this continuing silence from his mother mean? Had she been swept up into the horrors of which the others in the barracks whispered and muttered in the dark? The terrible thoughts flooded in, an invading army that his closed eyes would not keep out, could not stop; they advanced like a nightmare to the inevitable.

It was when he reached screaming point, flung away his arm

and opened his eyes wide in terror that he tried to tear his mind from the nightmare by focusing it on whatever he saw – sometimes the wasps that were building a nest in the rafters, watching them fly out into the light and return with balls of paper pulp hanging from the ends of their hair-fine legs, using their jaws to build the intricate little paper puffs like dried grey flowers. Or, if he rolled on to his side with an irrepressible groan, he could watch the columns of ants, each carrying a moist, soft, white egg into the dark cave in a crack between the floor and the wall.

The trouble with such fascinating sights was their silence, their tedium, the endless repetition of forms and actions that blurred and turned into an endless labour of human forms – bent, driven into black caves from which they did not re-emerge.

Nacht und Nebel. Night and Fog. Into which, once cast, there was no return. No return. No return.

Then he would heave himself up, search for a cigarette, go and look for a match. Extraordinary how a cigarette could retrieve a man from the lip of hell and insanity. Drawing upon it for his life, he watched the others, lying on their bunks, smoking, playing cards, talking and talking, incredibly enough, of food, always of food. How was it possible in this situation to think and talk of food? It was not that there was not enough food in the camp – there was. True, the meat was uneatable mutton that stank, and instead of eggs there was a dry yellow powder that looked like mustard gone mouldy and tasted of dust. There was no fresh coffee: the prisoners who worked in the kitchen experimented with all kinds of beans, roasting and grinding them, trying to persuade the others that what they made was drinkable, only no one ever agreed. But there were fresh vegetables, even illicitly brewed wines and fruit liqueurs. Yet their thoughts, their taste-buds, lingered over the food at home as if these comestibles were keys to the past, and in talking of victuals they were not just reminiscing over but actually eating, masticating the past, over and over to extract the last drops of juice, the last drop of flavour. Someone had only to mention marinated herring for them to start salivating, taste it again on their tongues, close their eyes and sigh, 'Ach, rollmops – and gherkins – do not forget the gherkins.' Arguments raged as they discussed the relative merits of roast herring and herring-in-aspic. Others said that before they died they hoped to eat one more meat pie, or *Wienerschnitzel*. Some pined for *Leberknödeln*, others for *Kartoffelpuffer*. Baumgartner's stomach rumbled as loudly as anyone else's but he was too ashamed to contribute to such talk. At least, he thought he was too ashamed and chewed a shred of tobacco when others talked, till one day someone mentioned salt rolls with poppyseed and he found his lips falling apart as he added, 'And butter – *auch Butter*', stuttering so that everyone laughed. That was the day when another roused himself to say, 'Butter? In Germany? They have no butter. They are starving. Our people are starving.' They would gladly have murdered him. Baumgartner would gladly have murdered too.

As the days filed past and seasons slowly evolved and died, the weight of time grew immense, crushing. To escape from it, Baumgartner began to search out company. He watched, to begin with, the fine long fingers that fluttered over a sketchpad held on the bony knees of Julius Roth when they sat together on the veranda steps, at the end of a devastatingly dry summer, to catch the evening air that they imagined might wander down the mountains that were invisible in the still-standing dust. Getting up to stretch his legs, he glanced at the sketchpad and felt an instant curiosity: they were not drawings of the landscape as one might have expected, or of the men who strolled around, but of objects and artefacts so far removed from their actual environment as to seem bizarre and fantastic – pieces of jewellery, oriental in their weight and lavishness, curios of brass and wood or glass, with no discernible purpose, even pieces of period furniture. Roth seemed to be furnishing some private museum in his fair, narrow head bent over the pad. Eventually Baumgartner could not quell his curiosity, and excitement. Pointing at a curved *chaise-longue* on which Roth was lavishing a wire netting of criss-cross shading, he spluttered, 'Like that there were many in my father's showroom – in Berlin. He would make like a fringe, small wooden bobbles here – ' he pointed with his nicotine-stained thumb – 'to follow the curve. Just for – for decoration.' He laughed guiltily, hoping he had not offended.

Julius peered at Baumgartner with his very pale, myopic eyes that were shaded by blonde lashes. 'Where? Along here? Mmm, yes, you are right – once I had one like that, sold it to the Maharani of Gwalior when she came to my showroom.'

'You had one – where?'

'The Maiden's Hotel, in Delhi. Have run it for years,' Julius replied with some pride, then went on sketching. Baumgartner could not tear himself away and, seeing his interest, Julius continued, in a high-pitched, tremulous voice like a pipe's, 'Mine I had upholstered in crewel embroidery from Kashmir – autumn colours. But the Maharani, she's probably changed it to brocade, or velvet. Oh, these rich customers, what can one not sell them!' He put down his pencil and began turning the pages to show Baumgartner. 'See, once I was asked to design the entire dowry for a princess from Rajasthan – carpets, furniture, carriage, costumes, jewellery. I am trying to remember everything – make a record of it – see.' He caressed the drawings with his fingers, delicately, with infinite approval.

'Is marvellous,' Baumgartner breathed heavily, 'marvellous,' meaning it.

'They came to me at Maiden's – rajas, *memsahibs*, all people with money. And taste. Of course, taste – that I demanded.' Julius put his lips together severely but then laughed. 'I wanted to catch the Viceroy. I must have the Viceroy here in my showroom, I decided. He was a keen *shikari*, I knew – so I ordered tiger skins, crocodile skins, elephant tusks. The tusks I had carved in a procession motif – you know, all elephants and howdahs in a line, smaller and smaller, so – so – so,' he showed Baumgartner with his hands. 'This, I thought, would bring the Viceroy himself. Or the Vicereine. Even better, no? They are so much more extravagant. But what happens? War! War is declared by these lunatics. And my poor elephant tusks and tiger skins are collecting dust – '

'Where? In Maiden's Hotel? In Delhi?'

'*Ach*, how can one know? How is one to find out anything?' Julius tossed his long hair distractedly. It was very light, flossy hair, Nordic in its fine spun silver fairness. There was not much of it – there was in fact very little, leaving pink patches of his scalp to show through. Julius complained it was the bad soap in the camp that was causing his hair to fall out. His white linen coat suffered the same indignities, but he kept it washed and mended and wore it over a succession of striped shirts that he somehow managed to have stitched in town and brought in on the tailor's bicycle. Constantly pressing down the tips of the white collar, or pulling at the cuffs, or stroking the fuzzy hair, Julius kept himself looking like a figure from a pre-war Sunday picnic, or coffee party, accidentally strayed into the dusty shambles of the camp.

Yet, when Baumgartner tried to picture his background, his antecedents, it proved impossible – he knew he would never have seen such a figure in Germany himself; where could he have sprung from and how had he come to be here?

In order to find out, Baumgartner felt he should begin by volunteering something himself. 'Like that – ' he pointed delicately at a drawing with his small finger – 'Like that glass bowl I saw in a window in Venice once – '

Julius looked up and beamed at him for a whole minute before he spoke. 'Baumgartner,' he said finally, 'you look like a beetroot farmer but you are – you are a *gem*. In Venice, he says!'

Baumgartner stumbled away, he could not bring himself to say more, for the time being at least overcome.

'Have you seen Julius's pictures?' he ventured to ask the barracks' scholar, Emil Schwarz, the bearded man to whom he had first spoken in Fort William, as they sat tearing off pieces of bread and dipping it into lentil soup in the shade of a miserable palm tree that had very little of it to offer; the heat of that summer was so great that the camp discipline had collapsed and melted and the internees could sit wherever they found some shade or a draught; there had already been several cases of heatstroke for the camp doctor Herschele to treat. 'He makes fine pictures, Julius – he was showing to me.'

He thought Emil Schwarz might be interested; not an artist but one who pored over books night and day, Sanskrit and Pali dictionaries, Buddhist scriptures, the Vedas, and Upanishads, and even more esoteric and lesser-known titles that he ordered through the library and were brought to him by the librarian's assistant, an impudent fellow who would throw them down in a cloud of dust, brush his hands and say, 'Carrying these in this heat is bad enough – but to read them also, you must be mad.' Emil would not smile; he never smiled – a painfully lean young man, his skeletal system visible as in a sculpture of the Buddha during his fasts and meditation, but with a beard of tar-black hair and mournful black eyes that were as Semitic as Baumgartner's and Julius's were not. Although he refused to smile, he was not unfriendly, and although he never initiated a conversation, he was willing to answer when Baumgartner made overtures, which was seldom.

To Baumgartner's astonishment, Emil pulled a face. 'I have seen them,' he admitted. 'What does he draw but objects he has stolen from temples and palaces and then sells for a profit? They are a thief's account book, a ledger that he keeps.'

'Oh no, no,' Baumgartner protested, not wanting the sugar-sweet Julius to turn out rotten at heart. 'No, what makes you think he is a thief?'

'I know it.' Emil waved a piece of bread in the air, then threw it to the crows that waited in a ring a few feet away from the palm tree and the two men; immediately they fell upon it, hoarsely cawing and struggling with their black wings. 'He used to show them to me in the beginning, till I began asking him too many questions. "Is this not from a Khajuraho temple? Is this not a Gupta head? And that looks like a Kushana." When he saw that I knew, he stopped showing them to me. Better so.' Emil gloomily watched the crows snatching at the piece of bread. 'A grave-robber, that one. He does not know the meaning of Indian art, only its value, in rupees. If you talk to him of iconography, of symbolism, of religion itself, he knows nothing – nothing.' Emil had himself been arrested in – some said a hermitage on the banks of the Ganges, others said the University of Benares; certainly either could have been his natural home and setting. It was strange how he turned even the internment camp into one by sheer strength of his brooding, uncompromising personality.

Although Baumgartner was impressed by it and attracted to it, he found himself spending more time in the company of the affable Julius. True, Julius treated him as if he were one of the facilities of the camp provided if you knew how to use them, but at this stage Baumgartner found any relationship at all a relief from the oppression of solitude, the tyranny of solitary thought. Good-humouredly, he shared his small ration of cigarettes with Julius, hung around the kitchen and begged for some of their soap so that Julius's shirts could be kept as immaculate as that dandy wished, and strolled with him down that central road that the homesick Germans had nicknamed the '*Bummel*', talking of furniture and furnishing styles while the white-hot sky softened into an evening grey, flared briefly into sunset flames, then blacked out till the stars and the lights of the small hill-stations on the Himalayan heights began to glimmer. It amused Baumgartner to think that here, in this square of dust enclosed by barbed wire and watched by armed guards, he was, with Julius's help, recreating his father's elegant, well-lit, stylish showroom. He might have been out strolling with his father on a Sunday afternoon, humouring him, keeping up with him, basking in the other man's attention and condescension. When Julius occasionally gave way to irritation – 'Oh, Baumgartner, but you are too, too ignorant; how can one speak to you of Byzantine, of classical, rococo and gothic art? *Mensch*, can we not have a little learning, a little culture around here?' – Baumgartner became suitably remorseful, as if his parent had delivered the scolding. 'I will try and find a book in the library,' he promised, but Julius found the idea amusing and began to laugh. Baumgartner brightened too – laughter was such a rare and valuable commodity; it might have seemed slight but, in that situation, it proved enough of a base for friendship. Their neighbours in the barracks were amused by this odd pairing; if they passed the two sitting on the veranda steps and smoking together, they would joke, 'How are the classes going? Will he make a good valet, Julius?' Emil caused Baumgartner a twinge by saying, sourly, 'So, the two of you have found something in common, eh? I wonder what it can be?'

Of course Baumgartner was not alone in searching for some ways to alleviate the burden, the tedium, the emptiness of the waiting days. Everyone in the camp was trying to fill, somehow, the emptiness of the space into which they had been swallowed. The Hut-fathers and the Camp-father who were elected by ballot had seen to that, and everyone had been assigned to a group, or a team. Apart from the physical labour to which they were consigned by the British authorities, they all became involved in some occupation that might give them the sensation of continuing the life that they had led in the world outside. Some had ordered and obtained books and were studying Sanskrit, Arabic, astronomy or homeopathy; they organised a series of lectures and demonstrations of eurythmics, theosophy as preached by Madame Blavatsky, the Mary Wigmore style of dance, aerodynamics, or anything at all. Those who had any qualifications were teaching others and those who had never felt the need for an education and did not do so now, worked in the carpenter's shed, making babies' cradles that rocked, music stands for the camp orchestra, bookshelves and ice-boxes. Apart from these legitimate and above-board activities there was an intense underworld of nefarious activity as well – the making of secret radios, or of objects for sale and barter like clocks and coffee filters. Baumgartner could not for the life of him see what use it was to make money or have money in the camp, but most were passionately devoted to the making and earning of what they believed indispensable to life.

It tired Baumgartner even to watch such activity. He found himself physically deteriorating, growing old at a rapid rate. There were the recurrent bouts of malaria from which everyone suffered, and the almost chronic dysentery. The doctors handed out quinine with only a glance at the sallow faces, the shaking and shivering patients; they hardly needed to take blood tests, and had not enough time for them. Dysentery left everyone pale and pinched in the face. Overcome by another bout, Baumgartner lay in a huddle, feeling the pain go through him in waves, leaving him sweating and exhausted. It was then that the pressing, stabbing anxiety about his mother became most urgent and his defences against it most weak.

Heaving himself off the bunk, he tried to carry it away into some place where he could mourn over it unwatched by the others, like a sick animal. He discovered that if he found a hoe, he could go into the vegetable fields as if he had official permission to do so, and try to calm himself with some mindless action of the hands like the opening and shutting of the channels that watered the potatoes at the farthest end of the field. He could no longer get to the ditch and the road that led to the village. He missed the sight, the friendliness of the scene.

It made him draw near to the fence that divided their section from the women's, and when he saw the pale blonde young woman in the adjoining enclosure bending to lift wet laundry out of a basket, then unbending to pin it to a washing line, he realised that it was for this form of living that he pined: simple, routine, repetitive, calm. Only later did he notice that she was also pretty – with the kind of looks that had been considered pretty in the Germany of his childhood: Teutonic, her hair almost fairer and finer than her blanched skin, the eyes

somewhat bulging and of a glass-clear grey, the lips such a pale
shade of pink that they were barely differentiated from the
skin. An utterly Nordic type of beauty, Baumgartner said to
himself. The movement of her waist as she bent over the
basket of washing and then straightened herself again, and of
her arms as she stretched a garment over the line had first
drawn his attention; now he found himself walking up and
down, up and down the same length of barbed wire fencing,
looking furtively every few seconds to see if she would emerge
with her tub of washing, then lingering to see her deal with it,
eyes narrowed against the white flood of the sun. She wore
faded cotton print dresses, the kind country girls might wear
in the lost Germany, and her bare feet were slipped into the
kind of slippers known as 'Burmese', although they were as
commonly worn by Indians. He dared not look at her face for
fear of bringing a frown to it, but kept his eyes lowered to the
feet going back and forth over the stubble of dried yellowed
grass, and the stocky, straight legs. He had not known women
like her in Germany, he had never lived in the German
countryside, and yet she seemed to embody his German
childhood – at least, he chose to see her as such an embodi-
ment, it was so pleasant to do so, like humming a children's
song.

Further back in the family enclosure, a young girl was
organising a game of '*Backe, backe Kuchen*' with the small
children who bawled back:

> '*Der Bäcker hat gerufen,*
> *Wer will guten Kuchen backen,*
> *Der muss haben sieben Sachen:*
> *Eier und Schmalz,*
> *Butter und Salz,*
> *Milch and Mehl,*
> *SAFRAN MACHT DEN KUCHEN GELB!*'

making it seem that Deutschland, the *Heimat*, was alive here,
on this dusty soil, in the incredible sun, even if it no longer
lived in its native home.

Baumgartner listened to them with half a mind, watching

the woman, wondering about her. What was her name? Who was her husband? Children she had. Sometimes they came out with her, a small straw-haired child whose nose ran over a sore lip and who wailed piercingly, clinging to her knees, lifting the print dress up as she did so, and an older boy who stood vacantly, sucking his thumb, his eyes roving over the field as if to make sure no one was watching or taking any part of this fair prize, his mother. Had his father set him to guard her? Where were they from, this German family that might have come from some village in Germany with a church, a bakery, a pond, geese, an oak tree?

When driven beyond endurance, he bent to break some small cucumbers off a vine and thrust them through the wire fencing. 'Here,' he muttered to the boy, 'd'you like gherkins? Ask your Mama to pickle them for you.' The boy stood frozen, staring at him and past him. The little girl stopped wailing and stared too. Then the woman said, in a voice so flat and harsh that Baumgartner quailed, 'Bring them to me, Rudi.' Then she turned to the girl and spoke to her in a language Baumgartner could not recognise at all.

As he backed away, having handed over the cucumbers to the child's sticky hold, one of his fellow prisoners brushed past him with a slop bucket, laughing. 'The missionary Bruckner's young wife – she's quite a plum, isn't she?' he snickered. 'Forgotten her German, speaks some heathen language these missionaries pick up in the wilds, but easy to catch.' He winked at Baumgartner. 'Was it with two cucumbers, or one?'

Baumgartner withdrew, offended, and tried to keep away from the fence, but lay on his back on his bunk, eyes closed, humming, fantasising about the missionary Bruckner's wife. Which church did they belong to? When had they set about converting the natives? He made up a picture of her touching the bowed heads of naked tribal men and women in grass skirts, and at night dreamt of her holding a great glass globe between her fingers in which candlelight was reflected and flickered. He was most surprised when one day, walking surreptitiously by, he saw a woman come out on the veranda of the family barracks and shout, 'Annemarie, O Annemarie,' and the young woman, about to pin a wet tablecloth on the line, lower it and turn around. Annemarie – he licked his lips to taste it, and found that, yes, Annemarie was perfect for this Norse goddess of the camp.

Perhaps the close proximity in which they lived made the men mind-readers. How else could they have guessed Baumgartner's reveries on those summer afternoons when he lay on his back, drugged by the heat, drawing whatever sweetness could still be drawn from the image? But gradually he became aware of the sniggers, the innuendoes behind their joviality. 'Something about these forest nymphs when they come out into the world, eh, Baumgartner? Can't speak a civilised language any more, more like the jungle folk with whom they have lived, but that's not bad, eh? A garland of flowers for the head, a little less clothing, and – ' Baumgartner was jolted into attentiveness and stared with such shocked eyes that they all laughed.

He began to notice the photographs that they all pinned over their bunks, which he had previously avoided looking at for fear of offending anyone. Now he realised that they were only too willing to hear questions which would release the memories that these photographs held in increasingly faded and smudged form. But Baumgartner would not go so far – he only glanced furtively as if looking in through windows, fascinated by what he saw, but certain it was not for him to share.

Trying to imagine the backgrounds of the different inhabitants of the camp was a popular pastime, no matter how often such carefully constructed scenes were sent crashing by the truth. Dr Herschele, who held the whole camp together, Jew and Aryan both clamouring for his attention rather than any other doctor's, so renowned was he for his diagnostic skills – 'he pulls up the eyelid, looks into the eye, and there he sees it – the disease – and is never wrong,' they said admiringly – became a kind of god to them. They were certain he had the most successful practice in Berlin, or Vienna. It was years before the truth broke – that he was really a veterinarian employed by a mission dairy to take care of the pigs.

It became the camp joke of course. After that, they laughed at their own gullibility and naïveté by building up the most unlikely, the most preposterous stories about each other's past: Julius was said to have been a transvestite, dressed in women's clothing and danced in bars in Hamburg, for instance – but what shocked them, and Baumgartner too, was the discovery that some of the prisoners had not only a past but a future too, outside and beyond the camp.

Baumgartner had somehow found his way into the vegetable field again, and was standing still and staring over the furrows at the sugar-cane growing beyond the fence when he noticed some of the camp guards, in their uniforms, walking along the path at the end towards the guard house. He shrivelled into himself, trying to become less visible, but they did not look his way. They were carrying a ladder and some paint pots and from the way they examined the fence posts, he could see they were there to do some of the perpetual repairs that went on. He stood still, staring through the shimmer of heat at the barbed wire, and watched as they turned out of the gate, past the guard-house into the dust road. Perhaps they had been assigned work on the outer fence, Baumgartner thought, and turned to trail back to the barracks.

But that evening, whistles were blown, guards running, searchlights turned on, the whole camp in an uproar. Hüber, Galitsino and the others in that group of hardy Austrian mountaineers Baumgartner had first noticed regarding the Himalayas with such strange professionalism, had escaped! Pretending to be workmen, just coolly walked out under the guard's nose! Baumgartner gasped when he heard – the shock brought water to his eyes and made him blink.

Posses were sent out in search all through the valley, the forests and the rice fields and the mountains.

No one slept, talking of the exploit or, in silence, imagining that escape through the dark forests, past tigers, on elephant backs, through rivers – who knew what, where?

When the commandant appeared unexpectedly at a meeting called one night and informed them that the escapees had been caught, and brought back, no one gasped or said anything. There was silence, the kind that follows a blow on the solar plexus, a kick in the stomach.

They learnt the details later. The men were given twenty-eight days in solitary confinement. That was not too bad, they thought, typical of that boneless British commandant. Everyone sniggered, delighted. The sniggers became roars of laughter when the men reappeared with their heads bald because the black dye they had used for their disguise had made their hair fall out. They were laughed at, but affectionately, even proudly. Everyone tried to get close enough to clap one or the other of them on the back, say a word or two. Baumgartner basked in momentary glory, having actually witnessed the escape.

When they broke out again the next year, there was no one to see them and they were not caught. That was more chilling. The rumours were wild, fearful. They had been eaten by tigers in the forest, trampled by elephants. They had drowned crossing a river, fallen off cliffs and been killed. What was frightening was that they had disappeared without a trace. It was like death. How many men in the camp would have chosen that? Baumgartner wondered, knowing he was certainly not one. He huddled on his bunk, finding its familiarity a comfort. He knew it was craven not to desire freedom, but it was true that captivity had provided him with an escape from the fate of those in Germany, and safety from the anarchy of the world outside.

As long as the news came in of German and Japanese victories, Baumgartner and the others in the Jewish quarter had good reason to feel thankful for the protection of the British-run camp, however sick with sorrow over the fate of their relations or of Germany, however restless and frustrated and bored by the lifeless monotony of the camp. At least it was a refuge, even if temporary.

Sitting beside Emil Schwarz on the veranda in the dark, waiting for a cool breath of air to make it possible to lie down and sleep, Baumgartner murmured something inaudible and incomprehensible about their contradictory situation. Schwarz, restlessly wringing his hands because there was no light and he could not read, seemed surprisingly to under-stand. 'Baumgartner, you should read – it is not such a bad thing to read, you know. Then you would see how Mann has described it all, all, just as you say, in *The Magic Mountain*.' But Baumgartner was not attracted by the title, it seemed to have no relevance to this flat, dust-smothered camp, and he thought it was just like Schwarz to refer everything in life to books as though that were the natural solution and end of it all. While Schwarz droned on about a sanatorium in the mountains, about the sick and the healthy, about sanity and lunacy, Baumgartner sighed, shuffled, smoked, slapped at mos-quitoes and wondered when it would be cool enough to go inside and sleep.

The restlessness everyone felt built up into a tension as the news of the war veered and changed. The Russians held at Stalingrad; America entered the war; there were the British victories that made the Nazis at the other end of the camp sullen, so ferocious that it was not safe to go near them. The possibility of a German defeat began to be whispered about in the Jewish quarter, secretly – and gradually less secretly, more surely. Baumgartner found himself shivering on a hot sum-mer night, as abjectly as a dog who senses he is about to be turned out into the street. He wondered if the long internment had not incapacitated him, made him unfit for the outer world. And what would they find outside? Germany des-troyed – no possibility of returning, so that he would have to accept India as his permanent residence. He wondered at his ability to survive in it, reduced as he was to such an abject state of helplessness, and the knowledge besides of being alone. He began to fear the time when he would no longer be in the company of Julius, of Schwarz, of the others in the camp who had become so familiar. It was not that any of them regarded him as a friend; it was that with them he could pretend he was not solitary. Outside, he would be that – a man without a family or a country. He could not stifle his unease and wondered if there was not that under the others' seething impatience.

It was yet another still, stifling day, grey and khaki, in an endless succession that threatened never to stop, but to go on till every man in the camp had grown old, died, and turned to dust in his grave, when a man suddenly ran screaming through the camp. 'Hitler *ist tot!* He is dead! He is dead!' Shocked by the suddenness, the loudness of the announcement, the men sat up in their bunks to stare at him. He had come to a standstill, stood trembling. 'It's true,' he muttered, 'the war is over. You can hear it on the radio.'

There was an odd silence. Baumgartner, and the other Jews, were tense, watching the effect of the announcement upon those who ruled the camp. They watched the way the whole machinery of the camp seemed to jar and stall. All the ordinary sounds – the hum that rose every now and then to an uproar and then wound down to a hum again – had stopped. The men could hear themselves breathing, sweating even. The siren had to be blown, and whistles and bells, to get them moving again, and humming. They began to go through the ordinary motions of the ordinary day again – lining up with their mess plates, eating, washing, sweeping, fetching water, but everyone's movements had become desultory, half-hearted, their voices dropped to an unnatural murmur. 'When will they open the gates and let us out?' one murmured to another, to be instantly answered, 'Don't be such a fool, Peter. After the last war, it took two years before they closed the POW camps. They have to decide what to do with us.' The young man Peter became agitated, even aggressive. He could be seen

thrashing his arms as he shouted, 'Why? Why? Why?' They
had to hold him and calm him. When he was silenced, his
friends led him off. Baumgartner watched. The bugles blew.
They were marched on to the parade-ground. Although
the British flag flew, the commandant seemed no more
in command than he had been before. He spent a long
time gazing vaguely into the distance as if waiting for the
mountains to materialise out of the dust haze. Finally, he
ordered them into the barracks. The men nudged each
other as they shuffled away: 'He doesn't know what to do
himself.'

They sat about in the barracks. No one seemed to want to
play cards. Towards evening, some roused themselves and
said, 'The *Kulturabteilung* has arranged a concert tonight. Shall
we go?' The others seemed irritated by the reminder. Some
opined it could not possibly be held, immediately others
replied that it had to be held. Bach must be played, Beethoven
must be played – for Germany's sake, for Germany's honour.
The members of the orchestra seemed undecided whether to
play or not to play, and listened with helpless expressions
while the men argued. Eventually they took up their instruments and shuffled towards the hall, somewhat guiltily. Then
the men followed, still arguing, but somehow needing each
other's company, wanting some kind of gathering. They
sprawled on the chairs that were lined up before the stage, but
the curtain would not rise. Eventually some began to drum
their heels. Others shouted.

What happened next seemed to Baumgartner, who stood at
the back, by the door, like a scene in a play – as if actors had
rehearsed their parts and were now playing them on the stage.
The orchestra appeared, sidling out from behind the curtain,
clutching their instruments. But they did not play, nor did
they make a speech. Instead, standing there before the grey rag
of the curtain, in their crumpled, faded, many years old
clothes, they held their instruments and studied their shoes.
Then one of them drew his feet together, straightened his
back, raised his face, closed his eyes and began to sing, in a

voice strained by emotion, the song of graves and funerals, of death on battlefields, of endings and defeats:

> *'Ich hat' ein Kamerad,*
> *Einen besseren find'st du nicht . . .'*

The men in the audience gave a collective shiver. Baumgartner saw some rise to their feet as if an anthem were being played. One by one they opened their mouths to join in:

> *'Die Trommel schlug zum Seite,*
> *Er ging an meiner Seite*
> *In gleichem Schritt und Tritt,*
> *In gleichem Schritt und Tritt.'*

Baumgartner stood, under the weight of their defeat, burdened by their defeat, finding it gross, grotesque, suffocating. He wanted to shout 'Stop!' He wanted to tell them it was their defeat, not his, that their country might be destroyed but this meant a victory, terribly late, far too late, but at last the victory. Of course he said nothing, he stood helplessly, only aware how crushed and wrecked and wretched a representative he was of victory. Couldn't even victory appear in colours other than that of defeat? No. Defeat was heaped on him, whether he deserved it or not.

FIVE

Baumgartner woke in a panic, feeling an iron weight press upon his solar plexus, press and press till it threatened to crack under pressure, and his heart hammered to get˚ out. He struggled and heaved, fought to get out from under it, hitting out with his arms.

Lotte muttered in angry protest. It had been her weight against him, leaning heavily, moist with perspiration.

Remorsefully, Baumgartner rubbed her rubbery red arms, then struggled out of bed, groaning, 'And no *Mittagessen*, no lunch, even have we had. Lotte, won't you make some *Mittagessen* now?'

She muttered something inaudible, and threw her head about on the pillow. Baumgartner sighed, straightened his clothes and stumbled towards the table. Still half-blind with sleep, he hunted in bread–bins and biscuit tins. 'No chocolate?' he whined. 'No chocolate even, Lotte?'

She suddenly jerked herself upright. Her eyes were red and her hair stood on end. She glowered in his direction, but without recognition. 'Chocolate – chocolate – ' she chewed the words with her gums, having lost her dentures in the pillow. 'You pig you, go out and eat chocolate. Don't come to me saying chocolate – chocolate – this time of day – this time of night – oh – aah!' she cried out as though an unseen weight had descended on her too, all at once, and collapsed on to the bed and slept on, suddenly immobile, noisily drawing air up her nose like a chimney.

Baumgartner removed his fingers from her tins and bottles, guiltily. 'Then I must go home and eat – so hungry, Lotte,' he complained, and fastened his buttons, buckles, smoothed his hair. Oh, he felt awful, awful. To sleep like this, soaked with gin, on a hot afternoon in Bombay – oh, it was stupid, stupid. He stumbled towards the door, and fumbled amongst the bolts and chains, rattled them helplessly, frightenedly, in a panic, wanting to get out.

The staircase was pleasantly shaded, silent, even if thick with cooking smells, but when he reached the door at the bottom on the stairs, the fresh air and the heat struck at him like twin knives. It was cruel, but he had to go, he had to walk back to his flat, get some food, he had to eat. And feed his cats. Thinking of them prowling around and crying with hunger, he struck the side of his head and spat, 'Ech!'

Ramu, seated on a chair at his door, asleep, opened one eye to see the old man stumble away, talking to himself. Before going back to sleep, he gave a wink, and a sarcastic, 'Hah – that *memsahib* – and the *sahib* – so old – still – hmp!'

Half an hour later Baumgartner staggered into the Café de Paris, a great sigh surging out of his lungs as he dropped into the nearest chair. Unlike the street outside, strident with afternoon light, the café was thick with shadows, green quiet shadows that seemed to be generated by the blaze and glare outside. The clockwise fans revolved at top speed, keeping flies at a distance. Thankfully, Baumgartner eased his feet out of his shoes. The summer heat always caused his feet to swell and of course to sweat – the odour would have made him flinch if it were not so familiar. He stretched his arms out and laid his palms flat on the cool marble top of the table, sighing with gratitude. As he did so, his eye fell upon a similar figure at the shadowy far end of the café.

It was the fair-haired hippy: he had not left. Moved, yes – he was no longer slumped across the table but sat with his back rigid against the wall, nursing one arm in the other, his chin lowered on to his chest. It was too dark to make out the expression on his face which was in any case obscured by the fall of his bleached hair.

Baumgartner quailed, and looked away. He did not want to have anything to do with this man, too blonde and too young to be of any interest to him. He twisted his head round to the counter, saw one of the waiters standing there, cursorily wiping a trayful of cutlery, and beckoned him. 'What is today's special?' he asked and when he was told, ordered, 'One plate, pliss, very quick. And water, pliss.' He felt dehydrated as well as starved. Such an afternoon. That Lotte. How did she live so? He shook his head and made grumbling, reproving sounds to himself. Feeling censorious, he drummed his fingertips on the table-top, waiting for the food to come. When it did, the waiter apologised that it was the last plateful, lunchtime was actually over and they had not started with dinner yet. Baumgartner, with his mouth full, made a reassuring gesture with his hand, wanting to be left alone to eat whatever there was.

While he ate, finding a great solace and comfort in the mouthfuls of rice and lentils and potatoes, Farrokh came out of his room at the back, still adjusting his pyjama strings and still unshaven. He did not really shave or dress till the evening. He stood at the counter, surveying his café with the look of a ruler, a despot, a very displeased one.

Coming over to Baumgartner's table with a surprisingly purposeful stride, he interrupted Baumgartner's reverie by asking, 'Mr Bommgarter, I can have word with you?'

Baumgartner's face fell – was he going to say the café would no longer supply scraps for Baumgartner's cats? Would Baumgartner have to look elsewhere for largesse, and establish working relations with a new set of benefactors so as to keep his growing family fed and contented? This was a constantly renewed fear. Putting down his spoon, he sat up meekly to hear.

But Farrokh, sitting down with his legs wide apart, and placing his elbows heavily on the table, lowered his face and brought it forward till it almost touched Baumgartner's nose.

At that range, every hair protruding from his nostrils, and every bristle on his jowls, was not only visible but magnified. 'Mr Baumgartner, what can I do? Please tell me – there is man from your country – '

Baumgartner drew back as if struck, wiping a bit of spittle from his cheek.

'That is only reason why I fed him,' Farrokh insisted. 'I know you, I know your country must be good country, so I gave food to the boy. Then he no pay. No pay, no money, he say, just like that – ' Farrokh pulled at his pyjamas to demonstrate the boy's insulting action. 'And he eat so much – he finish my *kofta* curry. Again and again he tell waiter, "Bring me *kofta* – more *kofta* – " Finished *kofta*. That is why none left for you, and you must eat potato.' He touched Baumgartner's arm in the soft, intimate way he had with his great hairy hands. 'And then – no money; so when I see policeman going down the street, I bring him in. I tell him everything, but policeman just look at the boy and laugh and go away, say I don't want to touch these druggies, these junkies, they are dirty men. What I to do? So I go back, catch hold of this boy and push him out. But what happen? He fall down. Just like that – in front of my café. Fall down, like dead dog.' His voice rose in indignation, like a woman's. 'People stop, stare. No one stop and stare if one of your own beggars drop dead in street. No, just step over him like he is a stone, or a dog turd and go away quickly. But when they see a white man with golden hair lying in the street, everyone stop, everyone cry, "Hai, hai, – poor boy, call doctor, call ambulance. What has happen, Farrokh-*bhai*?" And they all look at me as if I knock him down, as if I hurt him. *I* hurt him? I not even hurt my own boys when they fail exam, come asking for money. All kind bad things they do in school, out of school, but I don't beat them. I don't beat these worthless waiters who take my money and eat my food, then do no work. Why I beat this foreign boy then? I want to go to gaol? People must know this. You know this, Mr Bommgarter?'

Baumgartner nodded dutifully, and Farrokh felt he could go on.

'So I just go back to café, say nothing, and what these damn fool people of Colaba do? They *pick up that boy,*' Farrokh roared, his voice expanding and lifting so that it struck the ceiling and bounced back, 'they PICK UP that boy and BRING HIM BACK HERE!' He gestured violently at the figure in the corner. Although it nodded, it was clear the boy was too drugged to have heard, perhaps asleep in that rigidly upright position. 'Here he is again,' Farrokh cried in despair, 'and *now* what I do?'

Baumgartner looked away from the boy, from Farrokh, from his own hands bunched on the table. He was not interested in the boy, he was not responsible for him, why did Farrokh imagine he was? All he wanted to do was scrape up the last of the *dal* and rice on his plate and then collect the bag of scraps and go home to feed his cats. This he could not do in Farrokh's café unless he first satisfied Farrokh. 'Perhaps ask him where he lives, Mr Farrokh?' he suggested sadly.

Farrokh gripped the two edges of the table as if he wanted to break it in two. 'I ask already,' he bellowed. 'I *ask* and I ASK. But no reply. What I can do? Mr Bommgarter, pliss, go speak to him in his language – ask him what he *want?* Why he sit in the Café de Paris when he have no money for food, for tea? Why he not go? When he get up and go? Please spick, Mr Bommgarter, and tell him GO.'

Baumgartner looked desperately for some way to refuse. He had not the slightest wish to involve himself with the fair young man who might not be from his country and, if he was, very likely an Aryan who would not want to take any help from him. How to explain this to the good Farrokh? He sat looking helplessly at the oddly tortured position of the young man, crammed into a corner of the green-painted walls of the Café de Paris, and told himself, 'Perhaps he is Scandinavian – looks like a Swede – a Viking,' and very reluctantly raised himself from his chair and walked down the length of the empty café, watched by the determined Farrokh and an interested waiter at the counter.

At the corner table, Baumgartner came to a standstill, trying to think of something to say. Clearing his throat brought no response. Finally he bent and placed his hands on the table, and said softly, 'Is anything wrong? Can I help?'

He spoke unconsciously, without forethought, in German.

The boy opened his eyes. They were inflamed and unfocused. He closed them again. Baumgartner added in English, 'If you are ill, I can call a doctor. You need help?'

Without opening his eyes, the boy parted his lips sufficiently to snarl, 'Get out. *Raus*.'

Baumgartner instantly retreated. It was as he feared – the boy was German, a fair Aryan German, and wanted nothing to do with him. Well, that was that, then. With a clear conscience, he returned to Farrokh with a light step, shrugged his shoulders and explained, 'He say no, no help wanted.'

Farrokh frowned, his dark hairline, dark eyebrows, dark moustache all coming together in a ferocious black scowl. 'Then why he not get up and go?' he spat out, fiercely. 'What he sitting here for? Tell him get out.'

'He won't listen, Mr Farrokh,' Baumgartner pleaded, with a look at the remains of curry and rice on his plate, now congealed and uneatable. The sight of the food reminded him that he had to collect the bag of scraps for his cats. Perhaps it was necessary to make another effort for Farrokh before he could ask for it and leave. 'You want that I push him out for you?'

'Yes, I want,' Farrokh agreed fervently. 'My evening customers coming in, I don't want foreign junkie lying in corner. Not in my café. This family café. What they think? You think I have no *standards*?' He arrived at this impressive word by sheer pressure of rage and despair. Himself impressed by it, he continued, 'Other junkies will follow. This will become drug den. Not high-class two-star Irani restaurant for good families.' He was raving now, carried away by his highly coloured version of things to come.

Baumgartner began to feel aggrieved. Why was he being made responsible for Farrokh's status, for the Café de Paris's status? He came here only for the leftovers. Getting annoyed, he said shortly, 'Then let us go together and talk to him.'

The two approached the table in the corner together – one warily, the other threateningly – and Farrokh's heavy tread made the boy turn his head and look at them with a wan, uncaring air. 'I have said already,' he said in an unnaturally high-pitched quaver, 'I cannot pay bills. I am ill. I want only to sit here.' His teeth showed between his lips, like an animal's, in warning.

'No, *no* sit here if you are ill,' Farrokh began to roar, lifting his arms in the air. 'Hospital for ill people, not café.'

'Hospital is not for me,' the boy replied with something of a laugh that bared more of his teeth. Then he closed his eyes and leant his head against the wall.

Baumgartner found his concern aroused in spite of himself. The boy was not so different from a sick cat, he told himself in order to overcome the revulsion he felt from contact with this fair-haired boy that was instinctive and uncontrollable. To think of Nazi Germany now, after all these years, in faraway Bombay, it was absurd after all. Swallowing that revulsion, he asked, 'Shall I bring the doctor here?'

The boy seemed to be thinking it over and Farrokh stood and seethed. The café was quite silent, the street noises kept at bay by its thick shadows. Then the boy rolled his head from side to side in stubborn dissent. It clearly cost him a great deal to make that dissent.

'You need some medicine I can get for you?' Baumgartner tried again. He found himself pronouncing 'medicine' in the German way, and was irritated.

The boy opened his mouth, then chewed his lip, without any sound. His face became gradually clenched in a grimace, Baumgartner could not tell whether in a spasm of pain or at their enforced presence.

'You have a place I can take you to?' he ventured, remembering a charitable clinic where he had sometimes taken families of kittens he could not keep or those cats that needed surgery. Perhaps there was one for such strays as this boy here.

The boy laughed at that, spitting out the laugh coarsely, insultingly. He did not bother to answer, it was eloquent enough.

Baumgartner sagged. He was so tired, it was so hot, he wanted only to get home. 'Perhaps I better take you to my home,' he sighed sadly.

Immediately he felt Farrokh's large heavy hand clap him on his back with approval and heard him boom, 'Very good, Bommgarter *sahib*, very good. Maybe you spick same language. Maybe he tell you all his trouble. You help him, eh? You take him, eh?'

The boy struggled to raise his eyelids a millimetre or so and glare from under them at Baumgartner, again with the yellow flash of a sick cat. Baumgartner glared back. 'Come with me. It's not far,' he growled, in German.

When they stepped out of the café, Baumgartner lifted his head and sniffed a bit. The magic moment had come: it was four o'clock and at last the sea, the invisible sea of Bombay, had stirred, woken from its heavy, lethargic afternoon siesta and given off a faint wavering evening breeze. Although the heat still stood solid and livid between the walls of the buildings and on the soft, muddy tar, there was a quiver in the air, a scent of salt and freshness, and it was bearable again. One could look forward now to the whipping wind of evening and then the soft, muzzy night, and darkness.

Most of all, Baumgartner looked forward to coming home, and to bringing his cats some food. What had made him spend the whole day away from them? Such a fool. To sleep like that in Lotte's house, in Lotte's bed, all afternoon, he must be getting old, stupid. He shuffled forwards with the plastic bag of scraps he had been given hitting against his leg – Farrokh had filled it to the brim – and emitting odours that made passers-by stare. The boy plodded behind him, breathing heavily as though he were struggling up a mountain, and keeping his eyes on the ground and on his bare feet.

'Oh, I am sorry. *Entschuldigen bitte,*' Baumgartner apologised, stopping for him. 'Did not see – you have no shoes – the feet must hurt.'

The boy did not make an answer or look at Baumgartner but lifted his arms to adjust the rucksack on his back. Although he was tall and big-built, with the heavy square bones of an ox or a sportsman, he was clearly in very bad shape so that every movement caused him more effort than it should. Baumgartner found he had to slow down his shuffle in order to keep step with him. He found himself babbling, 'Just down the road – we turn the corner – we come to Hira Niwas. My flat is small – no sea-view like Bombay millionaires have – but is all right. So many years now it is my home, and I have place for everything, my cats including – '

The boy made no answer and eventually Baumgartner's babble ran out. In silence he trudged beside him, only putting out his hand to make him turn at the corner. The family that lived on the pavement outside Hira Niwas had gathered for the evening and looked at Baumgartner returning with a stranger. The boy seemed not to notice they were in his way and Baumgartner was terrified that he might knock over one of their pots and pans or trip over and break one of the strings that held up their shack. He drew himself in, tried to shrivel up and take the least amount of living space away from them who had already so little. As always, he felt his hair stand up on the back of his neck, and sweat break out as he passed them.

The mother was as usual washing her tin pots and pans in the thickly moving water of the gutter, with her sari twitched up over her knees and the knees jutting up over the ears as she squatted on the pavement. The child with the pot-belly of malnutrition and the light hair that stood up in twists, was beside her, sucking something brown and slippery in its hand. The flies crawled over the lip as well as the stuff and Baumgartner wondered if she had not swallowed a few. She flung it down in a fit and began to cry. At once the mother raised her hand and struck her across her head, screaming in the language Baumgartner had never learnt to understand. Now the child shrieked in outrage and the father, who had been sitting or sleeping inside the rag shack, pushed two of the rags aside and stuck his head out. From the inflamed pupils of his eyes and his dishevelled hair it was clear he had already started the evening's drinking. He flung some oaths at his wife in the language that was like pieces of stone, like gravel to Baumgartner's ear. She screamed back at him but also grabbed the child by its arm, pulled her over to her side and rapidly wiped her streaming eyes and nose with the end of the sari. Then she picked up the brown lump from the pavement and popped it back in the child's mouth. The man gave a roar and came out on his knees to jerk the child over to him and dig the lump out of its mouth and fling it away again.

By then Baumgartner had steered his guest past them and safely into the doorway of the building – one step lifted them from anarchy to security. As he led him in, he gave a furtive look over his shoulder to see who was responsible for the new screams that seemed to slash along the whole length of his back and enter the sensitive point in the back of his head: was it the outraged child or the infuriated mother? He hoped they had not noticed him or his guest. Although he barely acknowledged this to himself, it was true that he had fears – nightmares – of their coming after him one night. Why should they not? They saw him bring bags of food, knew he had a wallet in his pocket, wore a watch on his wrist, good shoes on his feet – old, patched, yes, but still shoes, more than they had or ever could buy – and he wondered what prevented them from grabbing him by his neck and stripping him in the dark. The nakedness of their street lives made him feel overloaded with belongings, and he felt their accusation whenever he passed.

Now he had to manoeuvre his guest past the watchman who looked on insultingly and refused to move his legs out of the way, and then guide him up the narrow wooden stairs with their uneven surface to which he was accustomed but others were not, and stumbled. 'On the third floor is my flat,' Baumgartner apologised. 'Quite high. Very dark here. You can see?'

The boy made no answer, might have been both deaf and dumb, but followed Baumgartner stolidly up the stairs, taking harsh, deep breaths as he negotiated the climb. What could the young man have been doing to be in such bad shape? Baumgartner wondered, and alternatives trooped up the stairs and into his mind, noisily. Drugs, drugs, drugs, they all said. Baumgartner shook his head. One should not say till one knew.

The cats knew his step. They seemed to hear it on the bottom step in the entrance hall, began springing off their chairs and beds and various roosts and by the time he was on the first landing, outside the Parsi family's flat with its daily renewed string of marigolds and its ricepowder picture of twinned fish on its doorstep, they began thudding against the door and yowling through its cracks in a frenzy. It was the sound of a welcome he so enjoyed that he began to smile and to hurry, but bumped into his leaden guest, apologised and forced himself to mount the last flight of stairs slowly.

The boy seemed sunk too deep in his private world, enclosed and stony, to react to the eager scratching and miaowing at the door while Baumgartner fumbled with a bunch of keys, but he could hardly ignore the furred, fighting presences that burst out as Baumgartner opened the door a crack and hurled themselves at all the legs and feet they could find.

Baumgartner was bent over them, crooning in German, 'Fritzi, *du alte* Fritzi, *komm*, Fritzi,' and 'Miess, Miess, let me go – I give you, Miess – ' and '*Ach, Liebchen*, Lise, Lise,' and only after a moment of confusion became aware that they were spitting and snarling and the boy was kicking them off like so many fur slippers. 'Pliss, pliss,' Baumgartner protested, getting off his knees to take the boy's arm. 'No need to be frightened – they only welcome us – you do not like them?'

The boy spat out a vicious 'No!' and reached down to scoop up the most obstreperous of them, the battle-scarred Fritz, and hurl him away violently.

Baumgartner felt inside him the somersault of fear, of alarm. The cats, too, were like a swarm of pigeons in a feathery flutter. All of them milled around, trying to get at Baumgartner's bag of scraps and at the same time scramble out of the young man's way. Baumgartner was hard put to it to keep them separated. Distractedly, he put the bag down on the kitchen table, then swung around in an effort to be hospitable, saying, 'Sit down, please – if you like, lie down a moment – I will – I will have some tea ready – please excuse – first my cats must dine – ' and then swung around again to tend to their feeding.

He emptied the contents of the bag across the table, got out the kitchen knife and began to separate the curried fish from the mutton fat and bones, the bread crusts from the rice and chapatis, flustered by their impatience and by his guest's sullen attitude in the middle of the riotous floor.

'Ugh,' spat the boy, 'it is – *stinking.*'

'Oh, one moment – one moment – I open the window,' Baumgartner put down the knife and turned to the window and undid all the rusty, difficult bolts and swung it open on to the lane which did not smell very much better. Then returned to his work, energetically cutting and chopping with the long knife while the boy stared angrily. At last the bagful of scraps was separated into small piles and Baumgartner could pick them up in his hands and put them on to the plates. The cats wound themselves around his legs, arching and rubbing and making small, scolding sounds, then gradually settling down to nosing through it all till they arrived at the delicacies they decided to accept.

The boy watched with a kind of stern disapproval. 'Something like I saw in the burning ghats of Benares,' he finally said from a corner of his unsmiling mouth.

Baumgartner looked up, puzzled, not comprehending such an allusion. Unlike the youths who came from the West now, Baumgartner had been to none of the tourist spots, not even Benares, never been drawn to temples or ashrams, an alien world to him, something he had walked past quickly, not entered, not even glanced at. So he could not understand the boy's reference but sensed in it hostility and censure.

'When the fires died, the man in charge of the burning, he took up a big stick – this big – and pushed it in the fire – and took out bits of meat – human meat – that was not ash and threw it down to the riverside. All the dogs waited there – and pounced – and fought – and ate these meats – these human meats – like *that*,' the boy laughed, jerking a finger at the cats. His laughter spluttered from lips that were out of control, were trembling. 'And in the temples – where the priests fed the beggars – you could see some fun. I have seen even a leper with no legs, no hands, fighting a woman with his teeth – that was fun!'

Baumgartner turned away. He carried Mimi back to her corner, laid her carefully in the nest made of his old shirt. He spent a long time arranging its folds around her so that they supported her chin, her head, and made her comfortable. Then he turned back to his guest, as to a bitter duty. 'Pliss, give me that rucksack. And sit down. I will cook a meal. You will have? Something to eat?'

'Eat?' the boy exploded. 'In the middle of dis – dis stinking –' he gestured at the room, the mess spread and heaped everywhere.

Baumgartner was struck into silence. He was not unaware of the smell: other guests had shown uneasiness and an eagerness to leave, at a time when he still had guests. Now, no one came any more. Still, he had not thought of it as repellent, unfit for the acts of life. Rather, it was to him a kind of fertiliser, with a fertilising action upon human behaviour. At least, it helped him to be comfortable, to survive, live, enjoy companionship. He felt his cats glide around his feet, wind themselves about his legs, heard their murmurs of recrimination, welcome, questioning, communicating, and wondered why he had introduced this lunatic into their midst, polluting it, threatening its rich, warm, natural life.

The boy was pulling off his rucksack. Flinging it on to the floor, he looked around the small room, almost dark with all but one of the shutters closed against the afternoon light, saw the divan with the faded print coverlet, and threw himself on to it. He lay there on his stomach, his legs sticking out at one end. Baumgartner could smell his body in its unwashed rankness; the cats sniffed, too, delicately, the small triangles of their noses creasing with distaste, perhaps mistrust.

There was no further movement, or sound from the visitor. Baumgartner stood waiting for a while, then turned around with a sigh and went to the kitchen end of the room. He began to clear away the remains of the cats' meals, rolling them all up in a paper bag and carrying them over to a plastic bucket under the sink where he dropped them. Immediately, the livelier of his cats – a scrawny rascal called Leo, and his black rival, Teufel, ran to the bucket, stood on their hind legs, dropped in their noses and pulled out the fish tails and strips of raw lights that he had bundled away. Spreading them on the floor, they ate with greater gusto than they would from china saucers. *Ach*, such naughty ones, Baumgartner smiled indulgently.

He washed the steel knife and put it back in its place on the breadboard. He wiped the table-top with a damp napkin. The familiar labour calmed him, and he glanced at the sleeping boy, thinking he must be overwrought: if he had been walking barefoot through India and seeing such sights as the one he described in Benares, then it was only to be expected. The boy needed sleep, a bath, and then perhaps he would want to eat. After all, the room was not stinking so badly as to keep him from sleeping in it, Baumgartner noted wryly, and went across to a cupboard made of wire-netting in which he kept his own foodstuff free from the cats and the flies. He rummaged around in a basket of vegetables to see what he had. Ah-ha. Yes, some bits of vegetables left from his last effort at marketing, and in the tins – he picked them up and shook them

– a little rice and lentils rustled reassuringly: enough, perhaps, for two plates of food. He would wash them and cook them and be very quiet so the boy would not be disturbed but sleep and get all the rest he wanted.

Then he caught himself: why did he bother about this stranger, unknown to him till this morning? He had felt no slightest stir of nostalgia when Farrokh had pointed out his fair head lolling helplessly on the table, or when he had glimpsed the blonde hairs gleaming on the wrists under the metal bracelet. He was not fair himself, nor had his mother been; only his father had had light hair of that kind. Baumgartner did not search out Europeans in Bombay for company. Why, he could not tell, but it was years since he had ceased to crave the sound of his own language, the feel of it on his tongue. Truth to tell, his years in confinement with fellow Germans in the internment camp had killed that need, or desire. Looking back, he saw that it was then he had decided that he would not wish to live in a pack, that he did not need the pack. Gradually, the language was slipping away from him, now almost as unfamiliar as the feel and taste of English words or the small vocabulary of bastardised Hindustani that he had picked up over the years. It was only Lotte who kept him in touch with the German tongue – but that was not why he went to see her. He saw Lotte not because she was from Germany but because she belonged to the India of his own experience; hers was different in many ways but still they shared enough to be comfortable with each other, prickly and quick-tempered but comfortable as brother and sister are together. But from other Europeans in Bombay – and there was a fair-sized population – he kept away, discreetly. He did not like their probing questions, their determination to discover his background, his circumstances, his past and present and future, before they accepted him. Why should Baumgartner be so secretive about his circumstances? He did not know – he shrugged – but it was so. He felt a fastidiousness about his private affairs and preferred to be either with someone who took it entirely for granted, as Lotte did, or else showed no comprehension and no curiosity, like his Indian friends – Indian acquaintances, he corrected himself, because – to be perfectly truthful – they stopped short of being 'friends'. To be quite candid, had he any at all?

The need to be candid made Baumgartner look down into his lap – he was sitting on a kitchen chair, waiting for the *pish-pash* to cook, and now he bent down and picked up the nearest cat – there was always one nearby. Holding its fur to his chest, he closed his eyes as a young man might with a photograph of his beloved held close. Here was all the friendship he needed – or wanted. 'Mmm, mmm,' he nuzzled into the grey fur, '*du Alte, du Gute, du.*' The cat growled a little, then began to purr, kneading his thighs with its claws, eyes narrowed into slits, and Baumgartner, laughing because the claws tickled, rumpled his fur the way he liked, drawing out louder and louder purrs till they almost deafened.

He sat there, quite contentedly, seeing the afternoon light at the kitchen window dim and withdraw, the building across the lane impress its shadow over it like a blind. The sound of the traffic rose to a crescendo as crowds left offices and went home in a cacophony of sound that entered the high room and reverberated.

Baumgartner got up and began to lay the table. It seemed very unnatural to him to put down two plates, two spoons, search for napkins, for a bottle of beer and an opener. This was not how he lived, Baumgartner the solitary. He had had enough of communal living in that camp to last a lifetime, he explained to himself and the cats. And yet he had led home this unlikeable lout in the disgracefully short shorts and the frayed shirt he wore tied at the waist like a girl. He had even permitted him to lie down on the divan and cooked a meal for him. Not because he was German, no, but simply because he was in need. Well, the man on the pavement downstairs, the family that lived there, was in need too; did he think of asking them up here and cooking for them? Baumgartner, Baumgartner, he reproved himself, tired and hungry and sad at the way the day had gone, picking open a scab long formed, revealing the rawness, the ugliness underneath. Farrokh had taken the boy for a German – correctly – and taken it for granted that Baumgartner, another German, would volunteer to take care of him – again correctly, for Baumgartner had. Or had he? He did not remember volunteering, and yet the boy was here. Certainly he had not refused Farrokh or prevented the boy from entering. As he would have had the drunk in the street been concerned. Why? Baumgartner, Baumgartner, he sighed, ask your blood why it is so, only the blood knows.

And that was stupid. Baumgartner slapped himself on the wrist, hard. Stupid, stupid, to talk of blood, thinking it was blood he had in common with this ruffian. It was not so. And he would turn the boy out to prove it was not so. Give him some food, then turn him out. What, at night? But why not? The boy was evidently used to living in the streets, would feel at home on them, would not need Baumgartner or the domesticity which he had insulted – so why suffer him?

The cats stirred at the sound of spoons and plates, some set up a plaintive miaowing as though they had not been fed already, complaining in the calculated tones of street beggars, or spoilt children. Baumgartner only smiled fondly at these sounds he loved, but they made the boy on the divan stir. After throwing himself around for a while, with grunts of protest, he finally sat up on the edge of the divan, his head hanging down on to his lap, rubbing his eyes ferociously.

After watching for a while, Baumgartner ventured to ask, 'Had a little rest? You would like to eat something now? I have a little food here ready – '

The boy made a grinding sound with his teeth, ran his fingers through his hair, leaving it in strands. 'Is a bathroom here?' he asked.

Baumgartner pointed at the door in the corner by the divan and the boy stumbled off. Then re-emerged to pick up his rucksack which he carried in, to Baumgartner's astonishment. After a while, he came out once more and asked for a box of matches in a low, distracted mumble. Snatching it from

Baumgartner, he returned to what seemed to be turning into his fortress. Baumgartner was a little puzzled, then felt impatient, knowing his *pish-pash* to be drying up to a point beyond the stage when it would still be edible. He busied himself like a housewife, adding bits of butter to it, going around opening windows, turning on lights, smoothing out the coverlet on the divan, but still the boy would not appear.

He tried to ignore the ominous silence that grew and expanded in the bathroom. He sat down at the table with the dish of *pish-pash* and the bottle of beer, clasping his hands together and determined to be firm and get rid of the boy as soon as he appeared. '*Ja, raus, raus,*' he was muttering to himself and to the cats, when the door was flung open and the boy strode out, seeming somehow a foot or two taller, his shoulders broader, his hair and eyes flashing, in every way increased, grown more vivid and insistent. He seemed lit up, electrified, so that whatever had been dormant now seemed awake – and screaming.

Baumgartner had lifted the beer bottle when he heard the door open, ready to pour out, but now he put it down and gaped in astonishment as the boy swung himself over to the table, laughing, his arms flapping on either side, then threw himself on to a stool across from Baumgartner and sprawled there in all directions.

'Ah-ha, so is the old man's dinner party, eh?' he snickered, slurring his words as though he had been drinking behind the door, and yet there was no odour of liquor and Baumgartner had to conclude that was not what it was. He smiled uncertainly, reached out for the boy's plate and filled it, apologising, 'A little *pish-pash* only. It will do? I have some more – and beer.'

The boy lunged forward and snatched the bottle from Baumgartner's hands, then – to his dismay – slammed it down on the table so hard that froth spewed from it and flew everywhere over the table like suds. His hand remained clenched around the bottle as though he wanted to crush it into a handful of splinters.

'Nah, none of dis – dis beer,' he roared, in a voice that was not only enlarged but also raised to an unnatural pitch, both shrill and resonant. 'Is rubbish only. Make the stomach sick. Sick. Throw away,' he screamed and, when Baumgartner was sure the bottle would be hurled at his head, he turned it upside down so that the yellow liquid streamed out in jets, flooding the table and falling to the floor where the cats scattered in indignation. Letting the bottle fall on its side, he brought the flat of his hand down on the table-top and swept the flood off, throwing it about like a naughty child playing with mud, in a puddle. 'Hah, that is how to do wiz beer – wiz dirty zings,' he bellowed.

Baumgartner sat upon his chair, paralysed and devastated, both hands holding the sides as though he himself were being shaken and scattered. Up to now he had imagined he was entirely in charge of this lifeless boy flung down limp upon his divan; now he felt himself taken up and threatened, violently.

The boy was laughing at the dismay on his face, laughing and laughing. His own face was very pale under the dirt – he had certainly not washed while in the bathroom; he still looked as though he had picked himself off a railway platform, an Indian railway platform, and his eyes were concentrated and pinpointed with an animal ferocity.

Baumgartner's consternation amused his guest as a fairground might amuse a high-spirited child: he laughed, giggled, pointed his finger and chuckled helplessly, then suddenly stopped, looking over the top of Baumgartner's head at the shelf behind him.

'What is *dat*?' he asked, jabbing his finger at what he saw.

Baumgartner stared at the finger that jabbed. Then slowly and carefully he withdrew his eyes, turned to the shelf. What could have caught this extraordinary fellow's attention? On the shelf Baumgartner heaped all the objects he did not immediately want – empty matchboxes, some photographs, an egg-cup, pencils and, yes, a row of tarnished silver trophies. Sadly tarnished – they had been left undusted and unpolished for so long. Embarrassed, Baumgartner turned to face his guest again. 'These trophies?'

'*Ja, ja,*' the boy jerked his chin up and down so that the uncut hair tumbled on his forehead and into his eyes. 'They are silber, man?'

Baumgartner nodded a modest nod. 'I think. I had a horse once – many races he won. A fine horse, Tiffin Time. It was in the year – let me think now – '

'You – you had a racehorse?' The boy's face was contorted with disbelief. He could scarcely control his jaw, it wobbled with amazement.

Baumgartner scratched the back of his neck in embarrassment: he was aware he did not look as if he were a racing man, as though he owned or ever had a racehorse. He chuckled to think of the days when he used to spend Sundays on the Mahaluxmi racecourse in the company of old Chimanlal, mingling with the Bombay society ladies in their silks and chiffons and pearls and the gentlemen in their white suits and field-glasses and gold cigarette-cases. He rubbed his feet together, under the table, chuckling. '*Ja,* it was so,' he admitted. 'Once I was in business, had also a business partner, a very good man – '

'But the trophies?' the boy snapped impatiently. 'Dese – silver cups – you won, your horse won?' It seemed a struggle for him to put together such disparate elements in his head.

'Together we had this fine horse, Tiffin Time. For two-three-four years he won many races, race after race. It was wonderful,' Baumgartner remembered, laughing. 'And my partner, he gave me the trophies to keep – he said I should have them – '

'*Pure* silber?' the boy pursued.

'*Ach,* I don't know, I can't say,' Baumgartner mumbled, embarrassed by the unlikely wealth piled up and gleaming on the dusty shelf along the dusty wall.

The boy shot up, throwing back his chair so that it fell on its side, and went round the table, supporting himself with one hand on its edge, to the shelf behind Baumgartner. He picked up the trophies, one by one, turned them about in his hands, turned them upside down, examined them. His lower lip was pushed out so that it looked thick and swollen and moist. He slammed them back on the shelf so that the pencils flew off and the egg cup rattled. He seemed furious now.

'*Ja, ja*, silber,' he shouted accusingly. 'Here, in dis house – all dese silber mugs. It is – fantastic!'

Baumgartner picked up a spoon, trying to distract his attention. 'Pliss, eat now before it is all cold,' he pleaded.

The boy would not eat anything. He walked up and down beside the table, his arms folded about him as if he were cold.

'You have no appetite?' Baumgartner asked sadly, looking at his dinner, shrivelled and dry, uneaten on the beer-washed table like wreckage in a flood. 'You have been sick perhaps? In – Goa?'

'Sick, in Goa?' the boy spat at him, 'Yes, sick in Goa. Sick in Benares. Sick in Kathmandu. Sick in Sarnath, sick, sick everywhere. Oh, I am *krank – furchtbar krank*,' he broke into German. It was like a crack in a poorly built dyke and now the flood poured out, streaming over Baumgartner and the cats and the dinner and the whole of the shabby dark room, filling it and setting it afloat on visions of places and people that had never entered before, even in nightmares.

In Benares he had lived with the *dom*s in the burning ghat. With them, he had piled logs of wood on the funeral pyres. Listened to them haggle and bargain with the families over the prices of wood, then the price of fire – even the fire was not given unless a price was paid. In the heat of the flames he had dried his clothes wet from bathing in the river. From the pyres he had taken the embers to light his cooking fire and make his food. When the fires died down, he helped to scatter the ashes and spear the bits of flesh and bone that remained and fling them down the steps to the river bank where the dogs fell upon the pieces and ate, growling with hunger and greed and possession. He had plunged into the river and bathed there amongst the remains of the carcasses, the buffaloes that came to drink, the widows who bathed in their white shrouds. At night he had slept in the courtyard of the palace of the *dom* raja, the head of the *doms* who was grateful to him for coming because no Hindu, no Indian would visit him or invite him or speak to him. He was rich, powerful; tigers of plaster and papier mâché guarded his palace by the river, but he had no friends on earth. Only he, he was a friend of the *doms*, of the *dom* raja himself.

'And – the bodies? Did you – also eat?'

'I was a tantric then – I was with the tantrics. With them, yes, I ate. I ate. Why? Why do you look like that? Is only flesh, only meat. For eating. For becoming strong. Strong.'

The tantrics he had met in the ashram in Bihar where he had lived on a rock, learnt yoga, meditated till one night the devil came to him, dressed only in white ashes, and shaken those ashes on his head. They had danced together on the rock, such a dance, to such music – the beating of drums, the ringing of bells that hung from the devil's neck – that the swamis who lived in the ashram had rushed out to see what was happening and begun to scream with fear at the sight. They had driven him out, with sticks and slippers, as an emissary of the devil.

'And you did learn yoga?'

'Yoga, yes. I learnt. And many more things. To become strong. To be like the devil.'

In Kathmandu he had loved a temple priest's boy, a boy whose skin was like honey and whose tongue was like a hibiscus petal, and grew his nails so long they were like knives. But he had stolen all his money, this boy, his belongings, shoes, clothes, even passport, and told the priest of their love so that he was beaten with iron rods, his bones broken, his blood made to run. In Kathmandu's dust was mingled his blood. From that blood, a special plant grew, like a sword with a cockerel's head. The cockerel crowed at dawn, it crowed the name of that boy.

'So one must be *strong* and destroy that love and I cut it *down*.'

In Tibet, in Lhasa, he saw the sight no man was meant to see. The corpses laid on the rocks under the sky, being cut into quarters with knives, into quarters and then into fragments, and the bones hammered till they were dust. When the men who performed this ceremony for the waiting birds saw that he was watching, they drew clouds into the clear sky, lightning out of those clouds, and made the thunder roll. Out of the cloudless blue sky they had loosed a storm upon Lhasa, hailstones the size of eggs, rain in sheets. He had danced in the rain and the hail. When he had turned to thank the magicians for this joy, he had seen them fly into the sky on a streak of lightning and vanish in flames.

'What are you saying? It is all dreams, my friend, mad dreams.'

'No, no dreams. No mad. Is true, *true*.'

In Calcutta he had lived with the lepers. They lived together on a refuse tip and lived off what they could scavenge from it. It gave off warmth at night and that kept them alive through a winter, the heat of that refuse decaying under their bodies. By day they fought with the stray dogs for bones, rags, bits of paper on which a little blood, a little egg, a little food was smeared. A leper girl had loved him – he was so white, she thought him pure – but, when her lip began to rot, he left.

'*Ach*, the poor – poor – poor – '

'Poor? Is not poor! Is great! Is wonderful!'

In Goa – hah, in Goa what had he not done? In Goa he had lived on the beach in a hut made of coconut tree fronds. In Goa he had bought and sold and lived on opium, on marijuana, on cannabis, on heroin – it was as plentiful as the sand upon the shore, and he had been as rich and as poor as a man can be on earth. He had lived with nudists, posed for tourists' cameras, sailed with fishermen, swum in the sea with dolphins and sea serpents. During the carnival he had not slept day or night, danced and drunk, drunk till the police had rounded him up with his friends and thrown them into prison.

'In a prison also you have been?'

'No prison for me – I am free wherever I go.'

In Delhi he had lived on the steps of the mosque, to sell the tourists cannabis and ivory as they came to take photographs. At Id, he had gone down into the bazaar to help slaughter the sacrificial goats and sheep, hundreds and hundreds of goats and lambs and sheep slaughtered for the feast, so that he had stood with his feet in blood, his hands in blood, all of him covered with blood.

In Lucknow he had walked in the procession at Mohurrum, beating his bare body with a whip, a whip with knotted thongs and slivers of blades inserted into the knots, chanting, 'Hassan – Hosain – Hassan – Hosain', while he cut and lashed his body till the blood ran.

'But you have no scars? No wounds?'

'No. I am whole. I make myself whole again and again.'

In Mathura he had done the *parikrama*, walked barefoot from temple to temple, bathed in the ponds, drunk from the wells, sung and danced the Krishna songs. At Holi, he and the pilgrims had pelted each other with coloured powders and coloured waters, till they were pink and indigo and purple. They had drunk opium in milk, eaten opium in sweets, smoked opium in pipes.

'So much drugs – what it will do to you?'

'It will make me – *ach*, great, and happy and great!'

In Rajasthan he had smuggled cases of opium on camelback, chased by the police across the desert sands. He had been lost in the dunes, he had met other smugglers – men carrying drugs, guns, gold. They had banded together, fought, parted, fled. Only the stars could steer you in the desert.

'Is not safe, such life.'

'But is fine, this life, very fine.'

In the Himalayas, in the snows beyond the monastery where he stayed, he had met and grappled with a yeti. The yeti had picked him up by his ears, lifted him off his feet, and hurled him down into the icy blue lake of Mansarovar. Pilgrims on the shore had saved him, helped him through the blizzard and brought him back to safety – to become a pilgrim like them, a worshipper. He was seeking now for other temples, other idols, other pilgrimages –

Stuttering to the end of his inspired recital, he began to run his fingers through his hair distractedly. Now and then he gave an uncontrollable shiver. He shot a furious, scornful look at Baumgartner. 'And you,' he sneered. 'So many years away – what have you seen? Where have you been?'

Baumgartner looked sheepish, felt confused, shy. 'Once – when I was a young fellow – many years ago – I was in Venice. *Ja*, seven days I have in Venice once. Ah, Venice.' He laid his finger beside his nose and his watery eyes gleamed. 'It was wonderful. *Es war prima.*'

The boy snorted. 'Venice,' he sneered, 'Venice is only drains.'

Baumgartner tried to protest but the boy was not listening, he was circling the table in a kind of frenzy. The cats hissed and sprang out of his way, sat on ledges and window-seats out of his reach, fastidiously tucking their paws under them and staring at him with eyes made huge by apprehension and disapproval.

'It will be all right,' Baumgartner tried to calm them, and him. 'I will see what is to do – it will become all right.'

The boy shouted '*Dummkopf*! Idiot! You think you will lock me up – in hospital? In prison? Police even cannot lock me up. I will run and become free – '

Baumgartner stumbled to his feet and tried to catch him by his arm, hold him, but was thrown off and nearly struck in the face.

'I go out – and come in, see? I am free, always. I can go out – and come in – then go out – like that, how I want. Now I say I go out – I have to – ' he stood for a moment, swaying, even put his hand out towards Baumgartner, but then pushed him away and made for the door.

'Where are you going?' Baumgartner called.

'Outside – I must – I have to – ' the boy gasped, groping at the lock. Baumgartner set him free. He leapt away, shouting, 'I come back later.' Baumgartner watched as he hurtled down the stairs, crashing from one flight to another. He leant over the banisters and called, 'And what is your name?'

'Kurt,' he heard the boy call – he thought he heard the boy call. Or some such name – abrupt, like a blow, or a slash.

Eventually Baumgartner shuffled back to his room, shutting the door behind him, feeling drained by all the madness. Mad, that was what the boy was, quite mad. In Germany he would have been a delinquent, a criminal. In India he was mad.

SIX

If the war was said to be over in the camp, there was no truce in
Calcutta. War raged in its streets every night and when
Baumgartner returned to pick his way through them, he
blinked uncomprehendingly at what he saw. The streets were
black with litter, the lights broken, the odour of decay strong.
At Howrah Station, he found himself shrinking, unwilling to
step into it. The city made the internment camp seem
privileged, an area of order and comfort. In a panic, he wished
he could flee, return to that enclosed world, the neat barracks,
the vegetable fields, the fixed hours for baths, meals, lectures,
drill, the release from the pressures of the outer world. They
had listened only to the overseas news on their secret radios, he
had not followed what was happening in the immediate
environs. What was it – a carnival that had ended in disaster?
Riots? Warfare? What could have blighted and blackened this
city so that its grim visage lowered out of the smoke and the
smog at him so threateningly?

In the hotel on Middleton Row, the manager sitting behind
the desk in the lobby was a stranger. Unlike the friendly,
talkative man Baumgartner had known before the war, this
one sat completely idle, his hands resting on his knees as if he
were a dummy. He even looked somewhat dusty. Baumgartner coughed to attract his attention. 'Hmm, can I see Mr Lobo,
pliss?'

'You are wanting a room?' the man asked in a sepulchral voice, reciting the words as if they were all he had been taught.

Baumgartner had made no plans and could make none till he had seen his business partner and learnt the state of the business. He feared from all the dire signs around that it could not be excellent. This would have to be tackled but for the moment he wished only to find Mr Lobo, to see if there were any mail for him and find out why it had never been forwarded nor his letters answered. Putting his fists, tightly rolled, on top of the desk, he said, 'I came to see if there were any letters for me – I am Hugo Baumgartner and I asked Mr Lobo to send me my letters. Mr Lobo is not here?'

The man looked down at the desk; he seemed to be thinking things over deeply. Finally he sighed, 'Mr Lobo gone away. He join Air Force. Gone.'

'When?' Baumgartner heard his voice crack, and he gripped the edge of the desk tightly; perhaps this was the explanation of that long silence during his years in the camp, too banal to have occurred to him.

'Long, long ago,' the man sighed tiredly. 'No come back, Mr Lobo.'

'But I gave him all my things to keep. He kept them? They are here?'

Against all his expectations, the man came to life. 'Mr Bommgarter – you are Bommgarter?' he mumbled and something seemed to stir behind his chalky forehead. He got to his feet and walked waveringly away to a cupboard at the end of the hall. There he stood, his knees painfully bent, searching along the dusty shelves, while Baumgartner waited in suspense. Finally he turned around and came back not only with the small valise into which Baumgartner had hastily thrust a few belongings before leaving, but also a packet of letters which he handed over with a look of much suffering. 'Mr Lobo tell me – keep everything for Mr Bommgarter. So I keep. What if Mr Lobo come back and say, "Did you keep?" Yes, I keep everything – for so long,' he complained, as though it had cost him an immense effort.

'Thank you, thank you . . . it was very kind, very, very kind.' Baumgartner stammered, but he was already leafing through the postcards, all written in a familiar handwriting. 'Pliss, allow me,' he murmured and, not noticing the man's outstretched palm on the desk, retreated to sink down into one of the brown leather chairs that stood about like empty bags in the lobby, and read the letters that had never reached him in the camp.

Strange. They were all postcards, and his mother had never been in the habit of writing on postcards: before the war, she had written to him on very fine azure blue paper with her old pen that obeyed the idiosyncrasies of her writing through long habit, splaying to breadth and squareness when she wished to emphasise something, then turning to a narrow edge for the fine flourishes.

He searched the dates for clues. There was one for every month from October 1939 onwards, for a year. Each bore a stamped message that read, '*Rückantwort nur an Postkarten in deutscher Sprache.*' What officialdom had they passed through, giving them this chilling aspect? 'Answers on postcards only, in German.' Only the endearments were familiar: '*Meine kleine Maus*', '*Mein Häschen*', and the signature: 'Mutti', 'Muttilein', 'Mü'. Apart from them, the messages were strangely empty, repetitive and cryptic. 'Keep well, my rabbit. Do not worry. I am well. Where are you, my mouse? Are you well? I am well. Do not worry. I have enough. Have you enough? Mutti. Mü.' Nothing more.

There was none dated later than February 1941.

He had to find a place fit for the cards. He could not live comfortably and luxuriously in the hotel, it would have tortured him to lie down in comfort, to eat and drink, when the cards were stacked in a corner, on a table, the numbers turned up for him to see whenever he looked that way or passed by inadvertently.

As he left, the manager regarded him gloomily from under the weak light, saying, 'Everybody leaving, everybody going. English soldier. American soldier, all gone. No more business – what to do?' Mournfully he watched Baumgartner pick up his bag and leave.

He found a room in a great decayed house off Free School Street, at the end of a narrow passage that had an overflowing gutter in it – 'In Calcutta a street gets flooded if a dog lifts a hind leg,' they said. There was nothing in it or around it that was not broken or decayed or stained – the high wall was crumbling, the palm trees were lopped, the portico was falling down, the light-bulbs were smashed, the banisters and stairs broken. The landlord, proud to have a foreigner for a tenant, sent him a string cot to sleep on – although he would have preferred to lie on the floor: it would have been more in keeping with his mourning for his mother. He kept his clothes folded at one end of it. There was an earthen jar for water, and a metal tumbler. He would sit on the edge of the cot – even the internment camp had not taught his German knees to fold up, so he could not sit on the floor – and look at his feet so he would not see the cards on the table. Their sparseness, their bleakness, their finality. He thought now that if he had been brought up as an orthodox Jew, he could have mourned her with ceremony; he would have followed the ancient customs, recited the ancient words of solace, and perhaps they would have helped to still the agony. But he was ignorant, and therefore helpless, held in the grip of an unexpressed sorrow. He had to allow the mournful blowing of conch shells and the chanting of Sanskrit prayers that drifted in through the windows at twilight suffice as a funeral ceremony for his mother.

He made no attempt to find and return to the Calcutta life of before the war. He kept away from Park Street, from Chowringhee, from Flury's and the Grand Hotel and Prince's and the 300. The Calcutta he lived in now – the Calcutta that had seen the famine of 1943, that had prepared for a Japanese attack, that had been used and drained by the war and war profiteers and now prepared for the great partition – was the proper setting for his mourning. The Calcutta of the black back streets, the steaming rubbish tips, the scarred tenements, its hunger, its squalor, its desolation. The hopelessness of it seemed right to Baumgartner; this was how the world ended, there was no other ending.

But time had to be filled, and the pocket too. This dreary belief – and the sheer habit of living – drove him through the debris of the streets to his former business partner's office. The street was like a tunnel, it was dark, the rickshaw could scarcely make its way through the crowds: everyone seemed to be on the streets; were the houses all bombed out? Baumgartner peered to see but nothing was visible through the thick, choking smoke except the mottled walls, the gaping windows and darkened doorways in which beggars slept. Habibullah's modest signboard still hung over one of them, although more askew than ever. As Baumgartner felt his way up the stairs in the dark – the light-bulb was either broken or stolen – he had a gradually decreasing hope of finding the office, still less Habibullah.

The latter loomed up from behind his desk like a ghost for all the vivid carmine dye of his tongue and lips, exposed in a welcoming smile, and the purple handkerchief that he tucked away so he could greet Baumgartner with both arms. He sent for tea, screaming at the ubiquitous urchin to hurry. 'And sweets,' he added, 'two plates of sweets from Ghani Ram's, don't forget.'

Then Baumgartner found himself the target for so many and such explosive questions that it was some time before he could calm Habibullah down and assure him of his survival, his safety, his well-being and the embarrassingly dull and secure years in the camp. Habibullah himself had stayed on in Calcutta through the threats of a Japanese attack that had made thousands flee the city and watched helplessly the disruption of life and its ordinary business. Naturally he had not received any of the letters Baumgartner had sent him. Now the war was over, Baumgartner gently suggested, moving the inkwells and the gluepots around on the desk delicately, he hoped to get back to his former business.

At the word 'business' Habibullah's attitude underwent a drastic change. The word was like a bullet that had shot him dead: he slumped over the desk, theatrically. When he finally raised his head to meet Baumgartner's eye, it was with sorrow and regret written all over his dark face. Baumgartner noticed now how lined and pouched it had become, all the old sleekness gone with Calcutta's bright lights.

'What business, *sahib*, what business?' Habibullah sighed, drawing out his purple handkerchief and toying with it nervously. 'Everything finished, gone.'

Baumgartner felt himself growing tense, his muscles, hands and knees all bunching together in a knot as if he were on the edge of an abyss and about to leap. The timber business was his livelihood, he had to have it. It was what he had returned to – it could not be gone. He had realised, while still in the camp, that a return to Germany was out of the question. Germany when it flourished had not wanted him and Germany destroyed would have no need of him either. If he were to remain in India he had to have the means to live in it (even if alone). He thought of the beggars in the doorway over whom he had stepped in order to climb up to the office, and the shrivelled, shrunken ghosts of people who roamed in the streets or slumped across the pavements, scarcely able to move out of the way of the rickshaws, trams and motor-cars. It began to seem as if the hopelessness of Calcutta was to become a part of his own experience now.

'But the war must have been good for your business, Habibullah,' he protested. 'Armies need timber. So many ships, and crates, and paper, and housing – they must have bought so much from you.'

'Yes, yes, yes,' Habibullah nodded from over the purple handkerchief, 'but all over, all finished.' He crumpled up the handkerchief . . . 'Now – nothing.'

'The business will – will go on, Habibullah,' Baumgartner tried to persuade him, and himself. 'How not?'

'Not for me, *sahib*, not for my family. For us – India is finished. Don't you know, every night they come and threaten us in our house? Every night they set some Muslim house on fire, stab some Muslim in the street, rob him too. Don't you know, *sahib*, they are driving us out?'

'Who?' asked Baumgartner, puzzled. In the camp, they listened only to the overseas news, they followed the war. Few had shown any interest in or awareness of what was happening in India. The freedom movement, the famine, the political revolution – no one had discussed that.

'These – these Congress-wallahs, *sahib*, the Hindus,' Habibullah hissed, clutching the handkerchief to him. 'They say they will kick out the British. Even the British are saying they will leave. And this man Jinnah, and his party – they are wanting partition, they are also wanting to leave. All Muslims should leave, they say. But – how? I have so much – my family, my home, my business – what will happen to it all, *sahib*?' he cried, nearly in tears.

Baumgartner said to Habibullah, simply and sadly, 'Tell me.'

It seemed that Habibullah was preparing to flee. He was negotiating with a Marwari businessman and planned to sell him his business while he left with his family for Dacca and what would become East Pakistan where there would be safety in numbers for Muslims. What worried him was whether he could take the proceeds from the sale of the business with him. In the midst of these worries, he groped for some light. Stretching his hand across the desk, he pleaded, 'Why not you buy from me, *sahib*? I sell to you, I reduce price for you, because I trust you, you pay in full – not like Marwari. You buy?'

Baumgartner unfolded his hands on his knees. They were damp with sweat. 'How can I, Habibullah?' he murmured. 'I have only my savings from before the war – and they will not be enough.'

Habibullah's harrowed face underwent a series of changes as it adjusted itself – from anxiety and tension to contrition and concern. 'My dear friend,' he said, in a low emotional voice, 'I am thinking only of self, not of other man's problems. Very bad, very bad.' He shook his head and went on to question Baumgartner and advise him with something of his authority if not his old serenity. His chief, reiterated advice was, 'Leave this city. It is no good. The Japanese have bombed it. In the famine thousands and thousands have died. The streets have been full of dead bodies, rotting. People had no rice to eat and rich men drinking whisky, *sahib*, that is how it was. It is still stinking of death, *sahib*, this city. And there will be more death, more death. I know it, I know it. I am leaving. You leave also, *sahib*. Go to Bombay. In Bombay you can do business and not be stabbed in the back when you are going home at night. Bombay had no war, no famine. Bombay is good city, *sahib*, very good city for you.'

'And what can I do in Bombay?' Baumgartner asked tiredly, the very thought of having to move exhausting him. 'How to start there?' He wanted to explain to Habibullah that their situation was not very different – and equally hopeless.

But Habibullah did not think so. From somewhere, he had retrieved hope, retrieved confidence. He spoke very firmly and precisely. 'Go to Chimanlal, *sahib*. He sent you to me. He is good man. A Bombay man, knows all Bombay business. He will give you business. He will help.'

'How?' asked Baumgartner.

'How? Are you not English, European *sahib*? Have you no European connections? You can help him with export business – '

'Europe has had a war, Habibullah,' Baumgartner reminded him. 'My country is – finished. What business can I do?'

But Habibullah had no more conception of Baumgartner's war, of Europe's war than Baumgartner had of affairs in Bengal, in India. Tapping his fingers on his desk authoritatively, he promised to write out a letter to Chimanlal about Baumgartner that would take care of everything.

'And in Bombay is your friend, Mr Bommgarter!' he

suddenly added with a yelp of exuberance. 'You will meet old friend again.'

'Friend?' Baumgartner was mystified. 'Who?'

'Lola!' Habibullah exploded. 'My God, you are not knowing? Madam Lola is married and living in Bombay. To who? To who? To Kantilal Sethia, Mr Bommgarter. Yes, yes, married, those two. When police came to tell Madam Lola she must go to camp like you, Kantilal did say, no, he will marry Madam Lola, make Indian lady of her, then no camp.'

Baumgartner found himself blinking, laughing with amazement and disbelief. 'Lola married – to Kantilal? Lola has become Indian lady?'

'No, no, no, *sahib*. So clever is that Kantilal, so cunning – he had *secret* marriage with Madam Lola, which is meaning not *real* marriage, only fake, *jhoota*. Fake priest, fake ceremony. All the time it is happening, *sahib*, all the time. These Hindu men not supposed to marry again, so what they do? They have fake marriage instead of real one. And you know what Kantilal do? He take Madam Lola to his house – *yes*, he take her to his own *house* – and tell his wife, this is governess for our sons, *English* governess. And poor lady, she cry and shout and scream, but what can she do? Madam Lola already standing there in the house, with bag and clothing and everything. Madam Lola has to pretend she English governess and give lessons to Kantilal's son. What lessons? I don't know, Mr Bommgarter, you must ask her. Singing lessons? Dancing lessons? I don't know. But already fighting is taking place. Mrs Sethia, she very very angry. Mrs Sethia is making faces and putting chilli powder in all the food and showing to Madam Lola the – what you call? – tongs, kitchen tongs? And Madam Lola getting frightened and running out of house, and all the neighbours looking and seeing. So poor Kantilal, he think better take Madam Lola away. Mrs Sethia he cannot send away, Mrs Sethia staying. So he take Madam Lola to Bombay, buy her nice flat. She say she have no money. He tell her give lessons, be teacher, but she say no, she will not be governess again. So Kantilal buy her shop – yes, yes, yes, I have heard this myself – he buy a shop for Madam Lola. In Bombay.'

Baumgartner found himself smiling. He found himself cheered, at least for the moment. Deciding to leave Habibullah in these good spirits, he got up and went, promising to think over the matter of Bombay.

Instead, he made his way to the old, crowded, slum-like house off Free School Street, in the lane too narrow for traffic but wide enough for people, pigs, stray dogs, even a few intrepid rickshaws. It was a complete contrast to the European quarter he had known before the war with its air of an eastern colonial port, its great houses with deep verandas and green shutters, high walls and tall palms, and the European life of Park Street with its hotels, confectionaries, bars and shops.

To enter this lane, Baumgartner had first to walk through the Anglo-Indian quarter that separated the European from the Bengali. Here the tailors' shops were hung not with the little blouses Hindu women wore with their saris but with the cheap frocks, skirts and blouses the Anglo-Indian clerks and secretaries wore to work. Even the butchers' shops were different and Baumgartner wondered why they made him so queasy, a German used to the sight since childhood. It was after a considerable time that he realised he had grown used to the sight of the Hindu butchers' shops with their goat carcasses and was now shocked by the huge carcasses of cows and buffaloes that hung in this Anglo-Indian, therefore Christian quarter. Even the dogs, he noticed, skirting one fierce gang that snarled and fought over a gigantic bone flung down by the Muslim butcher, were bigger, sturdier and more aggressive than he had seen elsewhere.

Baumgartner found no joy in the streets where he walked aimlessly, compulsively, in order to put off going back to his room. The congestion of the streets and the odours in the heat were overpowering; debris was piled everywhere – banana peels, coconut husks, ashes and cinders from the fires the householders lit in their small brick-stoves with cakes of cowdung soaked in kerosene, a lethal substance that let out billows of choking yellow smoke. In the evenings, the smoke rose to meet the mists that descended from the river and the swamps and mingled to form an impenetrable quilt that made one gasp for breath and cough.

Had it always been so? Baumgartner wondered, coughing into his handkerchief, or had he simply not noticed in the old days when he lived in the pre-war Calcutta of bars, dances, soldiers, prostitutes, businessmen, fortunes and fate? Perhaps if he went to the Three Hundred, to Prince's or Firpo's, he could find some of his acquaintances. But he could not bring himself to do so: that life and that time was a closed book, or like a pack of cards – finite in number.

Yet he remained there, hoarding his small savings, for more than a year, watching the fires that burnt in the city, their hot glow reflected by the smouldering mass of fog and smoke that buried them all and did not allow the flames to escape. At times there were screams to be heard in the dark and footsteps pounding along dark lanes just as in badly made thrillers for the cinema. Processions wound endlessly through the city, chanting slogans like dirges, slipping into sudden outbreaks of activity, to overturn buses and set trams on fire. Or there would be a strike – of taxis, of trams – and the streets would be deserted, waste paper slowly swirling from one end to the other, like ghosts or – again – like the cinema. There were barricades in the streets, police with helmets and batons and rifles, mobs sullen or infuriated – one could never tell.

Halted at a barricade, watching the police with their rifles at one end, the mob with their screams and gestures at the other, he turned in bewilderment to ask, 'Why?'

'They are protesting against the trial of the twenty thousand men who fought in the I.N.A.,' he was told by a fellow onlooker.

'The I.N.A.?'

The man looked at Baumgartner with fury. 'You do not know, about the Indian National Army and the war it fought against the British? In Burma and China? On the side of the Japanese?'

Baumgartner was speechless. Nodding rapidly and apologetically, he retreated from the barricade. He heard the increasing frenzy of the mob, the growing tension of the police, and told himself, 'Not here, not this, Hugo. No, no,' and slipped away.

His war was not their war. And they had had their own war. War within war within war. Everyone engaged in a separate war, and each war opposed to another war. If they could be kept separate, chaos would be averted. Or so they seemed to think, ignoring the fact that chaos was already upon them. And lunacy. The lunacy of performing acts one did not wish to perform, living lives one did not wish to live, becoming what one was not. Always another will opposed to one's own, always another fate, not the one of one's choice or even making. A great web in which each one was trapped, a nightmare from which one could not emerge.

He could only shuffle away down the side lanes, keeping close to the wall, his head lowered. That did not mean he did not see what there was – the misery, the filth. Empty ration-shops, hungry people outside. Those English newspapers that he read told him there had been a cyclone that had wiped out a year's crop of rice, that there were crop failures, shortage of grain, that the Viceroy, Wavell, had regretfully cut the caloric ration of each man to 1200. But out on the *maidan* where he sometimes drifted to hear the speakers who collected crowds whose size varied according to the volume and anguish of their voices, he heard talk of food stocks having been transferred to the British army, of scorched earth tactics by the British army under Japanese threat, of wilful destruction of resources. Moving from one group to another, listening to the speeches in their full flood of oratory and condemnation, Baumgartner retreated to the ranks of the peanut sellers and idle urchins, the pecking crows and stray dogs. Here, too, at any moment, someone might have grabbed him by the neck, seeing it was white. Rubbing the back of it, thoughtfully, Baumgartner shuffled away, back through the brown, stained lanes to the house.

On the twelfth of February the whole city closed down in a general strike after a tremendous rally in Wellington Square that Baumgartner did not attend. He stayed in. More and more now, he stayed in.

Not that the house provided any kind of shelter from the city. Down at the bottom of the lane there was a gap in the wall where the gate had once been and one entered through that into the walled compound that was really only partially walled since the wall had crumbled and in many places disappeared, allowing beggars, cattle, stray dogs and vendors of the whole locality to wander in and set up wherever they found space. There were always rows of supine bodies covered with white sheets so that they had the appearance of corpses in their shrouds but were only people lying in rows outside the house and its once gracious, now decayed portico – those who slept in the day were labourers who worked on night shifts, and those who slept at night were families that lived in the cracks and crevices of the building like so many rats, or lice, but came out for a little air after dark. Within the walls, sewing machines whirred, typewriters clacked, printing presses thumped, motor mechanics hammered at rusting automobiles, paint was splattered on tin and wood, chickens were plucked and slaughtered and, all the time, the single tap in the courtyard ran and ran over slabs of green and shining stones. Here women washed toppling mountains of pots and pans, filled buckets and kettles, scrubbed screaming children, bathed and washed their hair and carried on a seemingly endless war upon filth. The first sound of the morning, long before daybreak, was the chink of a metal pail set on the stone slab beneath the tap and then the rush of water as it filled. Late in the night when the last bit of washing was done, water still ran from the rag that was tied to the brass tap to prevent splashing and one might have imagined a perpetual stream ran through the courtyard. Yet nowhere could one see any sign of cleanliness – the tap only created a morass of mud and slime; children squatted anywhere to urinate or defecate; the washing did not turn the clothes white, only muddier. These clothes, that were washed daily and it seemed hourly, hung in long festoons from every window and balcony of the building, covering its mottled walls with flags – or shrouds – six-foot-long saris and dhotis forty inches wide. The whole building seemed to tremble and sway in every breeze as the garments flapped or floated or hung limp like the hide of an emaciated beast or the bedraggled feathers of a moulting bird.

Even when he had parted these curtains, entered the house, mounted the stairs, careful not to step on the beggars and lepers and prostitutes who inhabited every landing, and at last achieved the small cell that was his room, he had no sense of being walled away from the outer world as he had had in the camp. Here the world forced its way in without being asked: a hundred radios invaded it, either with the mournful songs so beloved of the Bengalis, full of regret, sorrow and sighs, or the rapid gunfire of news bulletins that marked the hours of the day and night. Always there was the nervous flutter of typewriters, the hum and whirr and clack of machinery. There were the inevitable sounds of quarrels and violence at night when the illicit toddy brewed in the closed sheds and garages and odd corners of the compound was bought and consumed; then wives were beaten, children threatened, or else the drunkards themselves abused and thrashed. (One of them howled customarily: 'Beat me, beat me. I am so wicked, you must beat me!') To sleep was only to know a tired semi-consciousness, stirred involuntarily by the sounds of human and insect life. Yes, that too, for in one corner of the compound mosquitoes bred in a still, scummy well and rose at dark to invade the house, defend itself as it might with the ringing of bells, the blowing of conch shells and the waving of joss sticks – the daily ceremony of dusk – and there devour its inhabitants till the early hours of the morning when they dropped off and flew sibilantly away.

In time his anonymity and the anonymity of his neighbours broke down, and identities, individualities were revealed.

Out in the compound a frail grey wisp of a woman in a widow's white sari pottered about with a watering can, irrigating the trees she planted compulsively all over the compound, only to have them eaten by the goats and chickens or trampled by the motor mechanics or the football-playing children. Whenever she saw Baumgartner, she came to him – she was very light-skinned, with the papery whiteness of the Zoroastrian and she seemed drawn to his complexion – and quavered tearfully about the latest losses: 'Six mangoes in a row I did plant, and today not one left – and last week my frangipani eaten by the buffaloes – ' while he nodded and nodded with weary sympathy. He watched her from his window as she stood over her wretched little servant boy with a surprising authority, ordering him to dig pits and plant the saplings she acquired from some mysterious nursery he could hardly believe existed in this city. Her doomed attempts to create a garden in this city-world awed him and horrified him by their persistence. Then he learnt – from a clerk who also sought him out more than he wished and tried to establish the bond of education by reading to him from the newspapers he carried around all day, and occasionally quoting poetry in a rhetorical thunder that sounded to Baumgartner uncannily like German – that she had once owned the house and still lived somewhere in its uppermost regions even after it had been sold and halved and quartered beneath her, and then the persistence seemed a mere habit of ownership. The clerk seemed to admire her proprietorial instinct but one who mocked it was a young man who lived in a kind of loft built above the landing outside Baumgartner's room. After watching one of Baumgartner's encounters with the landlady, he said sardonically, through his cigarette, 'These people who own land – they think even the grass grows for them.' 'And it doesn't?'

Baumgartner asked, smiling. 'No,' he snapped, 'the grass is the people's, the land is the people's.' 'Ah, a Marxist?' Baumgartner queried, and the boy nodded.

Sometimes he came down and asked Baumgartner for a match, then Baumgartner would offer him a cigarette as well. It turned out that he was not so young after all – had been involved in what he called, with dark pride, the 'Alipore bombing case' and been exiled to the Andaman islands for thirteen years – 'But how old were you? A boy?' Baumgartner asked, and the young man made a gesture of his hand by the waist to show how tall he had been then – and that was where he had learnt his Marxism. He laughed as he told Baumgartner, 'All British are highly educated, we think, but we used to order Karl Marx, Trotsky, Lenin, anything we wanted, for our library and they would get for us. They didn't know what they were giving us to read.' He had not only infinite scorn for his erstwhile captors but also an implacable hatred. The day he discovered that Baumgartner was German, he lit up with admiration as if in the presence of a war hero. 'But a Jew, a Jew, not a Nazi,' Baumgartner tried to deflect his misplaced ardour but this meant nothing to Sushil, who had renounced religion for politics and had no interest in Judaism; nor would he entertain any criticism of the German regime. 'If they had defeated the British, then they would have helped Japan to drive them out of India. They are our friends, Japan and Germany.' When Baumgartner stammered that they were not his friends, Sushil politely changed the subject, saying, 'Now I am not so political, now I want to learn other things.' He had learnt yoga in order to build up his body, and taken a course in radio mechanics. That was his greatest passion in life now and, released from the Andamans, he had set up an intricate array of radios in his loft in which the babble of a hundred voices thrummed, knitting themselves into a web of eery sound. Swinging himself up into the loft like a pilot into the cockpit of his aircraft, settling the ear-phones over his ears to emphasise this similarity, he would become engrossed as if taking off into space, bemused as a space-traveller, in a way that Baumgartner found enviable. From that abstract height he would occasionally smile at Baumgartner, say softly, 'Tokyo radio' or 'Voice of Moscow' and then his eyes would glaze over. Only sometimes his erstwhile friends would visit him, climb up after him, voices would be raised in argument, the air grow fraught in a way that would alarm Baumgartner. When they left, he would come to his door and call, 'Sushil, is everything all right?' and the boy would sigh, 'These men – old friends – they won't let me go. I want to listen to my radio, I want to learn more and more. Bombs, guns – those games I don't want to play any more.' 'Games, Sushil?' Another sigh. 'Ah, bombing here, killing there. It goes on all the time – why ask me to join?' Then he would settle the earphones over his thick black curls and cup his chin in his hand, pick up his pencil and notepad and seem to forget the earthbound world below.

So it might have continued if the city and pre-partition violence had not closed in upon his hiding-place. The nights were hideous with screams, gunfire, the sounds of rioting, the smell of burning. The days were strangely calm and empty. Baumgartner even went out sometimes, oppressed by the house, by his room, by the summer. There were times he felt he could not breathe the city air, that he was being suffocated, and then he would be filled with a panic to leave, to return to the camp and see if that orderly schoolboy world still stood, slip through the barbed wire and return to the barracks where he had lived in austerity and simplicity that had seemed his natural element – at least now, in retrospect, seemed his element. Then he found himself searching the streets for someone from that world with whom he might associate. He even wandered on to Park Street, the forbidden area of the past. Here, in normal daylight, he found himself staring in at the big plate-glass windows of Flury's. As if in answer to his enquiry, he saw a group of blonde women having coffee at a table and imagined one of them was Annemarie. Her pale hair, her fine neck, her back to him – surely it was Annemarie? He stood there, waiting patiently – impatiently for her to turn.

When she did, he saw of course it was not her. Annemarie would not have had coffee and cake in Flury's. Nor should he. He too turned and left, hurried back to the nightmare house where he lived, to which he now belonged.

That night the house itself was engulfed by a riot. He woke to screams as he often had before and only turned on to his back, resignedly folding his hands over his chest and preparing to postpone sleep till the latest domestic quarrel had died down. But when guns were fired, he jumped to his feet and went to the window to see the ghosts in their white shrouds fleeing and running pell-mell as men in theatrically blood-soaked clothes entered through the gap in the wall with torches and knives, screaming those slogans of religious warfare that were raised everywhere now. The buffalo calf in the shed bawled in hysterical fear to its mother who bawled back. Footsteps thundered up the stairs from below and Baumgartner hurriedly moved his chair and bag against the door, trying to secure it against intruders. The loudest scream came from his landing, from the loft above it – a male scream, somehow more intolerable than a woman's or a child's. His heart hammering inside him, Baumgartner moved the chair away and opened the door to go out and see – and met the marauders as they leapt down from the loft and ran down the stairs past him. When he climbed up to the loft and called, 'Sushil? Sushil?' he saw the radio buff's chair overturned and the boy lying face down on the floor. The blood streamed. Women came up the stairs, wailing. Pushing past them was the little landlady in white. She stood and stared at the corpse. 'Tcch,' she said, 'I always knew this boy was bad.' 'Madam,' Baumgartner stammered, 'the boy is dead.'

In his sleep, in his dreams, the blood was Mutti's, not the boy's. Yet his mother – so small, weak – could not have spilt so much blood. Or had she? The blood ran, ran over the floor and down the stairs, soaking his feet which stood in it helplessly.

When he went to see if Habibullah was safe and unaffected by the night's violence, he found the office empty, ransacked. A beggar picked through the rubble. Baumgartner asked him, in his cautious Bengali, 'Where is he, the *sahib*, Habibullah?' but did not understand the reply. Outside the morning street was normal, humdrum, except for the gutted buildings, the shattered glass and the smoke from the night's fires which were after all commonplace now. Baumgartner felt himself overtaken by yet another war of yet another people. Done with the global war, the colonial war, only to be plunged into a religious war. Endless war. Eternal war. Twenty thousand people, the newspapers informed him, were killed in three days of violence in Calcutta. Muslims killed Hindus, Hindus Muslims. Baumgartner could not fathom it – to him they were Indians seen in a mass and, individually, Sushil the Marxist, Habibullah the trader. He wondered if Habibullah had fled to safety in East Bengal and not left it too late. He must not leave it till too late. He must take Habibullah's advice, he knew, and leave for Bombay. He returned to his room, packed his bag, carried it down, went to Howrah Station – the rickshaw puller scuttled through the city as if in fear – and bought a ticket. He spent the intervening time in the railway rest room, unable to face the sight of the destroyed buildings or the panic-stricken population. Refugees from the city poured on to the station platform, filled it to overflowing with families and belongings, and in the end he had to fight through them, climb over them and claw past them on to the train that carried him to Bombay.

So Baumgartner came to Bombay. The glitter of the noon sun on the waves in the bay struck his eyes. It was reflected by the white walls of the houses along Marine Drive on which traffic rolled in an orderly way that suggested affluence and Westernisation of an order that Baumgartner had lost touch with in Calcutta. He was astonished by the way the streets sloped sharply and even curved; by the way houses were named, not numbered – all Europeanisms that he had forgotten, now brought back. He felt intimidated rather than reassured: he shrank, his eyes blinked. It made him realise how much a native he had become. Baumgartner, a native of Hindustan. He smiled, thinking of what Mü would have said to that. And yet he had not met a single snake other than in a snake-charmer's basket on the city pavements – he must tell her that. But – he forgot constantly, again and again he stopped and was brought up against the fact he could not admit: he would never hear from her again, there would be no more communication. He wrote to people, to addresses he remembered; he never had a reply; all of Germany might have been wiped off the face of the earth. That made him sort out the matter of his papers, his passport, his nationality, and found himself become an Indian citizen, the holder of an Indian passport. Holding it, he wondered if it meant that he would now never leave India and realised that, for all that it was a travel document, it did.

It was Chimanlal who made it possible for him to stay, who provided the mooring – instantly, generously, sympathetically. He had had Habibullah's letter, he said, but did not seem to require anyone's recommendation; he acted according to his own instincts, which were large, free, always hospitable. Putting aside his work, he took Baumgartner out to lunch. Himself eating only rice and yoghurt, he ordered for Baumgartner an excellent Parsi dish of mutton and dal at the Victory Club that looked out at the sandstone arch of the Gateway of India and the islands floating in the sea like upturned bowls of tan and ochre ceramic. The ships stood still on the sea, metallic and dart-shaped, but the boats bobbed lightheartedly up and down along the quay. There were still British soldiers in khaki swarming everywhere but Chimanlal said, with a clap of his hands, 'Like this – they will go. Soon all will go and we will be left alone.'

'You are sure?'

'Of course.' Chimanlal bounced up and down in his chair with confidence. 'You should have seen – if you had been here in February, you would have seen – the naval strike. Here, Mr Bommgarter, right here, on the HMS *Talwar*. The ratings went on strike because British officers were insulting them and giving them poor food also. Next day, twenty-two more ships in the harbour went on strike, and the men in the Castle and Fort barracks also. They flew our tricolour on their masts, Mr Bommgarter, I wish you could have seen, it was so fine. Then the army arrived, and there was fighting in the barracks, and the ships were providing artillery, and bombers were going to destroy the fleet. All of us brought food for the brave ratings, Mr Bommgarter. I offered them everything I had. But the strike spread all over the city – CPI called for a general strike – and there was fighting in the streets. Nearby, Mr Bommgarter, in Parel and de Lisle Road. Oh, we were winning, we would have won – but what did the Congress do?' He made a disgusted face. 'Gandhi-ji in his white cap – he came and said, "No fighting, no violence." And the ratings had to surrender, and it came to an end, our glorious revolt.'

Baumgartner made a vague, sympathetic gesture of his hands over the empty trays of food; he knew it was not for him, an outsider and a foreigner, to comment.

He did not need to; Chimanlal was ebullient again. 'But they will have to go – soon, soon. Now they themselves are saying they will go, they cannot stay. So you will see our flag flying soon, Mr Bommgarter – British flag will go, Union Jack will go, *our* flag will fly instead from the top of the Red Fort, and we will not sing "God Save the King", we will sing *our* own anthem written by our great poet Rabindranath. In Calcutta you must have heard of our great poet Rabindranath Tagore?'

Baumgartner nodded, but at the mention of Calcutta could not refrain from asking, 'And the Muslims, Mr Chimanlal?'

Chimanlal gave him a surprised look. The delight on his face became tempered. 'You are worrying about the *Muslims*, Mr Bommgarter?'

'I am worried about Habibullah,' Baumgartner admitted to that, no more. 'He was so good, so kind to me. He gave me much business – before the war, before I went to the camp. But last time I went to the office – he was gone. The office was burnt – I think looted. Where did he go?'

'Ah, my friend, you don't need to worry about Habibullah. Habibullah is much cleverer than Hindu *goondas*, Hindu thugs. He will have taken all his wealth with him – he must be in Dacca now, the home of his ancestors, happy and safe.'

'You think so?' Baumgartner looked doubtful. He had no reason to believe in such fairy-tale escapes. 'And his family?'

'His family also,' Chimanlal assured him in his sunny manner. He did not allow any cloud near him, repelled them by his warmth and the sunshine of his optimism, as Baumgartner was to learn over the years. Now he dipped his fingers in a bowl of water and wiped them desultorily. 'And Habibullah sent you to me, eh? We are going to do business together, eh?'

Baumgartner had his doubts, his uncertainties, but Chimanlal never entertained any. Baumgartner could not discover why he took up a homeless foreigner, not even one with the prestige of having been an erstwhile ruler, a part of the colonial might and power, but simply a stray, a pariah in the eyes of the raj, clearly the most powerless of all. Perhaps Chimanlal had a sense of history after all and felt it morally just to support someone who had been on the right side during the war, a fellow-enemy of the British. But such a motivation crumbled when Baumgartner learnt how hazy an interest Chimanlal really had in politics and history. Chimanlal had made his first fortune, he confessed, in the family's jewellery business, through another Jew, a Russian who had fled from the Bolsheviks by way of China and, landing in a small port on the coast of Gujarat where Chimanlal's family had its base, sold that family the gems he had brought in the linings of his jacket, gems he said had belonged to the Czar and Czarina of his abandoned land, and that Chimanlal was able to sell, on his behalf, to the Nizam of Hyderabad, earning a considerable commission for himself. Baumgartner wondered briefly if the fact that he had made this fortune through a Jew had influenced his generous behaviour towards Baumgartner, but found out later that Chimanlal's thinking was of a much more ignorant, uninformed and mercenary order. Who was that Russian Jew?

Baumgartner questioned. Where had he come from, how did he come into the possession of the Czar's jewels? Chimanlal was embarrassed, could not answer. He thought the man's name was Gin – Gin – Bug, something like that. Ginzburg? Baumgartner asked. Yes, yes, Ginzburg, came from Russia. Where in Russia? Chimanlal smiled, spread his hands, showed that they were empty of information. 'I am not educated much,' he told Baumgartner.

The freedom movement certainly had stirred something in his soft, pendulous breast under the crisp white cotton *kurta*, even if he had made much of his money by supporting the British war effort and supplying the British army. He told Baumgartner with pride that both Gandhi and Sardar Patel came from Gujarat, that he had heard Patel speak, when he was a young man, in his village, before he came to Bombay to run the family's jewellery business. And now the business had grown so much – jewellery was only one of his interests, timber another, but he also traded in leather, in bauxite, in iron ore, chemicals, aluminium, paper, spices – a whole empire of business, it seemed, and of course he could accommodate Baumgartner, quite easily.

He began, that blistering afternoon with the light coming off the sea like metal that had melted in it and was being drawn off in shivering silver sheets, by taking Baumgartner to a house, Hira Niwas, a tall stucco four-storeyed building in a dark lane behind the grandiose pile of the Taj Hotel, which was owned by a relation of his – he could have been merely a friend, but Chimanlal called every man 'brother'. He arranged for Baumgartner to rent a small flat in it for a price that was reasonable considering its location (he seemed to feel that as a foreigner Baumgartner could live nowhere but in the vicinity of the Taj). When Baumgartner had deposited his bag there, checked to see if water ran from the taps in the sink, if the shutters in the window opened and shut and if the door locked, he took him back again to his office which was in the more noisy and bustling quarter of Kalbadevi, near the huge Eros cinema and the Gothic walls of St Xavier's College, the

Parsi fire temple and the Parsi shops for little black caps, white vests and sticks of sandalwood, the Parsi dairy and sweet and confectionery shops, tattered secondhand bookshops, crowded tea stalls with glittering mirrors. Here he had a single office room, scarcely bigger than a cubicle, off a staircase in a seedy building that housed an Irani restaurant at street level, a tailoring establishment above it, a school for typing and shorthand, a dentist, a polyclinic and a dozen other small business establishments like his own.

He lowered himself on to a low divan spread with spotless white sheets, lounged against a white bolster under a lithograph of his patron goddess, freshly garlanded with marigolds and wreathed in spirals of richly sweet smoke from perfumed joss sticks. Perhaps she was the reason, Baumgartner thought, for Chimanlal's bland, imperturbable optimism and confidence and the good humour that he exuded like glistening perspiration (the office had no cooling arrangement other than the old and decrepit electric ceiling fan). Several times in the course of their talk he bowed to the oleograph on the wall, clasped his hands in prayer and murmured, 'If Lakshmi wills it, it will succeed. Everything is in Lakshmi's hands.'

Baumgartner found it disquieting to begin with – he had never left anything in the hands of the gods, and would not have known which ones to chose from the plethora available in India – or which of their many hands for that matter – but he found that if he were to work for Chimanlal, he would have to humour Chimanlal's beliefs and ways. Chimanlal showed him the ways in which he could be of use to him and how he could earn a reasonable commission, and he came and went with his orders and transactions, always doubtful if Lakshmi would guide him as well while he conducted Chimanlal's latest ventures – transporting bauxite down Goa's rivers to its ports on the Arabian Sea, setting up a factory for aluminium pots and pans in the hinterland of Gujarat – and was surprised to find he could secure orders and get business done so satisfactorily as to make Chimanlal smile broadly and turn around and bow to his garlanded goddess in thanksgiving so profound, so humble that it made Baumgartner look away in embarrassment.

On one of these business trips, Baumgartner found he had to change trains at a small junction out in the flat, red-soiled barren country where he would have to waste nearly a whole day. The train from Bombay deposited him there on a blazing morning with the sun pouring on to the corrugated iron roof like smelt from a foundry, then drew away, leaving him on a wooden bench, mopping his neck with a handkerchief that grew quickly soiled and grubby, and idly watching a miserable pair of rhesus monkeys in a small pipal tree that they had stripped of leaves, grooming each other with dissatisfied expressions on their small pinched faces. Other travellers lay on mats or bedrolls spread out on the station platform, only once in a while raising a hand to brush away flies or languidly wave a palm leaf fan. Coolies in their red shirts sat on their haunches smoking *bidi*s and waiting for the next train to arrive. A station-master in a white uniform badly in need of washing, ironing and mending, came out of his office to advise Baumgartner to eat. 'It is not good to sit for so long without food,' he reprimanded Baumgartner, who was surprised: surely the station-master ought to know his timetable and understand the reason why Baumgartner had such a long wait. To placate the man – perhaps he was preventing him from going off to enjoy his own lunch – he got up and went to a food barrow where a vendor served him with some potato fritters in a leaf cup. Afraid that the station-master might be watching, Baumgartner tried to eat them but the chillies defeated him and he let them drop under the bench. Instantly a stray dog dashed up and snatched it as though a whole horde were after it, and some crows did soon alight to try and get a share. Baumgartner took a cup of sweet milky tea from the vendor and drank that, although it made him mop his face even more frequently. The afternoon slowly dragged itself over the breadth of the corrugated iron roof, then finally began to fall

westwards. There were still some hours to wait – Baumgartner's train did not arrive till late in the evening. Why had no
one warned him? He felt anger at being sent off uninformed
and unprepared but, as usual, the anger rebounded on him, its
ultimate cause.

It made him get to his feet and walk down the length of the
platform and out of the station. Behind the station sheds and
yards there was a township of a sort – some stucco houses with
doors painted green and blue and pink, several shacks of tin
and rag and cardboard. Open gutters ran outside them along
which children squatted, women washed and dogs lapped.
They looked up in suspicious amazement to see him pass but
he tried not to meet their eyes, to walk on. The vendors of
cigarettes and soft drinks called to him from their barrows but
he wanted neither. There were grain and oil stores, the usual
workshop with lathes and sparkling welding machines. String
cots were dragged out into the dust of lanes, and cooking fires
lit. When he had walked past and left behind these habitations,
he came upon some cattle foraging for fodder in the dry,
friable soil of the barren land, a herdsboy sitting on a stone,
whistling. He walked on, leaving them behind too.

The road petered out into the stony dirt. There was no sign
of fields, of agriculture, or irrigation or habitation. There was
the red sandy dust, and the black volcanic rocks. The dumb
unrelenting flatness of the iron earth at last gave way to a slight
swell. Baumgartner, unable to face the walk back through the
township again, decided to climb that low hill, if such a name
could be given it. Who knows, he sighed, perhaps on the *other*
side there was something to see – golden valley, flowering
grove or still pool. He had to laugh at his own stupidity. No,
of course, there would be nothing but this red dust, this black
stone, sun and barren space. But perhaps the hilltop offered
something – at least there was a tumble of rocks to be seen on
it, crouching like a beast for protection from heights, views,
space. He would go up and sit there for a while. The dust crept
into his shoes, lay in a red film on his socks and trouser cuffs,
and the stones stubbed against his toes. Still, a little movement

could be felt in the air – not exactly a breeze, but at least a stir, and it gave him the energy to complete that climb.

Yes, there were rocks piled there on the bony spine of the hill. Baumgartner surmised that they had been placed together to form a kind of cave. It was clearly no temple of famed carvings and fabulous idols such as heaped the rest of the country with their artistic splendour – no, it was Baumgartner's luck to have come to a part of the country that had been left out of such abundance – but he felt it must be something ancient and primitive anyway.

He stood for a while on that mean summit, while a pair of kites wheeled in the colourless, featureless sky as if they had sighted him and were wondering if he was worthy prey before they swooped. Baumgartner remembered stories he had heard of eagles who were fed at a temple, who flew free and ranged everywhere but returned every evening to be fed by the temple priest. Where was that temple? Not this one, of course. No one could have heard of this one, there was nothing to say about it and it was probably nameless. He was, in fact, not quite certain that it was a temple at all. True, now that he had paused and looked about him, he could see that there was a path of sorts leading from the small town across the flat land to this hillock – he saw its grey trail through the rusty earth from this height. So it was used, people came here, to see – what?

Finally he lowered himself to fit the crack that made an entrance into the rocks, and found that if he overcame his squeamishness about dark places, it was possible to enter. He edged his large bulk into the small space bravely and for a moment struggled with a vision of having his face clawed by escaping birds or – worse – bats. He could smell them, that rank urinary odour that one could expect in such dark caves. But he heard no squeak of bat voices or flap of bat wings; they had left only their odour here. Or was it that? Could it perhaps belong to something else – like an idol?

Although his eyes were growing accustomed to the dark, he still could make out nothing in that inner chamber. There was no vent or shaft for light or air. Although it was so well sealed from the heat of the sun, it was not cool either; on the contrary, the heat seemed to thicken and congeal here, like spilt blood, into a dark clot.

Very cautiously Baumgartner moved forwards, his feet feeling the uneven surface of the stone flooring. When he thought he was in the centre of the chamber, he stopped. Actually, it was something that stopped him, but he could not tell what. Neither his feet nor his outstretched hands struck anything. He had heard nothing. But he was certain there was an object there. Trying to stand still and breathe calmly, he told himself it could be an idol. What kind of idol? Could it be that black, engorged penis he had seen in roadside shrines, or an oxen hump, placid and bovine, some swollen udder of blood? He strained his eyes to see but his eyes had never met with such total blackness. The darkness itself was a presence. Abandoned the temple might be but he could swear it was not empty. Something was blocking the chamber, emanating a stench, and watching *him*, with an uncanny stealth, not betraying itself by the slightest sound or motion. The silence thundered in his ears. After listening to its beat for a long time, he finally lowered his head – he could hear the small bones of his neck grate against each other – and down by his foot he made out a flat slab of black stone and upon it a rounded projection, also of black stone. The reason he could make it out in that thick darkness was that someone had smeared it with red powder, or paste, which reflected some small trickle of light that came through the slit of the entrance. Something fragile and dry lay curved around it – perhaps a marigold garland, dried up. Perhaps a snake skin, or even a snake. What did this black stone profess to be that it was so honoured? Baumgartner would have liked to know. The chamber seemed to hold a secret. If Baumgartner could find out that secret –

He swivelled his head slowly, listening to the bones creak. But there was no one to tell him – no priest, no pilgrim. No voice, no song, not even a dim inscription scratched into the black fur that coated the stones.

He was certain now that there was nothing here but what he could dimly make out. Then what was it that was so stealthily watching him, breathing so malignly down his neck, raising the small hairs on his back as if he were faced with danger, with death? It had to be something, even if only a deadly spider, or scorpion. But it was not that kind of fear and Baumgartner knew it was not a spider or a scorpion. It was just a stone. A black blob, spat out by some disdainful god, to land at his feet and then solidify, blocking his way.

Definitely he had a sense of being stopped. He was to go no further. He had arrived at the final barrier. And what was that – death? Was this temple occupied by death? Was it the scene of some hideous human sacrifice? One read of them, from time to time, in the papers. Even of cannibalistic rites, tantric magic. Had some drugged creature, animal or human, been dragged up here to be decapitated, to spill the crimson stuff out of its unstoppered self and water this immutable black blob of god-spit, god-sputum? Perhaps it was death that lay there in a heap, a heap of death piled up, as casually as dog's turds, saying to Baumgartner – the end, no more.

But Baumgartner would not have its no. He turned and scrambled out of the narrow exit with such speed that he scratched his arms against the stone, hurt his knee against its rib, and fell out on to the hillside as if ejected by whatever possessed or inhabited that temple. Indigestible, inedible Baumgartner. The god had spat him out. *Raus*, Baumgartner, out. Not fit for consumption, German or Hindu, human or divine.

Half-way down the track, laughing in humiliation and mortification as he rubbed his scratched elbows, Baumgartner knew he had been expelled from some royal presence. Go, Baumgartner. Out. He had not been found fit. Shabby, dirty white man, *firanghi*, unwanted. *Raus*, Baumgartner, *raus*.

When freedom came, Baumgartner was again on the fringe, looking on the Independence Day celebrations from a distance, finding himself smiling at the flags, the balloons, the slippers flung up in the air in rejoicing, and then wondering why he smiled. When communal riots rent the new nation, making Bombay bulge with the refugees who streamed in from over the border, he skirted their shelters, avoided the sights. He was glad when Bombay settled back into its familiar activities of trade and commerce, committing itself again to the possibilities, the opportunities, the sanguine nature of a port.

It was that aspect of the city that Chimanlal exemplified. Deciding that he would never fathom Chimanlal's motives, that under all that bland guilelessness there was an unfathomable guile, Baumgartner simply accepted when Chimanlal, coming down the stairs from his office, found him lunching in the Irani restaurant below off a piece of bright yellow cake and a glass of tea and insisted he leave that and come home for lunch. It was the first of many invitations, many visits which allowed Baumgartner to see another reason for his rocklike complacence, his confident calm.

In a small flat at Teen Batti that firmly turned its unlovely back to the view of the bay and preferred to face the raucous street instead, in a room painted green and blue and lit with strips of neon lighting, the two men sat together on a swing with a shiny red plastic seat and with small coloured bells attached to strings wound around its metal stand, till the women – Chimanlal's wife and daughters – came out of the kitchen where they had been cooking, filling the apartment with the odours of *asafoetida*, garlic and hot oil, and placed steel trays of food on the table for them. Even after many visits Baumgartner never felt at ease, either on the swing or at the table. To begin with, he was too aware of the immense amount of labour and preparation that had gone on in the kitchen in his honour, and then of the unfamiliar food itself, alarming in its complexity. Himself used to eating pieces of bread or bananas when he was overtaken by hunger, unable to understand the need to combine ingredients and flavours and set them afloat in oil in little stainless steel dishes on a tray, he fumbled, ate with a clumsiness at which the women curled their lips in sarcasm not untinged with distaste that he saw before they had twitched their saris over their diamond-studded ears down to their diamond-studded nostrils and gone back to the kitchen for the second helpings that Chimanlal called for with an affectionate authoritarianism as of a genial tyrant who cannot conceive of not being loved and honoured.

It was with his only son, the youngest child, that Chimanlal became entirely human in Baumgartner's eyes – by which he meant vulnerable. He would have the boy woken up and brought out to meet Baumgartner, clinging to his mother's or his sister's hip, rubbing his eyes and whimpering with unspent sleep while Chimanlal chuckled and clucked and made a series of bird or animal-like sounds, almost unable to summon up ordinary speech to deal with a being so extraordinary, in his eyes close to celestial, his only son and heir. Seeing what the boy meant to Chimanlal, on Independence Day Baumgartner bought the child a paper flag of the new Indian tricolour and also a present. It was a tin motor car, the kind that could be wound up with a key and sent clacking and rocking across the terrazzo floor, and Baumgartner bought it for a few annas on the pavement where hawkers were doing brisk business that day, but it succeeded phenomenally – not only did the spoilt baby stop wailing and play with intense concentration for an unprecedented ten minutes, but Chimanlal, throwing himself back into the swing-seat and then forwards across his knees with joy and hilarity, looked at Baumgartner, wiping tears from his eyes, with unconcealed love. 'Hugo *bhai*', he called him thereafter, 'Hugo brother', and invited him to join him in his one weakness, his sole vice, making Baumgartner feel as if he were peeling off layer after layer of a large and shining onion to arrive at its sweet yellow heart.

Standing beside Chimanlal in the members' enclosure – a Chimanlal transformed by the fineness of his white Sunday *kurta* and dhoti, the touches of gold about his body –

Baumgartner could not help exploding with a laugh of delight
when the starting gun was fired and the horses released like
pellets from their barrels. With that gun, with that shot, the
memory came to him of how he had lain face down on the
polished parquet floor of the Berlin flat. Hammering his heels
and howling in outrage because his father, so elegant in his
light suit and cravat, refused indignantly to take him along to
the races. Mü had set him, when he was worn out by kicking
and screaming, on her lap by the window, wiped the last traces
of his tears with her tiny lace handkerchief that smelt of
eau-de-Cologne, and jumped him up and down on her knee in
an attempt to amuse him with a game of:

> 'Hoppe, hoppe, Reiter,
> wenn er fällt, dann schreit er.
> Fällt er in die Hecken,
> fressen ihn die Schnecken,
> fällt er in den Klee,
> schreit er gleich: O weh . . .'

and then he had struck out at her, at her breast, in fury at being
thought so small and easily bought over. To have lost a day at
the races, the real races, and for her to imagine a baby game
would do instead, had been intolerable. She had put her hand
to her breast where he had hurt her, her face shocked at his
violence. That was how he remembered the scene now, and
also remembered his body rolled into a ball at the bottom of
his dark, damp bed, while he clutched his right foot and his
right hand with his left, and muttered like a wizard, 'Mick-
muck-mo, make it so – '

Thirty years the wizard had taken, but he had waved the
wand at last, and now here he was at the races. Papa, he wanted
to shout, Papa, what do you think? He wanted to lift his arms
and wave – and he did, exuberantly – Papa, do you see me
here, at the races? And what would his father have made of the
Mahaluxmi racecourse by the Arabian Sea, the dome and the
towers of the Haji Ali mosque a purple silhouette against the
orange sky of the west, the stands that milled with the silk saris
and gold and diamond jewellery of the Indian ladies, and the

dark, hysterical men who trampled the beds of flowering cannas and pressed against the white fence to see the horses flying by on the circular track that began in Berlin and ended here in Bombay which became, by magic, the Berlin of thirty years ago?

They went together, every Sunday afternoon during the season – Chimanlal delighted to have a companion, for he could not have brought his Indian associates – he would not have wanted them to know that he had a gambling streak, it would have laid him open and made him vulnerable – and Baumgartner, constantly rollicked by delight at having arrived at the scene where he had wanted to be as a small, obstreperous boy. Slow, slow as a snail, slow as a turtle, Hugo, he told himself, but with quivers of laughter and pleasure. And the horses, the splendid horses, they swept up and they swept by, with the speed that is most affecting of all to the slow. When at last he ventured, after several visits, to help Chimanlal lay his bets, he found he had a gift – he who had never imagined he had a gift of any kind – for picking the winners. Again and again the two of them went up to collect their winnings, divided them, left rich. Chimanlal could not understand it, for Baumgartner swore he had no method at all, did it entirely by intuition that could fail at any moment. On the last race of the season, the big one, they won such an overwhelming amount that they did something that would have seemed incredible to both of them at the start of the season – they bought a horse. After two years of training in Poona, it went on to win several races in subsequent seasons. Again and again, Chimanlal was called to lead the horse, mounted by his jockey, a wizened monkey in pink and lilac satin, to receive the silver trophy. Swamped by gratitude, Chimanlal pressed these trophies into Baumgartner's arms, insisted he take them to his flat. 'I will come and visit you, I will have a drink in your house, we will drink to our horse and our luck,' Chimanlal said. He did not understand Baumgartner's reluctance to carry the shining objects down the street to his flat, stared at by all the goggling onlookers on the pavement, and he did not want them in his own house. Baumgartner was not sure if his womenfolk knew of his weakness – probably not.

Yet he never failed to share his luck with them. Whenever he won, he would stop the taxi that was carrying them back from the races, at Crawford Market, and in the small, mirror-backed stalls across the street, he would buy large bags of salted pistachio nuts, almonds and raisins from Kabul, walnuts from Kashmir, *chilgozas* from Ladakh, and chuckle, 'This is for my son. Today I must give my son a present. You buy also, Hugo *bhai*, buy,' but Baumgartner stood on the pavement, his hands behind his back, watching him make these extravagant purchases, and merely shook his head. There was no one for whom he could buy such gifts, and why should he take large bags of dried fruit back to his empty flat in Hira Niwas?

But it was when he was thoughtfully walking back from one of these Sunday expeditions – extraordinary how low his spirits fell after having been raised so high by the sight of those horses and the memory they called forth each time – having insisted on Chimanlal letting him get out of the taxi and walk across the Oval, past the cricketers and footballers and peanut-chewing strollers, to Colaba Causeway and from there to Hira Niwas, that he saw a cruelly maimed cat dragging its broken leg and halved tail along a gutter and, instead of averting his eyes from a sight so repugnant, followed it anxiously to make sure no dog was attracted to such easy sport, and no boys stoned it to death. Why should it not die? Surely death would be preferable to life in the Indian streets, he argued, and yet – when it came to the main road where traffic raced at it murderously – he bent and lifted the beast, holding it to his breast even though it twisted and turned in his hands and sank its teeth into his wrist. It was too weak to do much damage, its mouth hung open and drooled uncontrollably, and its eyes already had a warning glaze of white drawn over them. The watchman at Hira Niwas and the children of the building who were playing their eternal games of bat, ball and stones on the pavement, all stood and stared as he stumbled past them apologetically, but he kept the cat carefully wrapped in his arms and carried it up the stairs to his flat where it stretched out on the newspaper Baumgartner spread for it, and died.

After that, he searched the streets for a replacement for the first cat in his life. They were not so easy to find. Even if they were everywhere, especially in the vicinity of the cafés and restaurants where he had his meals and cups of tea, they were by no means inclined to respond to his polite blandishments and enticing calls; they glared at him suspiciously and sprang aside if he came too near. He was abashed to find he was less attractive to them than a life in the harsh streets, but told himself they could not possibly know what comfort, what care waited for them in his little room.

In the end, shamefacedly, he was reduced to capturing kittens, separated from their parents, crying indignantly in the dustbins where there was so little sustenance. The first pair that he caught spat and hissed and scratched his arms up to his elbows, but he found their fury enchanting, contained as it was in such small – and in spite of the filth and the fleas – elegant bodies. Also, they were easy to win over when he had found them scraps of fish from the kitchens of the Taj and the smaller hotels and restaurants around. After that, there was no stop to the cat family that grew and multiplied under his roof.

Now there was a reason, even a need, to hurry back to the flat. The more crowded and messy it grew, the more comfortable Baumgartner felt in it, but he had to admit that his visitors did not. Poor Chimanlal held a handkerchief to his nose when he came to have a drink with him after a good Sunday at the races.

'Next Sunday you have a drink with me at the Turf Club,' Chimanlal said on the landing as he left, and Baumgartner had to agree, knowing how the fastidious vegetarian had suffered.

It was on the Turf Club lawns, amongst the members in their hats and saris that floated in the evening breeze lifting off the

Arabian Sea and drifting across the racecourse, now emptied of the crowds and given up to the walking and dog-owning fraternity of Malabar and Cumballa Hills, that Baumgartner was startled to see a familiar figure – a head taller than anyone else present.

It was Julius – an elegant, evidently affluent Julius, garbed in a fine suit of silk and linen, a poppy-red handkerchief in the pocket of his cream-coloured tropical suit, a panama hat in his hand, but it was unmistakably Julius, and Baumgartner broke away from Chimanlal's side and hurried to him; it was so long now since he had hoped and wanted to meet someone from the internment camp days, but suddenly that old wish woke and washed over him.

He remembered that long mane of light flowing hair Julius had had in camp with its spun-silver fairness. Now it was almost all gone, leaving his scalp showing through in pink nakedness, all except for one strand that remained, just above his right ear. Julius had made the most of this remnant, and grown it to shoulder length so that he could comb it right over down to his left ear. It was like a somewhat slippery and precariously balanced boater of new straw that had to be constantly adjusted by his long nervous fingers. Its silveriness had greyed a bit, or dulled; it looked dusty now.

But, 'Julius,' Baumgartner exclaimed, putting out his hand, and Julius stared at him with those nervously blinking, pinkish eyes of his for a whole minute or two before he recognised Baumgartner and from his expression Baumgartner could see that he was noting his shabby clothing, his dusty shoes, his increasingly slack and lumpish figure and faded eyes. After that initial shock and hesitation was over, Julius gave a cry of welcome, more high-pitched than ever.

On hearing it, his companion who had kept her hand lightly on his arm but had been turning her head to scan the crowds, searching for the known and the celebrated, stopped and tilted her straw cartwheel hat in order to smile at her companion's acquaintance with a cool politeness. Baumgartner saw – as disbelievingly as if it were on stage, in a theatre – that it was no other than Gisi, Gisela, Lily of Prince's, Lily of the cabaret, Lily of the Lola-and-Lily duo. He also saw that in spite of his scruffiness and early middle age, she had recognised him by the way her glassy grey eyes not only widened but turned briefly upwards into the painted silver lids before rolling down again and regarding him levelly, hostilely. She had allowed the brassy blonde of the cabaret girl's hair to fade to a refined mouse-grey shaded with silver; her eyes were still extravagantly rimmed with kohl, as dramatically as when she had been a dancer, but her lips were no longer painted such a vivid scarlet; instead there was a pearly lustre like a paste spread over them. Her dress looked cool, expensive, silken and elegant. She smoothed down the full skirt that billowed in the sea breeze with a gloved hand and turned her head from side to side, smiling a society smile that focused on no one and was directed at nothing and everything, signifying a well-bred tolerance under evident boredom. She was not going to recognise Baumgartner.

'Hugo, old man! If it isn't Hugo! My old companion from those unspeakable days – '

'*Ach*, Julius,' Baumgartner murmured, shaking hands that were sweating with discomfort and dismay, 'they were not such bad days – '

'Not such bad days!' Julius's high-pitched voice rang out, scandalised, making several heads turn their way and Lily frown as lightly as a pencil sketch, so well bred had she become. 'To be virtually in a prison for six years – and he calls that "not bad"! If that isn't just like you, Hugo – to you even prison is all right and nothing is really bad, eh? But Gala, my dear, he helped me survive, you know – he was someone to talk to in the wilderness. And we must talk of so many things, Hugo,' he babbled. 'Did you know that the man who escaped, that fellow Hüber, he wrote a book about the whole experience? But, Hugo, it must be read – a man we knew, shared the camp with, he goes and writes a book about it – is it not fantastic?' His companion's hand on his arm evidently began to exert more pressure than normal. Breaking off, he looked down at her taut face worriedly and what he saw made him trail off. 'Gala, my dear, let us have Hugo over to the house – we can have a proper talk then, can't we?' She turned her face to him bluntly, closed her eyes and nodded as if under torture. 'Tonight, eh? At tonight's party? We have a few friends coming – it will be delightful – my dear man, here is my card. You see, I run a little art gallery now. And you? Your address, your telephone number?' and Baumgartner, hastily pulling out one of his business cards from his pocket, pressed it into his hand, mumbled goodbye, and fled.

After drinking a celebratory beer with Chimanlal and returning to his flat, he found that the telephone that so seldom rang was ringing and ringing when he opened the door. Apologetically pushing past the cats that came to greet him with scolding cries, he picked it up and held it to his ear. Lily's icy tones came over to him like steel needles entering his ear.

'Mr Baumgartner? This is Gala von Roth. I am afraid my husband made a mistake at the Turf Club this evening. He was not aware of my guest list. I already have one unattached gentleman to make up my table, and cannot have two since only one unattached lady is coming, the Maharani of Bitnore who is here on a visit. I regret very much – I feel so ashamed – but you will understand. Another time, of course. Very soon perhaps.'

Baumgartner was smiling to himself, listening to Lily's voice. He was remembering that cold, tuneless voice singing, at Prince's, with such abandon, such determination:

'Lola and Lily
Are fifteen and free,
O Lola and Lily – '

and suddenly burst into a laugh he could not help.

It made her break off her polite nonsense and gasp at his audacity. But it had startled her, prevented her from slamming down the telephone, and in that moment of shocked silence Baumgartner laughed, '*Ach*, Lily, it was nice to see you today at the Turf Club. It does not matter about tonight, of course. But when I saw you, I wanted to ask you something.

You know perhaps where is your old friend from Calcutta, our Lotte?'

The silence grew and thickened. Baumgartner half-expected her to slam down the telephone but the shock seemed to have made Lily clasp it as if she were paralysed. He smiled, thinking of her frozen face, her eyes half-closed in torment, the black kohl gleaming wildly around them. Painted hussy, he thought, chuckling, Shanghai Lily, that is who you are and I know it, when she said, in a clipped cold tone, 'You have a pencil and paper? This is the address. Take it down, please . . .'

'Hugo, *mein Geliebter?*'

'Lotte, *Liebchen*, where are you?'

She told him and he groaned to find it was only down the road from his flat, at the other end of Colaba Causeway. 'I can come on my feet, running,' he said, 'is so near, Lotte, so near, and we did not even know.' 'Come, come,' Lotte shouted over the telephone. 'I am waiting, my Hugo.'

There she was, in a cotton dress with red and pink and violet flowers all over it, her red hair even redder now with a generous dyeing with henna, her toenails and fingernails painted a livid pink, all beckoning him eagerly as he came up the stairs to find her standing at the door, laughing. They embraced with a warmth that had no hesitation and no embarrassment about it, was made ardent by their long separation and by all they had shared in pre-war Calcutta. Lotte patted Baumgartner's cheeks, held him by his shoulders and laughed with joy as she looked at him.

'So long since I see *ein Deutscher*, a German. So long since I see *anyone* in this prison house Kanti keeps me in,' she explained, drawing him in.

'Very nice prison house,' he teased her, looking around. Flowered curtains flapped wildly in the sea breeze, a servant boy came in on silent bare feet and put a tray with glasses on a brass table by a set of cane chairs on which cushions and magazines lay carelessly scattered. 'Kanti is kind.'

'Kind, he says! *Mein Gott*, you call that *kind*? To keep a woman locked up alone and waiting for him?'

'It saved you from the prison camp, Lotte,' Baumgartner reminded her, standing by the table, waiting to be asked to sit down.

She did not ask him; she grabbed his wrist and pulled him down on the sofa beside her. 'Tell me, tell me, Hugo,' she begged, 'and I will make you a gimlet like I make for Kanti – '

'Where is he?'

'*Ach*, don't ask me where he is. He leaves me here like a widow and lives in Calcutta himself – he has business there, you know,' she said vaguely as she leant over the table to mix drinks. 'You met him there? He told you where I was?'

Baumgartner explained how he came by her address after more than five years in Bombay. She clapped her hand over her mouth and giggled till her eyes ran with bright tears.

'Gala – Gala von Roth!' she choked. 'Is it not too fine! Is it not wonderful!'

'He was only Julius Roth when I knew him in the camp,' Baumgartner smiled.

'*Ach*, it is wonderful – *von* Roth! And he is not any more Julius – too Jewish – so he is Julian. Very English, you see. Not a bad thing to be English here in India, you know, Hugo. And first he started with an antique shop in a hotel lobby, and that Gisela, she went around saying it was her collection of Chinese art they were selling, that those plates and dishes were left to her by her father, a collector in China he was supposed to be. Of course I knew she bought it all in auction houses in Calcutta, on Russell Street and Middleton Row. All those English people leaving the country, in forty-seven, the auction shops were full of fine furniture, fine china, everything selling real cheap, and our Gisi, clever Gisi, buying and buying. Clever she is, that one. Then she and Julian – that is how she calls him, Julian – they sold it all in the hotel lobby. And the profits went into an art gallery – that is what they call it: "art gallery". All these new young Indian painters – no one knew any Indian painters, before, eh, Hugo? There was that crazy Margarethe

Bumuller who painted all the politicians in Delhi, made them look like Roman emperors, and there was Fritz Langheim up in Darjeeling, painting monks and monasteries – but where were the Indian painters? But now they are there, you know, and they like hanging up their pictures in a foreigner's gallery, that makes their art so *international*, like they are artists of the world. And Gisi tells me Julian is selling a lot – Indian people are buying Indian art now like they used to import from Europe before. So they are making money – the von Roths.' She bent over with giggling. 'One day let us go together, Hugo. We will go and have coffee in the hotel lounge, eh, and just stroll by the gallery, eh? If Gisi won't let you come to the house and have you talk with him, no matter, we will have our talk in the gallery. I think he will like it better – if *she* is not there. Most of the time of course Gisi keeps a sharp eye on her Julian – and on the sales. Let us go and see them *both*. What can she do? She cannot throw us out, can she, with all her young Indian painters watching? She likes to be their patron, pats them on the heads and calls them by nicknames, and tells me, "*Ach*, Lola, they *love* me, these Indian painters, they know how much I help them, they know I can make them famous *internationally*." "Famous where?" I asked her,' Lotte cackled, 'in Shanghai?' She swilled her drink about the glass so that the ice cubes clinked and the gin splashed. In her delight at gossiping, her delight at having such trusted and familiar company as Baumgartner, she swung her bare legs on to the sofa and over on to his lap, wriggling her toes luxuriously. 'We will make a nice pair in the von Roths' gallery, you and I, Hugo,' she drawled. 'Let us go tomorrow, eh?'

'When will Kanti come again?' Baumgartner asked her, eyeing her feet in his lap and wishing she would remove them. So many years of seeing women who were clothed from head to foot and who even drew their garments over their faces rather than look at him directly or be looked at by him had had their effect on him, he found. He now found Lotte's behaviour bizarre.

'Kanti?' she huffed. 'Who knows when he comes? Business,

business, nothing else matters to the man. Then he gets tired, then he needs a change. Then he wants a little song and dance, a little drink with Lola, and one fine day he turns up at my door and wants me to go down on my knees and touch his feet, so grateful I am supposed to be for his visits.'

'You, on your knees?' Baumgartner chuckled at the unlikely picture.

'Yes, yes, but not so often. Mostly I am alone. All, all alone. *Ach*, Hugo, but now I have *you*.' She leant over and nibbled at his ear. 'Never did I think I would see my Hugo again – and here he is, here he is,' she cried with such genuine, such open delight that Baumgartner put his hands over her toes and squeezed them in silent response.

The tenants of Hira Niwas received notice to quit. The landlord, a choleric old gentleman whose face expressed an animal frenzy at being thwarted in his aim of pulling down the old, four-storeyed house to build a new twenty-storeyed structure and so become a millionaire, tramped from flat to flat, waving the notice he had received from the corporation, stating that the building was unsafe and must be vacated before the next monsoon.

No one paid the slightest attention. Monsoon after monsoon washed over Hira Niwas, leaving it more slimy, green, decayed and odorous but still standing – even if propped up with a forest of bamboo poles on the ground floor. The family that lived there had the bamboo poles growing out of the chipped terrazzo floor of their living-room, their bedrooms, and weaved their way in and out between them nonchalantly; the sweeper swept around them, the children raced their pedal cars and scooters amongst them. Sometimes a little plaster fell, occasionally a whole brick, but miraculously – not more.

Baumgartner learnt to confront the landlord, now severely handicapped by a stroke, with the same sneering equanimity that the other tenants displayed, and did nothing to find himself another flat. How could he, in Bombay, where the rents were fixed by racketeers, smugglers and film stars? It was out of the question. He shrugged at the landlord's shrill hysteria and turned back into his room before the old man caught a glimpse of the family of cats that stirred and pullulated in its damp green confines like a blanket of living grey mildew. Baumgartner could contemplate homelessness for himself but not for his cats. '*Mein Kätzchen,*' he crooned, picking one up and gazing ardently into its face.

His room filled and overflowed with them, with their scrawny progeny; daily he made the rounds of nearby cafés and restaurants where the kitchen staff got to know him and kept aside scraps for him, making faces at each other behind his back and sniggering, '*Pagal sahib, billé-wallah sahib,*' for Baumgartner grew shabbier as he grew older, no longer noticing if his shoes had soles that flapped or if the buttons on his shirt were missing or even if they were clean and washed any more; after all, the cats greeted him exuberantly whether they were or not.

Lotte sometimes wrinkled her nose and tugged at a torn collar, saying, '*Ach*, Hugo, can't you buy a new shirt sometimes?'

It was not that he could not, but he had simply got out of the way of shopping, of spending money. And although the years were jogging by now at a comfortable pace and with an evenness that he had not known at any other stage of his life, it was partly because he did so little business for Chimanlal now. It was not only that he disliked leaving his cats to go on business trips but also because Chimanlal's son was growing up and spending more time in his father's office, learning the business, and there did not seem much for Baumgartner to do any more. Baumgartner marvelled that such a youngster should be trusted with so much work already but Chimanlal sighed, 'If I do not trust my own son, Hugo *bhai*, who can I trust?' Baumgartner noted that he did not sound as if he meant the words – they were wrenched from him. Chimanlal was not well. He had a bad colour and Baumgartner told him he should see a doctor whereupon Chimanlal turned to the oleograph on the wall, still hung with a fresh garland and wreathed in clouds of incense, and said, 'This is my doctor, Hugo *bhai*, it is Lakshmi alone who will look after me.'

He went away frequently on pilgrimages, taking his wife, daughters and daughter-in-law, to visit temples and saints in distant caves or mountain-tops and in ashrams. He returned small, starved, wretchedly ill but ecstatic – he had had the *darshan* of yet another deity, yet another holy man, and how could that not have a good, a benign effect on him, he asked Baumgartner whose expression stated grave doubt. Chimanlal expressed regret that he had never been able to make any dent in Baumgartner's wary agnosticism. Baumgartner's fumbled, embarrassed replies to Chimanlal's questions about Judaism, about how a Jew could believe in the same Moses, Abraham or Jacob that the Christians did, had brought about an early end to anything like the theological discussions in which Indians revel – and he never went so far as to ask Baumgartner to accompany him to a temple or on a pilgrimage – to his profound relief.

He was also immensely relieved when Chimanlal told him that he was seeing a doctor and taking medicine, but the relief was momentary for he went on to learn that the doctors were sometimes homeopaths, sometimes *ayurvedic* doctors who treated him with nameless pills and powders, herbs and roots that seemed to do him no good. 'But I am much better now,' Chimanlal insisted, 'and much stronger.'

For some time they kept up their Sunday visits to the Turf Club, laying their bets with an ever greater caution and discretion.

It was at a race meeting that, one afternoon, Chimanlal collapsed against a fence and fainted. Baumgartner held his head in his lap till an ambulance came and removed him to hospital. He fetched the son, who threw furious looks at him as if he were responsible and then turned him out of the ward, insisting that he be left alone with his father. Chimanlal was operated on for a tumour that night and did not regain consciousness. Baumgartner joined the mourners at the cremation, standing at the edge of the crowd, all of whom shrank away from him, horrified by the presence of a foreigner, a *firanghi*, at such an intensely private rite. Hearing the babbling chant of the priests, seeing the confusion around the pyre, smelling the odours of burnt flesh and charred wood under the noontime sun, Baumgartner too wished he had not come, and shuffled away.

When he visited Chimanlal's office, he found the son installed at a new stainless steel desk, painted grey and provided with many shining locks. Baumgartner was somewhat reassured to see Lakshmi in the usual place, below the tube of neon lighting, but was soon to find that nothing else was. The boy peremptorily wound up the last bits of business Baumgartner still had with the office and more or less dismissed him with a curtness that betrayed years of pent-up resentment and jealousy. When Baumgartner thought to ask a question about the racehorse he and Chimanlal had jointly owned, the boy gave up his cool self-control and began to shout, 'What are you talking about? What joint ownership? Show me one paper – ' he banged the table with the flat of his hand, making Baumgartner wince – 'Show me one paper you have signed or my father has signed – '

'No, no, there are no papers,' Baumgartner told him, leaning forward to calm him. 'Your father and I - we were friends – we didn't draw up any legal papers – it was just an understanding, a friendship – '

'My father is no more, Mr Baumgartner,' the boy said stiffly. 'He has left for his heavenly abode.'

Baumgartner understood that with Chimanlal's death all connection with the firm, formal or friendly, had ceased, and got up to leave. The boy did not wish him goodbye.

The next time Lotte pulled at a thread dangling from his cuff and complained about his ancient shoes, Baumgartner told her, 'But Lotte, I am not earning any more. I am retired, you know, old retired man now. So I can't buy clothes and look like a fancy man still.'

'*Mein Gott*, when were you ever a fancy man?' she cried. 'I am only asking that you don't look like a beggar.'

'*Ach*, a beggar,' he said dismissively. 'I have enough, don't worry. More than many people, Lotte.'

He meant the people who filled the streets of Bombay these days like so many rags or scraps of paper. There seemed to be a drought every year in the land and the pavement filled visibly with a migrant population from the fields and villages. One family had taken up the length of the pavement just outside Hira Niwas. Overnight their tins, rags, ropes, strings, papers and plastic bags had been set up to make a shelter and when the tenants woke next morning, they found a cooking fire burning, tin pots and pans being washed in the gutter and some were actually witnesses to the birth of a new baby on a piece of sacking in the street. The doorman, himself a migrant but an earlier one, driven here by an earlier calamity, now possessor of a job and an official status and therefore infinitely superior to them, yet not so superior as to run no risk of contamination from the starved and the luckless, cursed them from his safe perch in the doorway, and the tenants stopped on their way in or out to express their horror and contempt for the ragged creatures who hardly seemed human to the citizens of the *urbis et prima* of the west. The migrants seemed neither to hear nor speak but Baumgartner, for one, shuffled past with his head bowed and his eyes averted – not to avoid contamination as the others did, but to hide his shame at being alive, fed, sheltered, privileged.

Lotte clicked her tongue with displeasure whenever she had to pass them and told Baumgartner she preferred it if he visited her instead. She herself looked increasingly less affluent, even haggard, the henna dye no longer concealing the grey roots of her once carroty hair, while the printed cotton frocks she wore were faded and no longer replaced. She still had her long, fine legs and liked to pick up her skirts and point her toes and do a little pirouette to remind herself of her halcyon dancing days but – if she had had a few drinks – these were not so successful.

Instead of going back to Hira Niwas after his morning gin

with Lotte, Baumgartner took to staying on for the afternoon. They would sit at the round brass table and play card-games that were very boring since they were only two players, so boring that they found themselves yawning behind their hands till Lotte finally flung down her cards, pulled her skirts up over her thighs and flung her head back over the sofa, crying, 'Oh I am so sleepy – these hot, hot afternoons – I am going to bed, Hugo,' and would go off to her room where he heard her switching on the electric fan and throwing herself into bed with a great thud. He would shuffle off his shoes, lean his head against the sofa, fold his hands over his stomach, and have a nap himself.

Then she called from the bedroom, 'Don't pretend you are sleeping there, Hugo, you old goose. Come along and lie down and be comfortable with Lottchen.'

He stumbled to his feet and into the bedroom and gratefully lay down beside her in the darkened room. She flung her arm across his chest, murmuring, 'Old goose, Hugo,' and then edged her leg closer to his, finally rolling against him. He responded to her affection with some reluctance, he would have preferred to sleep chastely at one end of the big bed, feeling more as if they were brother and sister than anything else. Then the thought of having had Lotte as a sister, in that shining flat in Berlin, with Mutti as their mother, overcame him and made him snort with laughter into her grey and red curls and draw an arm around her.

On hot summer afternoons she might push him away and say petulantly, '*Ach*, Hugo, you are sweating – and you never wash your shirts even.' He only laughed and did not mind, perfectly content to lie on his side of the bed, dozing till they heard the servant boy making tea in the kitchen at five o'clock, when she gave him a fierce kick with her naked foot, hissing 'Get up – go to the bathroom as if you were there for a wash – Raju must not see.' But by the casual insolence with which he flung down the tea tray beside them, Raju showed that he had of course seen, and knew. Lotte was terrified. What would Kanti say? What would Kanti do?

Actually Kanti visited her less and less, kept away by ill health to begin with and then by religion. He worked very little, leaving all his business to his sons, and even if he came to Bombay he spent all his time by the little altar he had set up in one corner of the bedroom, Lotte complained, praying and fasting and observing all the rituals of the Hindu year.

'Repenting his wicked ways?' Baumgartner asked mischievously, giving Lotte a little nudge as they sat drinking their gimlets in his flat, and Lotte gave his hand an angry smack so that his drink spilt.

One night, Lotte, very drunk, arrived at his flat and insisted Baumgartner go out with her. She directed the taxi to Julius and Gisi's flat which they found lit up for a party. Whilst Baumgartner protested, 'Ach, Lotte, I don't want to go – please let us go home – ' she dragged him on to the pavement outside their window where she stood screaming, 'Shanghai Lily, hey! Hey, Shanghai Lily!' and when he tried to pull her away, turned and hit him. He walked off and left her. Two policemen arrived in a jeep, jumped out, grabbed her by the arms and lifted her into the jeep. She was taken to a police *chowki* and accused of drunken brawling: it seemed Gisela had telephoned from her flat and complained. At dawn, Baumgartner was rung up and told to come and bail her out. Making her bathe and shower in his flat, then forcing her to eat a bowl of cornflakes and milk, he reproached her for her drunkenness, genuinely shocked by her behaviour.

'Ach, Hugo,' she protested, looking at him with a suddenly thin and pale face, 'it was because of *you*. What I can't take from Gisi is how she treated *you*,' and he did not know how to show his emotion so he took the napkin and wiped her chin on to which milk had trickled like a child's.

They never spoke of that episode again though it was the precursor of others. Kanti's illness and death made her seem to lose control over herself and she became defiant. In the small room she moved to after settling a case brought against her by his sons, she seemed to get into perpetual rows with the neighbours. More than once the police had to come and intervene so that the neighbourhood brawl did not turn into a riot, a sequence of events only too common in Bombay, and Baumgartner was occasionally summoned as a mediator. 'A *memsahib* using such language,' the scandalised policemen told him, and he was ashamed. He became nervous of any involvement in Lotte's affairs, wished he could keep to himself, but there was too long an association, too deeply ingrained a habit, and gradually, as she became drawn into her new neighbourhood and its own cast of characters and their affairs, violent and otherwise, the von Roths at least ceased to be a thorn in her side; she no longer felt any interest in them. The art gallery in the hotel lobby had closed down to make way for a boutique where silk scarves and sequinned purses were sold at greatly inflated prices to foreign tourists, and the von Roths ran their business from their own flat that Gala kept barred to all acquaintances from their past after the disgraceful affair of the drunken Lotte.

'Hmff,' sniffed Lotte after a very unsatisfactory conversation on the telephone that was all that Gala permitted her, 'she doesn't want us to see the flat is not so grand as she pretends. Julius is not doing so fine any longer. Indian painters have Indian patrons now – rich businessmen, industrialists – big men, not like my poor Kanti. They don't want a European telling them what is good, what to buy, by now they have their own taste. So old Julius is finding business poor.'

'How do you know?' Baumgartner asked, genuinely curious.

Lotte plucked her skirt over her knee. 'She told me,' she replied, 'that Gisi.' When Baumgartner looked dubious, she exploded, 'What do you think? That we don't talk together any more? After so many years, so much we have been through together? Who will she talk to if not old Lotte from Calcutta? Everyone thinks that she is so clever – but I know she is just an old goose.'

Baumgartner felt too tired to dispute this. 'Oh, they will

find some way to live,' he sighed. He had not been to the races since Chimanlal's death, and he had last seen Julius in the street outside Akbarally's, with a shopping bag about which he had seemed suddenly embarrassed, mumbling something about having to help Gala with a party she was giving that night. His clothes had looked frail, as during the years in camp; he still had his flossy hair carefully combed over his progressively balder scalp and looked more than ever like an old sheep. 'Poor Gala,' he piped, 'the heat is so bad for her. You know she cannot stand the climate. Oh, Hugo, why did we not go back? We should have gone back long, long ago,' he mourned, making Baumgartner want to snort, 'Go back *where*? To what?' But he did not – it was against the rules.

'Of course they will somehow live,' Lotte said. 'You think our Lily will let him sit and do nothing – like *you*?'

Nothing, then, was what life dwindled down to, but Baumgartner found he enjoyed that nothing more than he had enjoyed anything. Perhaps enjoyment was too strong a word for such mild pleasures as he now knew – watching his cats devour a bag of fish he had brought them, dozing with one of them on his lap for company, strolling down to Lotte's for a drink – but they suited him. He felt his life blur, turn grey, like a curtain wrapping him in its dusty felt. If he became aware, from time to time, that the world beyond the curtain was growing steadily more crowded, more clamorous, and the lives of others more hectic, more chaotic, then he felt only relief that his had never been a part of the mainstream. Always, somehow, he had escaped the mainstream.

SEVEN

The boy was very late.

Baumgartner had cleared away the dinner, scraping the uneaten *pish-pash* into the cats' plates, washing the dishes and putting them away. He himself had lost his appetite – if one left the eating too late, one found the appetite had dwindled and gone. Now he sat in his old cane chair by the door that opened on to the narrow balcony and looked at the racing papers of the week before. Although he had not been to the races since the day Chimanlal collapsed at the Turf Club, he still bought the racing papers from the urchins who swarmed around the cars waiting at traffic lights and peddled their wares at the top of their cockerel voices. To begin with he made a great show of cleaning his spectacles, adjusting them to his ears and nose, then studying last Sunday's programme, running his finger along the list of names as though he were looking for prospective winners. But it was only an act, put on to show the cats he was a busy man with his own life, not entirely at their service. One came and lay across his feet, something he rarely did in such hot weather. Another stood by his knee, dug her claws into the material of his trousers, managed to inject their tips into his flesh, and then dropped away, visibly pleased at having left her mark. A third climbed on to the chair back and balanced there till he fell on to Baumgartner's neck, then sprang off with a yowl and retired to the balcony. Baumgartner knew he was being summoned.

Folding up the racing paper and putting it away with a show of reluctance, he went out on to the balcony that overlooked nothing but the narrow, enclosed lane and the blank wall on the other side.

He never could make out why the builders had attached these ledge-like balconies to the walls of Hira Niwas. Other tenants used them to hang out their endless washing, but Baumgartner never had any washing to hang. Like the others, he stored his junk on them, old boxes and tins and empty bottles – and of course the sand trays for his cats. It made a playground for them when they felt active, and the way they climbed on to the boxes, or wound their way in and out of the iron balustrade made him protest. 'Now what if you fall, eh?' and bent down to hold them away from such danger, at which they mocked.

It was absolutely dark in the lane, the single lamppost having had no bulb for at least a year. People from the street sometimes came to urinate against the wall and rubbish drifted in and accumulated undisturbed. At the end of the lane, where it opened on to the street, Baumgartner could see streetlights shining on the family that lived on the pavement. They were unusually, probably only momentarily, quiet. He could see dark shapes crawling in and out of the low shack, and hear voices and the sounds of cooking and eating. Baumgartner could hear the hiss and splatter of oil, the eternal clinking of pots and pans in the flowing water of the gutter. In the darkness, so little illuminated by the dim lamp, it made a scene both melancholy and comforting. It was a scene that was linked for Baumgartner with the one he had observed through the barbed wire fencing of the camp – of women going to their cowpat heap to fetch dry pats for fuel, Annemarie hanging up the washing, and further back in time – his mother putting steaming dishes on the table, preparing him for bed . . .

Yet only five minutes walk would bring one to the Taj Hotel, lit up and swinging with the life of money, business, trade, success; the stretch of Arthur Bunder Road and the waves of the sea battering the stone wall, the flood-lit Gateway of India, the evening crowds strolling, eating spicy snacks at pavement stalls, sitting on the parapet and looking out at the lighted ships in the bay, waiting for night to bring a little cool with the sea breeze. The life of Bombay which had been Baumgartner's life for thirty years now – or, rather, the setting for his life; he had never actually entered it, never quite captured it; damply, odorously, cacophonously palpable as it was, it had been elusive still.

If he had earlier been grateful, now he was depressed. Fatigued, probably. Picking up Teufel under his arm, he went back into the room and shut the door. He looked at the clock on the shelf amongst all the tarnished trophies and saw it was late, very late. How long should he stay up and wait for the boy? Would he return at all? His rucksack lay on the floor beside the divan and so Baumgartner presumed he would return for it, but it could be tomorrow, or the day after. A boy like that, such a wild fellow, he could not be expected to bother about his belongings.

Baumgartner sighed, and went down on his knees with a great groan to put the scattered belongings back into the rucksack and put it out of the way so that no one should stumble on it in the dark. He tried to pick up objects and shove them in without looking but if the objects were as extraordinary as syringes and phials then he could scarcely ignore them. His round, fat face looked furrowed as he handled the slim, sharp objects of glass and metal: they looked dangerous, they felt dangerous, he wished he did not have to touch them. Nervously he looked up to see if the boy would not burst in and accuse Baumgartner of – of what? What could old Baumgartner do with these things? They belonged to the young, they were a part of another generation's existence, not his. He pushed them into the rucksack and buckled down the straps so they would not fall out again. Then he lifted the bag and leant it against the wall by the divan. Immediately Teufel, the most curious of the cats, slid across to it and began to examine it delicately, sniffing with his fine nostrils and shaking his whiskers at the peculiar, unaccustomed odours, then suddenly pouncing at it as though it was an interloper, a beast, digging his claws through the canvas ferociously, then falling away.

Baumgartner laughed at his antics. '*Ganz meshuggeh, du,*' he smiled, feeling much better, and went into the bathroom to change into his pyjamas.

Coming out, he looked sadly towards the divan on which he always slept. Could he not go to sleep now that he was so tired and it was so late? Would the boy come tonight and demand to sleep here? Surely not. Baumgartner sat down and pressed his hand against his eyes which grew blurred and watered when he was tired. '*Ach*, Mieschen,' he sighed to the soft grey one who came and rubbed her cold nose on his wrist, willing him to lie down so she could curl up on his chest, 'we are not used to entertaining guests, eh? Not made for guests over here, eh?' He rubbed the flat head between the two sharp ears, and she pushed hard against his hand in an ecstasy, purring in a way that acted as a soporific on Baumgartner.

Finally he lay down on the divan – just for a little while, he told himself, and to keep himself awake he reached out for the packet of cards on the low table that he often read at odd hours of the night when he could not sleep. They were very old now, these cards, the paper brown and flecked and very brittle, but somehow the ink had lasted and he could still trace the writing on them with its cryptic messages: *Do not worry, my rabbit, I am well. Are you well? Keep well, my mouse, and do not worry – I am well* – and then they stopped. There were not many of them. Once again he had come to the end of the small collection. There were no more. After that – *Nacht und Nebel.* Night and Fog. Baumgartner put them carefully back on the low table, in a small pile where they always lay. Switching off the lamp, he lay with his arm over his eyes and in the dark could still see the script, spidery and fine. Gradually the words ran into each other, became garbled. They made no sense. Nothing made sense. Germany there, India here – India there, Gemany here. Impossible to capture, to hold, to read them, make sense of them. They all fell away from him, into an abyss. He saw them falling now, white shapes turning and turning, then going grey as the distance widened between them and him. He stood watching as they fell and floated, floated and fell, till they drifted out of sight, silently, and he was left on the edge, clutching his pyjamas, straining to look. But there was nothing to look at, it was all gone, and he shut his eyes, to receive the darkness that flooded in, poured in and filled the vacuum with the thick black ink of oblivion, of *Nacht und Nebel.*

Kurt returned many hours later. The family on the pavement was asleep, lying wrapped in sheets that the darkness made white – all except for the drunkard Jagu himself who still had something in his bottle to finish and sat with it between his legs, his back against the lamppost. Kurt, seeing its glint, stopped. The man looked up at him, at the strange face, distinctly white, foreign. The shorts, the bracelet, the dishevelled hair marked him out as a type that had become known on the streets of the city. Hip-py they were called, the two syllables separated to make the scorn heavier.

The two men regarded each other in the dark, the only two awake and alert at that hour. Kurt finally spoke, not expecting to be understood but knowing that there were certain words that everyone knew who belonged to the city, any city. 'Ganja? Hashish?' he asked, in a low and rasping tone because his throat was sore from wanting. 'Grass? Brown sugar?' He put out his hand to emphasise his want.

The drunkard jerked into action. Lurching to his feet, he began to swear at Kurt, clutching his bottle and guarding the last drop fiercely from this hungry-looking *firanghi.*

Kurt shook his head and spread out his hands to try and calm him. 'No want, no want,' he growled 'Ganja? Grass? LSD?' He made jabbing motions of one hand at the other.

Jagu gesticulated more angrily, righteously even. The woman stirred in her shroud and muttered some angry words, trying to silence him. The man swung around to abuse her for interfering. Kurt left them to it and walked on.

He went up the stairs into the hall of the brown stairs and the bright odours. The watchman was not on his stool; he had gone off either to relieve himself in the street or play a hand of cards with the other watchmen. The single unshaded bulb hanging by a dirt-encrusted cord shone with a wicked brilliance. Kurt went up the stairs heavily, grasping the sticky banisters to help him mount them, his legs having the curious sensation of giving way under him, his feet of slipping in different directions. He panted laboriously, his breath coming with difficulty as he mounted the first, second and then the third flight of the old rotten wooden stairs. On every landing, a closed door, a steamy silence. It was very late.

On the third landing there was no light, the bulb having fused and not been replaced, but some light from the hall below filtered up and Kurt peered at the small handwritten label pasted on the door. *H. Baumgartner*. The name made his mouth twist with sarcasm, with ferocity. To come half-way across the world and meet H. Baumgartner, what an irony. Then he bunched his lips together and paused as he got a small penknife out of his pocket and inserted it into the keyhole. Sven, in Kathmandu, had taught him the trick – if the knife had a sharp enough point, and was pressed and turned in a certain way, it could open almost any lock, but it had to be sharp and fine enough to enter the lock at a certain point: was it? Kurt tried to control his large hands that seemed clumsy tonight, as difficult to bring under control as his legs and feet – like them, his hands seemed colossal, weighty and with a will of their own. But he managed – it was a trick he had used so often after all; he gave a snort of laughter, thinking of Sven, of Kathmandu, of Freak Street, of ganja, the smell of it, the dry, leafy, clinging smoke and sweetness. He put his tongue out between his teeth as he tasted it, and tested the lock. With scarcely any effort, just a wish, it sprang open. There was a click and Kurt heard a sound in the flat responding to that click, but only a very soft sound, very light, quickly fading. Baumgartner's cursed cats of course, he thought, and swore. Pressing the door open a slit, he peered in. After the shadowiness of the landing, it did not seem impenetrably dark – some light from the street came through the open window. In that light he saw the sliding, slinking shapes of the felines as they raised themselves or lowered themselves to examine the visitor. He restrained his impulse to lash out at them with his bare feet.

He stood for a while in the doorway, staring into the darkness and the dusky shapes, the moving ones and the immobile ones, familiarising himself with it all before he took his next step. His rucksack was gone from the rug, he saw, and also made out Baumgartner's thick, lumpy shape on the divan, limp with deep sleep. He turned his head very slowly and made sure that the silver prizes on the shelf were still there. There was little light to see by, but he could make out their sizes, their shapes, their number. He slid his penknife back in his pocket and shut the door behind him, so silently that the shape on the divan did not stir.

He walked silently across the floor to the kitchen table. The cats sprang out of his way, like furred moths flying up at a touch. He saw the table-top was blank, cleared away as might be expected from a fussy old bachelor. But what he looked for lay there as if at his request – the long thin kitchen knife with which he had seen Baumgartner cut up the disgusting putrid flesh for his damned cats. The memory of that repulsive meal and of the stupid slow warty old man fussing over the caterwauling beasts made him lift his lips off his teeth as he reached out for the knife and picked it up with silent fingers. He stood holding it still for so long as to make the cats stop pacing around him, worrying at these unfamiliar movements. Then he turned and glided over the floor towards the divan, ready at any moment to stop and freeze or else leap into frenzied action.

There was no movement. Baumgartner slept on, his hands clutching each other under his chin as he lay, curled on his left side. His right arm had sunk down over his chest to meet the left arm, leaving his ribs as well as a triangle of chest exposed, the flesh soft and yellow, like tallow, where the pyjama top was open. His mouth was open, too, and his breath came and went, the lips moving faintly as cats' whiskers move, but without their sensitivity to what was happening near him. Baumgartner slept, in ignorance. Ignorance was, after all, his element. Ignorance was what he had made his own. It was his country, the one he lived in with familiarity and resignation and relief.

Kurt steadied himself, drawing his feet together, straightening his legs, both to ensure his balance and give him a position of strength. He brought his hands together so that both clasped the hasp of the knife and it seemed to take long moments before he could get his grip right, place his fingers in correct alignment, summoning up all his faculties so that they gathered in that one shaft. Then, with great speed, he raised the knife, then bent, and plunged it in, deep into that soft tallow so that it shuddered and let out a kind of whimper, or just a gasp, but some kind of flutter. It had to cease, it had to be made to cease. Withdrawing the knife, he plunged it in again, and again, and again. With increasing slowness, and increasing weakness, till all movement came to a halt – the rocking, the quivering, the flutter, the gasp, all ended.

Then the silence and the concentration and the control all broke together. The cats were leaping like black flames around his feet, yowling maniacally. Jumping over them, he hurried to the shelf, sweeping off all the tarnished silver trophies with ringing sounds of metal on metal, clanging and clanking, one against the other, as he filled his arms with them, carried them to where he had seen his rucksack leaning against the wall and, falling down on to his knees, shoved and pressed and pushed them all in. In that kneeling position, he swept his hands over the small table – Baumgartner might have left his watch there, or his wallet. Whatever there was, he scooped up and crammed in, throwing aside bits of paper, cards, letters that he certainly did not want. When he got up, he found a black fluid running down his knees to his feet. Trying to wipe it off, he stared at the body on the divan – yes, that pale mound of yellow tallow was oozing with something dark, liquid. It was not like blood, it was like a diarrhoea of blood. God, why didn't he stop that? Kurt felt a bubble rise in his throat that he had to choke back. Then he bent to swing his rucksack on to his back. He was breathing hard as he buckled it back into place, fumbling with the straps, getting it all wrong. Hell, he cursed, and hurled aside some furry body that had come too close, and bumbled his way to the door. He spent a minute struggling with the lock, lurching past the doorposts, sudden-ly clumsy again, out of control again. His feet no longer floated; now they were like stones and fell from one stair to another, thundering on them like an avalanche descending. Surely everyone would wake, fling open their doors, look out and see –

Kurt fled, so fast that he did not see if the watchman was on his perch or not, but he did note the white bodies stretched on the pavement because he had to avoid them, and the figure slumped against the lamppost that suddenly jerked itself upright on seeing Kurt escape from Hira Niwas with a sack. Pushing past him, Kurt vanished.

Clutching the empty bottle by the neck, Jagu approached the doorman and taunted him. 'Thieves come and go and you sleep your ganja-sleep, eh?'

The watchman, who had been dozing, snapped shut his mouth and woke with a jerk. 'Shut up or I'll crack your skull for you,' he growled.

Sighing, shifting and preparing to chat the small hours of the night away, Jagu looked down for a clean strip of marble on which to sit, then saw the stain – a footprint marked in fresh blood.

Seeing him double over, his greasy hair falling over his face and his eyes bulging, the watchman drawled, 'What's the matter – taken sick?'

'Fool,' Jagu muttered, 'come and see,' without really wanting to draw attention to, himself not even wanting to take notice of, this evidence of a violence he knew, he felt, had been committed. Before the watchman could get off his stool and come down to look, he had already started running – first down the road after the *firanghi* who had just left with a loaded sack, then wheeling around and turning back to Hira Niwas as though he had gone mad, screaming, 'Blood! Bloodshed! Blood!'

The watchman had seen what Jagu saw. Clutching him by the arm, he wrenched him around and clapped his hand over his mouth. 'Drunkard, idiot, swine,' he hissed, 'what are you trying to do? Bring the police here?'

'Pol-pol-poliss,' the drunkard whimpered, covering his cut lip with his hands. 'You saw? You saw?'

'Saw *what*?' the watchman spat at him. He too wanted to see nothing. He would be dismissed, he would lose his job, his family would starve –

Jagu clung to his arm. 'We must go up and find out.'

The watchman swore and spat and shook his head but it did not help: he had to go and see.

All along the worn terrazzo flooring of the hall there were the bare footprints marked in blood, as well as a trail of dark drops. On the wooden staircase these became brown spots. The two men followed them up to the third floor landing where Baumgartner's door stood open. Then they faltered, hung on to the staircase, stared at each other. Now it was Jagu whose courage failed: he realised at last what the police would surmise. He had been hauled up to the police station before at the first report of a theft, a burglary, a rape, a brawl, anything at all in that quarter. He knew he ought to leave, to run. Rouse his family, pack his bags and bundles, and leave, silently in the night. Yet, in spite of this urge based on both common sense and experience, he felt a totally senseless curiosity and concern too.

'Which *sahib* is it?' he whispered to the watchman. He had

never been in the building before but he knew, somehow, which one – 'the *firanghi*?'

The watchman nodded. 'Old fool,' he muttered, 'he and his filthy cats – '

'The one with the plastic bags? That beggar who eats other men's leftovers?'

Then they heard a sound inside that made them stiffen with fright – it was a wail, high-pitched and quavering. Jagu swung around and made as if to roll down the stairs but the watchman held him by the arm, explaining, 'The cats – ' and together they ventured in.

It was a little while before they found the light-switch. As they stumbled around in the dark, cats brushed against their legs, hissed, spat, leapt out of the way, lashed their tails and made warning sounds; their eyes were everywhere, huge, shocked, triangular and brilliant.

Jagu spat. 'What a stink. Did the *sahib* never throw out any rubbish? Smells like the municipal rubbish dump.'

'Maybe the dead body,' the watchman muttered, not wanting the prestige of Hira Niwas lowered in the eyes of a common street drunkard. It was he who found the switch, illuminated the room and saw the sight.

They kept their distance. Neither would approach. At the door, they argued. Send for someone – but who? The landlord did not live in Hira Niwas. Which of the neighbours – ? Who knew the *sahib*? The watchman had seen a blonde woman come and go, on foot, she must live nearby, but where? The watchman clutched his head as if a piercing headache threatened to split it – and actually it did – when he remembered seeing Baumgartner go into the Café de Paris at the corner so frequently that he must surely be known there. Giving Jagu a push, he said, 'Go, go to Caffeydepree, go call the owner. Tell him to come.'

Jagu shrank away from his touch. He retreated on to the landing and stood there in the shadows, sweat pouring from his body copiously, rankly. 'No,' he refused, shaking his head violently. 'No.'

'Then go and call the police,' the watchman exploded. 'I have to stay here and guard – I am the guard – '

Jagu rolled his eyeballs at him. 'Mad,' he accused. 'I – I go to the police?' and he pointed at his chest dramatically.

Neither would go. They stood staring at the wrecked room in the blank artificial light – the objects flung down from the shelf and scattered below it, the knife on the rug, stained, with the papers and cards swept off the small table by the divan, the thing on the divan – a nondescript bundle of old, stained clothes that someone might have thrown down, a part of the general litter. Except that it oozed the filthy black stuff that was spilt everywhere. The cats who had been springing from one corner to another as if demented, now sat frozen, staring from under tables and chairs at the two men. Only when the window became a frame for greyness instead of night did they realise the need to make a move. By then they could hear people moving about the building, doors opening, cisterns flushing, bathers hawking and splashing, a radio blabbering. Finally the watchman decided to fetch the nearest neighbour and Jagu sank down on to his haunches by the door to wait.

The neighbours came. For a while frenzied words flew over the drunkard's head – 'But – you haven't called the police? You saw the murderer? You didn't chase him? You didn't call? You fools, you idiots, you'll be made to pay – ' and then there was silence as they rushed away in different directions, thundering up the stairs and down them and along the passages, leaving the watchman to come and huddle beside Jagu, equally guilty. They waited like criminals in prison for the gaoler.

People came streaming in, adding up to more visitors than Baumgartner had had in years. Farrokh, who had come in his pyjamas and slippers, unwashed and unshaven, stood in their midst, his face sunken and devastated. He had been brought to help – but what help could he give now? Others, more energetic, less hampered by emotion, seized enthusiastically upon the first likely suspect – Jagu, who was still squatting in a corner, too frightened to slip away as he knew he ought. Fastening on to his hair and neck, they shouted in triumph, 'Here he is – we have found him – the murderer!' The watchman made a feeble attempt to intervene, protesting that it was Jagu who had alerted him in the first place, but no one listened; they marched Jagu down the stairs and, seeing the police van draw up at the pavement, threw him inside. 'Take him to the *thana*,' they advised the police, 'and interrogate him.'

Jagu's family, gathered by the door, set up a great wail. The woman tore her hair and beat her breast in lamentation. A policeman gave her a push in the chest, saying, 'Murderers, thieves, pimps, all of you – you'll be cleared off the pavement and sent back to the thieves' village from which you come. This is the end of all of you,' whereupon she fell at his feet, trying to prevent him from driving away with Jagu, and received a kick on her back in return. Jagu, totally paralysed with fear, lay moaning in the van.

Two Dobermanns leapt out, held by two policemen who seemed scarcely able to restrain them as they scampered up the stairs. This created instant pandemonium amongst the feline inmates of the flat – they jumped on to cupboards and curtain rods and stood there, arching their backs, spitting and yowling and slashing out with their claws if the dogs approached. Both the Dobermanns and the policeman re-treated, apologetically, telling the watchman they would wait outside till the flat had been cleared of these defenders of Baumgartner's realm.

The watchman turned to Farrokh in appeal. How was he to get the cats out of the way? Farrokh stared at him and at the cats, equally helpless. But one of the neighbours ran down and out and returned with two ragged boys with sacks. They earned their living, they claimed, by picking through the dustbins on the streets, and they were quickly persuaded to catch the cats and put them in their sacks and remove them – 'far away', the watchman recovered sufficiently to say, sternly, and Farrokh, tender-hearted, retreated on to the balcony rather than watch. He stood there with his head bent, listening to the furniture falling, the boys shouting, the cats spitting as they dashed from cover to cover. The situation grew worse when the fire brigade arrived: someone had called them on the telephone, thinking that the crowd at Hira Niwas could only mean a fire. Shown into the flat on the third floor, they discovered that all they could do was help in the cat hunt. One cat, cornered on a window-sill, leapt out of the window and fell to its death.

He – it was the lamed Fritzi – missed by inches the bald, perspiring head of the landlord who stepped out of his car and hurried in, moaning and wiping his face. 'Never in all these years,' he groaned as he stumped up the stairs, 'in all these years – in Hira Niwas – has such a thing happened.' He appeared to blame Baumgartner entirely, although he had a few words of abuse for the watchman who cowered when he saw him enter. But for all his disgust and distress, he did walk across to the telephone and, remembering that it was Chimanlal who had brought Baumgartner here for a room, rang his office and drew a reluctant assent from the son to come and see to his late father's murdered friend.

The police returned, timidly, without the Dobermanns who had lost heart in the search and could not be made to mount the stairs again. They helped the rag-pickers to secure the sacks and saw them off the premises thankfully. Farrokh re-entered the room, wiping his eyes which watered from the glare on the balcony, and protested mildly against the wreckage, the broken glass and the overturned furniture, but the police paid no attention – they were pleased, it seemed, to see so much havoc, it made a good case against the murderer.

'Sahib,' the watchman made a quavering attempt, both hands folded together in a prayer for an audience, 'sahib, Jagu saw a man – a firanghi, a young firanghi – run out, with a sack – '

Chimanlal's son pushed him roughly aside as he entered. He

was dressed for the office in a safari suit with brass buttons that shone. Holding his handkerchief to his nose, he complained, 'The stink – what is stinking in here?'

Farrokh had heard the watchman's words and asked, through lips stiff with fright, and foreboding, 'You saw – he saw – a young *firanghi*, you say?'

'Such filth!' Chimanlal's son exclaimed, looking around him. 'Tchh, how these filthy foreigners live!'

'It was not like this,' Farrokh protested, 'it was someone else – '

'It was getting worse and worse,' the young man insisted. 'Whenever I saw him, I found him looking more like a beggar.' He glanced across at the divan, then draw his handkerchief over his nose quickly. 'What is that doing here? Call the police. Get it moved to the morgue.'

The police, who were still waiting for their chief to come and begin the investigation, explained feebly that they could not disturb the scene of the crime.

'Don't talk rubbish,' the young man said crisply. 'Get the hearse and have this – this body removed at once.'

The police, looking almost relieved that someone should have given an order so clear and precise, saluted and went tumbling down the stairs 'to make arrangements', they said.

'But – should we not call his friends?' Farrokh protested, turning away from the murder and the murderer to what seemed now of greatest urgency. 'There are no relations but friends may want – '

'What friends? He had friends?' the young man asked with contemptuous disbelief.

'Yes, yes – there is a *memsahib* – she lives in Colaba – I know her – she comes many times to my café with Bommgarter *sahib* – '

'*Memsahib*?' the young man's face searched for an expression, found none. How could any *memsahib* be involved with something so soiled, used and useless, ready to be dragged away for disposal?

But Farrokh became stubborn. Pushing out his lower lip, he insisted. He gave instructions to the watchman to go and fetch Lotte. The watchman turned to the landlord to ask for permission to leave the scene – 'duty' was the word he used and kept repeating, in order to mend his spoilt image – 'my duty' – when a neighbour, an excitable young man who could scarcely wait to take some part in this drama, offered to go and made off instantly. The thought of breaking the news to a *memsahib* galvanised him: it would be better than any play on television.

While waiting for the chief police officer to arrive, Chimanlal's son walked around the room, inspecting the battered objects it contained. He asked Farrokh to put everything in a box that could be taken away by the police. 'Clear this flat, it must be handed back to the landlord, no one is going to pay the rent.' At the mention of rent, the landlord pricked up his ears and began to take a lively interest. 'Perhaps the furniture can be sold,' he speculated, 'and the rent owing to me can be paid out of the proceeds.' The police guarding the scene objected to anything being disturbed, even more to anything being removed.

'*Sahib*,' Farrokh appealed to the landlord and to Chimanlal's son with a gesture of his open hands, 'Bommgarter *sahib* is still here – he has not even left yet.'

Then Lotte arrived, dragged out of her sleep and brought in by the excited neighbour. So fast did she come, hobbling, that she broke the heel off her red slipper. Then had to limp. Still, she burst in, clutching the hair that stood up on her head with one hand, the open front of her cotton dress with the other, herself looking the victim.

The crowd waiting in the room could not have asked for more: it was all they could have desired, the drama, the theatre, the raw emotions, everything. Speechless, yet audible in their horror and excitement, they watched the *memsahib* arrive, hobbling on broken red heels, holding together a torn red dress from which the white flesh spilt. It was wonderful, perfect – the *memsahib* giving a scream, clapping her hand to her mouth, standing struck, rushing forward, throwing herself on the corpse, weeping, 'Hugo, Hugo, *mein Gott*, Hugo! What have you done?' *Memsahib* on her knees, dress rucked up to the thighs, red hair flying forwards, face buried on the old man's chest, sobbing. Farrokh standing by, wringing his hands, whining like a character on stage, 'Old *sahib*, good *sahib* – taking tea in my café every day, every day for twenty years now – ' then going down on his knees too and crying like a baby. All the crying anyone's heart could desire, loud and shrill and scandalous. The audience shivered with delight.

The police chief shouldering his way in, swaggering, shouting, 'What's this? What is going on? Clear the way. Clear the room,' and policemen swinging out with their batons. 'Move back, move back.' Even photographers on the scene – click flash, click flash. A chance of getting one's photograph in the papers. Everyone surging forwards with new enthusiasm. Police batons flailing. 'Clear out. Out.'

In the moment that the room was cleared of all crowds and even the police were outside, Lotte cast her eyes around the room in despair, saw the blood-stained postcards scattered over the rug and – partly in order to tidy up, tidy the room and restore it to normalcy, and partly out of a desperate wish to keep something of Hugo for herself – she threw herself on her knees and hurriedly, frenziedly gathered them up and hid them in her blouse. When the policeman opened the door again, she saw the crowds had been driven on to the landing, on to the staircase, into the hall. None willing to leave. Too much going on, too much still to happen. Jostling and gossiping, waiting and straining.

Finally the corpse being carried out. Everyone lurching forwards, holding their breaths, letting it out in a long communal hiss. The corpse – yes, dead, without any doubt dead. Wrapped in white sheets, the bloodstains hidden, but still a corpse, dead, heavy, wobbling. A certain respect due there. 'Make way, make way,' and people falling back. No one wanting to touch, to be touched by death, by the dead. Hands and handkerchiefs rising instinctively to mouths, noses. Not to breathe, not to breathe in death. Everyone drifting out on to the pavement to see it lifted into the hearse, to see the hearse go. Standing in the sun, speculating on the murder, the murderer. But the heat driving them away. Like knots of ants, unknotting, straying up and down the road, disappearing. Other things to do, after all. Have to get on, with living.

'Thieves!' Lotte screamed at those that remained in Baumgartner's room. 'What have you done? Who has done this?' She gestured at the wreckage left behind like so much debris after a riot.

Farrokh shook his head. Chimanlal's son blustered, 'It must be cleared. The flat must be handed over. The police must cordon it off,' and the landlord nodded his head, 'Yes, yes, yes. Yes, yes, yes.'

'Clear it away? Where will it go? Who will take it? It is Mr Baumgartner's flat, these are his belongings,' she shouted at them, her throat raw from weeping, her face and eyes as red as her anger. 'Everything is his, no one can touch it.'

The police officer, Chimanlal's son and the landlord kept away from her, by the door. Exchanging looks they chose the police officer to speak for them. 'Madam, it is property of the police now. Police will keep till case is closed.'

'Police? You thieves are going to keep Mr Baumgartner's property?' she screeched. 'No, I will not permit! I am Mr Baumgartner's friend – oldest friend – '

'Oldest friend,' Farrokh burst in passionately, 'yes, yes.'

'And I will not permit you to touch – '

Then Chimanlal's son took over, realised he must take over. Strolling across to her, he spoke levelly, keeping his tone sensible. 'No, madam, sorry, it has become police property because it is a police case. This murder.'

Lotte glared at him with a face crumpled with crying. She bared her teeth as if she would bite anyone who came near. But instead she nodded, kept nodding as if she were suddenly so old, she had lost control. Swinging around to the empty soiled divan, she muttered, 'Yes, yes, I go now, I go, too.'

•••••••••••••••••

By the teapot, on the table, she spread out the cards, sniffing at longer and longer intervals. She moved them about till they were all in an orderly row before her. All. Each one stamped with the number: J 673/1. As if they provided her with clues to a puzzle, a meaning to the meaningless.